The Boys of
<u>C</u>hi <u>O</u>mega <u>C</u>hi <u>K</u>appa
Freshman Initiation

An Erotic Anthology
Edited By

Mickey Erlach

Herndon, VA

Herndon, VA

Titles Edited by Mickey Erlach for STARbooks Press

Contents

STICKY RICKY'S SLEEPOVER
By Jake Harding

The situation at Ricky Stanton's sleepover becomes out of hand. Beer bottles clink together as brothers become intoxicated. Jerseys are removed and yield steel-solid torsos. Twelve of us sit in front of a fifty-two-inch Sony and watch our team's tight-end and quarterback pat each other on their bulbous and sexy-firm asses.

The frat house smells of sweat, beer, and semen that lines boxer-briefs. It's semi-trashed with popcorn debris, a bucket of chicken wing bones, two pizza boxes, and couch pillows scattered everywhere. It looks as if a hurricane has moved up from the Gulf and ravished our Theta Chi house. But none of the wreckage matters though because it's the best football game of the year, and Smithton College is on its way to pure victory!

I sit in my designated recliner with my legs slightly open. I kick back, enjoy my hot brothers, and the game with such zeal.

The nineteen-year-old icy-blond twins – Stang and Chip Colterwood – with their impeccably chiseled frames, cheer with excitement as the Stallions gain another touchdown for our college. Masculine yelps and howls fill the room. High fives are shared, and chest-bumps are not uncommon. One of the twins – Stang with his rearing mustang tattoo on a right bicep – calls out to me, "Jude, do you want another Rock?"

I nod my head and smile, wish for his crimson-red lips to wrap around my twitching wanger, but comprehend that this isn't going to happen, since he's straight. Within seconds, he hands off another Rolling Rock to me and smiles at my good looks: coal black hair with slim sideburns, tight jaw, impassive jade-colored eyes, twenty-one-year-old dashing smile that's quite narrow, and swollen crotch that, when excited and hard, is ten inches tall and two inches wide.

"Thanks, dude," I call out and crack open the beer.

"Anytime." Stang continues to concentrate on my chiseled looks, possibly salivating to kiss me, but I'm a little too drunk to tell.

My view focuses on Ricky Stanton in the center of the room; he holds his own long-neck Rock as if it were one of the twins' erections. He's the hottest guy in the frat house. My Italian frat brat from head to toe, model perfect in every way with his superstar, or porn star, looks. Ricky has a banged up knee from a car accident at eighteen and doesn't play football like most of the guys in the house. Truth is he loves the sport and wishes he were the superstar quarterback for the Stallions and wants to show off for us on TV right now. Ricky's incapable of action on the field though, but not in front of the Sony, since he jumps up with excitement and roots our team to an expected win.

There's lots of good Ricky stuff to go around, though. All the queer guys I hang with drool over the jock and melt for his muscle-toned body. Ricky has this skin-flick appearance that we go nuts over: twenty-one-years-old, pumped to the max, just under six foot, midnight blue-colored eyes, cocoa-colored hair, matching goatee, totally ripped to the core in all the right places, and downright just man-toy gorgeous. We all agree that Ricky's dessert at every meal, the finest prick of energy, and completely untouchable, since he, like the Colterwood twins, is straight.

Every few weekends, Ricky has a sleepover at the frat house. All the charming, hot, steamy, and sexy-sweet fellows of our fraternity show up for an afternoon game of touch football behind the frat house. When evening approaches, this same lot of succulent jocks and boyish cuties retire into the frat house to watch our hometown Stallions whip the asses of our rivaling teams at away games. What transpires is essential to how men really get along behind closed doors: a serious ritual of male companionship and unexpected bonding. Pizzas are delivered by cute twinks, beer is necessary, and man-sweat lingers heavily about the room like mold in the bathroom. Honestly, the evenings turn out just right and perfect; college men in bliss.

Single Ricky is a good host who just happens to be monetarily loaded. He serves beer, an assortment of subs, and other various man-foods for our animated football frenzy. Of course, there is too much drinking – Ricky leads the pack – and one predicament of questionable behavior among horny men follows another. We become slap-happy with each other as opened palms playfully snap off tight asses. Packages are rubbed, biceps are touched, and surprisingly jerseys are removed and expose a circle of just-right chests that look straight out of Corbin Fisher. It becomes a half-naked and rip-roaring event of inebriated men and testosterone-induced conduct.

Once things really get out of hand, our responsible and semi-drunk host collects truck keys in a Stallions' ball cap. He surprisingly and playfully flicks hardened nipples on ripped and bulging chests, and exclaims, "No drinking and driving tonight, dudes – it's a sleepover!"

For the next hour, the Stallions' game is the center of attention. Three consecutive touchdowns are scored by our home team. The blond twins, beautiful creatures with model careers, bond mysteriously in a twosome-huddle to my right. Inexplicably, they jab each other with teasing punches and cheer the Stallions on. Ricky gets in on their hyped action and calls out with a thunderous roar, "Dudes, we are going to the championships!"

Of course, the Stallions win the game. The score ends with solid triumph: 28 to 13. The boys are wild and in rare form. They consume more Rocks, cold pizza, and celebrate a wholesome victory. I find their romp tantalizing and mysterious, obsessed with their actions. A new party breaks out with house rock. It's pure magic as half-drunken guys dance together while Lady Gaga sings something about a disco stick.

The twins huddle together to my right and whisper secretly to each other. Both glow with exuberant smiles. I see their golden and hairless chests touch, and nipples press to nipples as their connection continues. Diligently, I gaze at their semi-hard, seven-inch throbbers in tight, ivory colored Rufskin shorts as they rub against each other, which leaves me stimulated and on fire, unlimited eye-candy just for me.

What the Colterwood twins discuss is kept from my ears, though. I'm skeptical about the steamy-hot brothers and sense they are up to no good. As a rocket builds in my jeans, which desires to shoot a pre-load into Unico briefs at any second, I observe the twins in an unbelievable and unexpected action, and close in on innocent Ricky Stanton.

It's pure exhilaration what happens next. It's cock-ripping good, if the truth be known. Stang positions himself directly in front of Ricky as Chip cuddles up behind our host. Neither is threatening. Both are terribly sexy with their ice-colored hair and fall-into eyes. What they accomplish with Ricky's chiseled and shirtless torso is blissfully chaotic and rod-blowing. The underwear models with their perfectly sculpted chests body-slam Ricky, compress him between their magnum nipples and innocent force. It's a threesome before my eyes; grown men sticking together. Simultaneously, the twins yell with heated energy, "Winning slam!"

What is so shocking and different with this particular "winning-slam" in comparison to the ones I have witnessed before is that the mischievous

3

twins break free from Ricky's fine body, and other man-handling actions transpire. Adorable Stang gently caresses Ricky's denim package, palm against hidden cock and balls, and slowly raises his fingers to Ricky's fuzzy navel, lined torso, across one pec, and perfectly erect nipple. And, behind sweet and innocent Ricky is a preoccupied and daring Chip, who grinds his pumped crotch into our host's tight end, holds Ricky by the hips, and licks the nape of his neck ... steadily, continuously, and passionately.

Certainly, these are cock-hardening events that can prompt me to slip out of my jeans and Unico briefs and fondly begin to bring my ten inches of meat to life. Instead, I watch and learn this arrangement among men, stroke beef through briefs, work pre-spew to the tip of my pole, and cause a wet spot to form on the fabric.

Obliviously Ricky – who is just so sweet you can take him home for Thanksgiving and other holidays – cheers wildly to his twosome attack, "That was the best win ever!" referring to the Stallions' success and not the twin-sandwich he so easily became only seconds before.

Just when I think things are about to calm down at Ricky's sleepover, the evening's activities heighten my homo-interests to the fullest. The twins convince Ricky Stanton to pass out on the frat house's living room floor instead of his private bedroom. Ricky, without any hesitation or conflict whatsoever, possibly feels buzzed and light-headed from the Rolling Rocks, agrees to the manly arrangement on the floor, a newly devised sleeping plan among half-naked men.

Cute Ricky, before he settles between the ripped and beefy twins, turns to me on my comfy chair and asks, "Jude, do you wanna join us?"

"I'm good right here. Thanks."

"Suit yourself," enchanting Ricky supplies and cuddles on the queen-size comforter, stuffed alongside two pieces of man-toy fun.

I expect the threesome to fall asleep rather quickly together, but mistakenly and unintentionally – by pure accident, mind you! – the appetizing trio dangle limp arms over tight torsos, succulent looking thighs, and boxer-covered guy-packages. Ultimately, I gaze at the paradise and harmony on the floor as careless palms find blond treasure trails, cocoa-colored pits, and pumped biceps. Unmistakably, the men giggle in a feisty evening blur, dramatic, intoxicated, and enjoy the moment together as fingers meander wildly over tight backs, ladder-like abs, and stiff cocks; a festive night game on the frat house floor called Sleep Teasing.

What transpires among the studly and chiseled men is more dick-riveting than what I merely perceive. The twins are impeccably mischievous and fake sleep, unaware that I'm still wide-eyed and awake. Sweetly, they have lighted smiles on their edible mouths and continue their evening plot to seduce Ricky Stanton. And because I'm not tired, I become eager for their nightly game, soothe an upright woody in my briefs with both hands, and breathe slowly and softly ... ready for whatever is about to come next.

Ricky is already asleep on the floor. He rolls between the twins, which prompts some friction between the three men. An eight-inch long thumper now rests against his stomach and covers his navel. The sight is XXX stuff all the way. Ricky lies on his left side, snuggles against Stang's behind, and unintentionally pokes his massive porn-rod into Stang's tight ass.

Stang cannot handle many more pokes and prods, though. He smiles greedily in my direction, simply rolls over on his right side, and faces Stanton. His lips are only inches away from the middle-man's, ready and willing to kiss him. Of course, it is shrewd Chip who wants in on the action and rises to the occasion. Chip gently pulls Ricky towards him by Ricky's tight ab-covered stomach and positions the dark and sleeping meat on his back for easy access.

It's enigmatic what the sugary-blond twins create with Ricky's Italian skin. With Stanton on his back, still engaged in sleep, a busy Stang begins to lick Ricky's dark and solid nipples with his extended tongue. His brother, Chip, dives for Stanton's cocoa-colored treasure trail, kisses its length from north to south, and eventually meets the tip of his sultry tongue to Ricky's now exposed cock-head that peeps out of tight boxer-briefs. Chip, exceedingly experienced in this new sport of intimate licks, flicks his tongue against Ricky's piss-hole, closely and wholeheartedly with a rhythm that leaves Ricky Stanton to twist awkwardly in half-sleep, slowly wake up, flutter his eyes open and closed, and groggily blurt out, "Dudes, what's going on?"

Stang pulls off an erect nipple and responds, "You're dreaming, Ricky ... Go back to sleep."

"I'm what?" Stanton asks, sleepily.

"We're having a post-game with you. Just enjoy it."

"Enjoy what?"

Stang looks devotedly into Ricky's dreamy eyes, smiles broadly, and whispers, "It's post-game action, Ricky. And, you're our star player."

What is so hot about this connection of men is that Chip continues to suck on the tip of Ricky's pole and carries out an efficient and rod-eating moment. He goes to town on the eight inches of spike with ease, consumes the fully exposed tackle now, massages its stem with his elongated tongue, and opens his mouth and busy lips. Endlessly, scrumptiously, and eagerly, he pushes his mouth over every inch of Ricky's slick stinger, caresses its veined hardness, and fingers the man's fuzzy ball sack with stray and manipulative appendages.

One stroke. Two strokes. Three strokes. I can't take it much longer. These boys have me harder than hard. Quickly and rapturously I pump both palms on the inflated protein between my Unico-covered thighs, flattered with the moment, totally equipped for heated action with them. I'm ready for my spout to shoot a load onto their model-like skin, bursting too soon. I hold back though, breathe in and out, slow the strokes down … and watch, engrossed and obsessive with their movements, covertly attracted to their prosaic measures.

Ricky now becomes somewhat flustered beneath the twins. A confused smile of contentment surfaces over his face as Chip works his cock and Stang continues to lap mercilessly at not one nipple, but two. Ricky, unable to hold a pre-load in, is still somewhat dreaming. He lets out a slight grown, arches his packed buttocks upwards, allows Chip to come off the shaft for air, and shoots three droplets of warm jizm onto the plan of his firm chest, almost tagging Stang in the face.

Stang pulls away quickly and responds with a laugh, "Dude, now you're getting in the game."

Chip adds, "He's a pro at this … ready for anything that comes his way."

I imagine both twins going head to head after the three bubbles of spew on steamy Ricky's chest, licking their plump lips, butting heads together as their busy tongues lap up bubbles of the sweet goo from my friend's torso. This is only my imagination, though. Instead, what really happens is rather mundane: Stanton finds a misplaced frat boy T-shirt nearby and wipes the gooey-mess away.

A surprised Ricky, dazed and confused, begins to sit up now, but is gently pushed down by Stang, who instructs, "The game's not over yet, guy ... It's just getting started."

Jesus ... have mercy on me. The scene is too wild and untamed ... too possessive of my skin. I watch the twins eat Ricky whole after they strip him out of his boxer-briefs. One twin (Chip) pushes the host's legs apart and dives his tongue into the depths of Ricky's bottom. He causes Stanton to groan and moan as Chip caresses his hole with continuous laps. The other twin (Stang) pivots himself over Ricky's hard shaft and digests inch after inch of the wood into the depths of his throat.

Ricky becomes sexually flustered, just like me. He cannot take much more of this flesh-chore. He murmurs inconceivable cheers as the twins do their impeccable skin-deeds. Ricky spreads his legs wide and wider – very similar to mine in the chair – and allows Chip to direct his tongue into his insides and lick his hole passionately. And Ricky, totally into this party of three, attempts to push his ass upwards, shoves his log deeper and deeper into Stang's opened throat, and works himself into a slippery and sultry frenzy of man-lust.

I want in on the action but keep my distance, and manhandle my goods. I push my jeans and Unicos down to my ankles and off, bolt my hips upwards, and spread my legs apart, just like Ricky. Our movements are synchronized like intense lovers as we thrust together, fully captivated by the accomplished twins. We work up and down, moan and hum, willed to blow our loads at any second.

It's Chip who pulls off the inexperienced and fully awake Ricky now. His twin follows and rises from the rocket between Ricky's legs. Chip nicely instructs, "Ricky, do you want to be our quarterback now?"

Ricky, who is sweaty and heated and throbbing-hard between his legs, looks puzzled as he asks, "What kind of quarterback?"

Chip goes to his twin over a still Ricky, and asks, "You ready to show him, Stang?"

Stang shares a ravenous smile, lights up with new excitement, turns his head towards me, and peers at my vertical cock in bare fists. He replies, "Let's get the audience cheering, dude ... I'm ready whenever you are."

The trio are my heated, lustful, naked, and strapping friends on the floor. It is pure bliss in the drunken moonlight as Stang rolls a Hot Rod condom down over his nine inches, squeezes some lube from packet he just happened to have nearby on his stick, positions himself behind Ricky's tight ass, and gently tells the star of the masculine show, "Spread your legs a little, I've got to make a play here."

Ricky listens, now on his knees with one twin in front of him and the other one behind him. Slowly he moves his right knee to the left and permits Stang's hefty entrance.

Unbeknownst to Ricky: Chip plants and pivots his hard branch into Ricky's mouth; he pushes inch after inch into his throat, and Ricky sucks on it with desire.

They are intimate but not forceful. Ricky loves these moments between the Colterwood twins. To my knowledge, he is not the experienced lover.

What unravels before me is chaotic bliss, a sexual frenzy between three men in the middle hours of the night, which leaves me breathless and stunned.

Ricky spreads his ass cheeks for Stang, who is busy as ever. Stang enters his find with ease, pops four plump inches of his heated pick into Ricky's behind and slowly pumps three more inches into the bulbous ass-chute.

Chip is preoccupied with the back of Ricky's head and pushes it towards his crotch. He meets the man's mouth with blond pubic hair. Ricky's chin is slapped by Chip's swinging balls again and again and again, and adds a sense of chaotic delight. Perfection.

"Deeper, Stang ... Push it in him deeper," Chip coaches.

Stang responds while he carries out this upbeat instruction, "Like the good quarterback he is."

"Inch after inch, Ricky ... Take it like you want it," Chip groans and rocks steadily into Ricky's mouth.

A skin-game among the threesome unfolds. It's a dude-sandwich and Ricky Stanton becomes the meat. The act is something I have never viewed in real life: three frat brothers labor over each other; a trio of sweat-slicked jocks fucking; men who are entangled with tongues and mouths and cocks and assholes. Filth and desire on the floor. Blonds seduce their find. Twin-prey is devoured. All mine to view ... entirely.

Ricky does not fight off these restless actions. Instead, he gags on Chip's nine inches that press down the tense length of his throat. My eyes view the hard cock that hangs between his legs. Stang pummels his ass, bashes himself into it, and eventually pulls out. All three men sweat and vibrate together, groan, and moan. My interest hangs on the shaft between Ricky's stiff legs, an eight-inch item that is untouched and veined, harder than hard ... delicious looking.

I am astonished as the cock stands stiff against Ricky's chest. A string of white and creamy goo drips out of its cock-head and stretches to the comforter. How yummy the evening treat looks! How scrumptious! Motionless on the chair with my rod ready to burst between my legs at any given second, a wrinkled crescendo is just about to erupt. Now, my hands continuously work my own ten inches as I observe the restless twins while they pump Ricky wildly from both ends. One slaps his ass as the other pulls Ricky's head towards his concrete goods ... rapturously.

It's Stanton in the middle whom I have my money on – coming first; this is my gut feeling. The poor dude is so excited about getting it on with the model twins that he can't possibly keep his load in any longer. By the look of his wide eyes, poker hard shaft, and his bobbing and pulsating ass, I believe the frat boy is ready to cream right on the comforter, and shoot the rest of his load, submissive to the moment.

Stang Colterwood doesn't let this happen, though. Stang pulls out of Ricky's suctioned ass, rips the condom off, drops it to the floor, and explains to his twin, "Let's flip him over so we can shoot our loads on him."

After Chip pulls out of the dude's mouth, the twins gently and aerobically lift Ricky Stanton up, flip him over, and delicately place the guy on his back. Chip stands on Ricky's right side while Stang stands on his left side. Both leave Ricky to stare up at their chiseled bodies and identical shafts and lined torsos.

Ricky, to my utter surprise, calls up, "Bring it on guys ... I thought you'd never get around to this."

This, of course, is my cue. A generous attraction that I can't miss out on. With a shaft stiff between my legs, I stand up and move over to Ricky on his back. Politely, the twins leave room for me between Stanton's spread legs. And like a fraternity only intended for the hottest and intimate dudes, we look at each other with tense smiles, hands positioned on man-poles, and understand each other's motives this evening … ready for our shared show.

Four guys pump their rods in feisty motion: up and down, ferociously, groan and hump, their fists busy at work. Four asses push into hands as we prepare to blow our loads. I see the twins at work: masterful hotties operate their identical rods, cut chests slick with perspiration, wild fire in their grey eyes, hips move backward and forward, both of them stare at each other as if they are mirrors, ready to shoot at any second. And, here is Ricky on the floor: bucks his ass, both fists planted on cock-skin, rolls the excess flesh up and down on his thick shaft, his face completely flushed and sweaty, and his chest heaves.

"You look good," Ricky says up to Chip.

Chip responds, "You look better."

I am too stunned with the trio, hypnotized by their ripples and perfection, thrust my meat intoxicatingly, and succumb to my own needs.

Beneath me, Ricky groans, "I'm shooting now, dudes … and there's no stopping me." Of course, he's the first one to blow his load. My attention is quickly drawn to a spray of quarterback sap that flies out of his rocket and creates white lines along the middle of his chest and …

The twins shoot next in synchronized motion. They groan simultaneously, thrust asses forward, and call out each other's names. Juice blows onto Ricky's perfect chest, and covers his lats and abs and nipples and pubic hair with thick white cream. Both twins smile from ear to ear, obviously happy and enthralled by their tedious labor.

Unable to hold my load any longer, I murmur again and again, "What a show, guys." I feel an emphatic rush burst through my staff and release an arc of Jude-ooze on Ricky's body. I decorate him with white liquid, blow my own mind, and shoot another arc on his skin. Here, I listen to him groan with deep satisfaction as droplets splatter against his chiseled chest as he becomes sex-spent.

Ricky smiles up at me, dazzled by all of our performances, and shares, "You three rock."

It's not over, though … seconds pass as we laugh together. The twins and Ricky have an ulterior motive. After a quick clean-up with cotton towels, they tackle me to the floor and begin to wrestle with me. The trio huddles overtop my bare skin and begin to lick its every crevice and crease with their hungry mouths. Here, under their greedy care, I am enjoyed as a post-midnight snack, seduced by their busy fingers and cocks ... until I end up blowing another sticky load once, twice, three times by dawn's early light.

KAPPA SIGMA RAU-RAU-RAUNCH
By Michael Roberts

"Good eeeeeeeeeeeeeeeevening!"

Apparently, this was his attempt at a Bela Lugosi impression.

It wasn't working.

Lugosi was tall and slender; this guy was neither. And I don't think that Lugosi's Dracula was dishwater blond and wore half-glasses. When the imitator spoke, even a faint illusion was shattered; his voice had none of the correct accent or mellifluous menace.

"Welcome to our parrrrrrrrrrrrty," he said. As he rolled the last word, his false vulpine teeth came loose and fell down his throat, and he went into a coughing fit. Behind him in the entranceway to the fraternity house, two of his brothers smiled knowingly and moved behind him less than promptly to pat his back less than gently. When he recovered and tried to thank his somewhat reluctant saviors, they were gone.

He picked up the plastic that popped out of his mouth, which looked disgustingly wet – the fake dentures *and* his mouth – and said, "Welcome to Kappa Sigma Rau," in what I assumed was his real voice, that of a friendly Peekapoo. "Didn't you understand the theme of our Halloween party – vampires?"

"The theme of the party," I said, in a manner intended to be affably condescending, "was announced as 'The Undead.' I chose to attend as Professor Lonagan."

Professor Lonagan taught linguistics, required in several college majors, including mine. I was currently in his junior seminar, something to do with the evolution of the English language, but it wasn't clear what.

Some of his students *weren't* required to take his classes but signed up just to watch him became almost fatally frenetic about arcane fricatives, umlauts, and Chaucer's final *e*.

I was fit enough to approximate Lonagan's slender frame, and with the appropriate jacket with leather patches at the elbows that had faded to gray and horn-rim glasses and my hair uncombed in his styleless disarray, I was a reasonable simulacrum of the good doctor.

For some reason, the unusual doorman looked discomfited.

"Well, I'm – F – Ferd ..."

"Hello, Freddy," I said, putting forth my hand, not at all certain that I wanted to shake fingers that had been adjusting his soggy oral appliance.

"No," he said. "Ferdie."

"I see," I said and shook his warm, damp hand.

"And you're ..." he said.

"And I'm what?" I said.

"Your name is?"

"My name is Gavin."

"Nice to meet you," he said and pulled me into the foyer and closed the outer door. "I'm Ferdie."

"I'm sure you are."

He steered me toward the living room of the fraternity house, still holding my hand, which had become nearly sopping, his and by absorption mine, and said, "Of course you know," and of course I did because I was staring at Professor Lonagan.

He wasn't in costume but was attired as usual.

"Of course I do," I said feebly; I suddenly had difficulty breathing.

"Of course you do," said Professor Lonagan, so dryly that he seemed to expel a little puff of sand. "Hello – Gavin."

"Hello, Pro ..."

After a few seconds of weighty silence, Ferdie, perhaps discerning that I was in a tad of a dilemma, said, "Professor Lonagan is our faculty advisor."

"It's nice to see you again, Pro ..."

"Indeed," said the professor. "It's nice to see *you* again – Gavin."

He paused. He smiled. He *was* in costume – sort of – one extended tooth dangled in the middle of his uppers. I *thought* it was phony – but perhaps I hadn't previously been paying attention to Dr. Lonagan. It was all very disconcerting.

"I look forward to seeing you in seminar Monday."

"I ..." I said.

Professor Lonagan sidled away.

"Come in," said Ferdie.

The living room was full.

Kappa Sigma Rau was a fraternity for less desirable males – those with slide rules, thick glasses, bad haircuts, pants too short or too long, a lack of social graces, an unhealthy interest in academics. So if the two frat brothers who had desultorily rescued Ferdie seemed indifferent (and I had known that they were frat brothers because they, like Ferdie, wore pocket protectors as part of their holiday couture), that was indicative of how low Ferdie was on the social ladder – if indeed he were not lying on the floor beneath the ladder. Kappa Sigma Rau was not one of the most popular groups on campus.

But the Halloween partygoers were numerous because carousing is the main collegiate curriculum to a majority of students, and a celebration anywhere with anyone anytime is to be enjoyed. And the evening was young, and more interesting parties were scheduled later.

The celebrants dressed in various vampire regalia. Some were Lugosi wannabes or Boris Karloff knockoffs. Some were generic neck nuzzlers. Unlike me, they had exercised little creativity.

I saw a few of my Alpha Theta Tau fraternity brothers. I waved at them, but formidable football player Trent was entrancing some wide-eyed coed hanging on him and his every word and his impressive biceps; handsome basketball player Carlton demonstrated for a spellbound group a game-winning maneuver; and magnetic rower Henry was bouncing on a sofa with his usual excess of energy, hands flying, barely missing the young woman opposite him, possibly explaining an esoteric theory of rowing as she seemed to be wondering if she should be intrigued or alarmed.

I tried to converse with some of the attendees, but even so early, several were already inebriated to the point of incoherence; others' idea of

15

repartee seemed to be a vapid grin. A Boris Karloff leaned forward, I thought, to follow one of my points and passed out in my lap. I removed him and began to make my departure.

Doctor Lonagan was in the hallway. "Good night – Gavin," he said, my name sounding sepulchral, and I gasped, "Good night, Pro ..." and hurried to the front door, not quickly enough to avoid the doorman, who had reattached, crookedly, his ersatz teeth and wanted to wish me a "Merrrrry Halloween," as if Dracula had zinged Santa Claus.

I said, "Thank you, Freddy" and rushed down the sidewalk. He called after me, "No, Ferdie!" and I shouted back, "I'm sure that's true," and turned the corner and escaped that pestilential stretch of Fraternity Row.

On that Monday, I was in Professor Lonagan's class. When I entered the room, I didn't see him and hoped he was ill, and then I heard my name in his subterranean tone ... "Hello – Gavin." I whirled in alarm and nearly knocked him on his scholarly ass.

"I – I ..." I said, envisioning my grade point total declining so far that I would become ineligible for even a course in remedial alphabetizing.

"That's all right," he choked, not entirely convincingly, and righted himself, "ah – Ga – Gavin" – the reading of my name like something out of Edgar Allan Poe.

As the discussion progressed, he kept looking as if he were going to call on me, then would skid to some other student. I was prepared to expand fluently on his questions, having spent Sunday buried in the text and his numerous handouts, but my eloquence wasn't allowed expression. He at last bested me by looking directly into my eyes and saying, "What do you think about that – Ferdie?"

I whirled around, and there was our maladroit denizen of the fraternal night in mufti, preening in gratitude at finally being caught by Lonagan's spotlight, saying, "I'll be happy to respond."

But while Ferdie was being ostentatiously obsequious, he was also explicating sound points about the subject at hand.

When I looked at Lonagan, he was actually smiling. I hadn't seen that in the time I'd known him, and I found it surprising and obscurely alarming.

"Good, Ferdie," he said, and at that moment, the bell sounded, and the seminar was concluded.

On my way from the classroom, Ferdie bumped into me and accompanied me out onto the quad, chattering animatedly at a speed that should have gotten him ticketed. His diatribe was an amalgamation of admiration for Professor Lonagan, fascination with the seminar's subject, self praise and self criticism about how well he thought he'd known today's segment until Dr. L called on him and then he wasn't sure that he knew anything at all but was so grateful that he'd been able to discuss the question to the professor's satisfaction ...

At that point in his monologue, I was several steps behind him; he finally realized that I was not next to him, braked abruptly and whirled. I pointed to the door of a building and mimed that I had to go inside to my next class, "Leading Trends in Literary Thought as They Apply to Today's Exigent World," in which the instructor was comparing Stephen King and Albert Camus.

He shrugged, making a little grimace of sadness, and called, "Goodbye, Gavin," and I called, "Goodbye, Freddy," and he called, "No, no, Ferdie," and I called, "I'm sure you're right" and fled through the door.

# # # # #

I had eluded Ferdie twice, and I recognized that continuing to elude him would take a great portion of time and effort.

At the next meeting of the seminar, Ferdie engineered himself into the seat beside me, which he then continued to occupy. He was smiling at me vacuously – I suspected that he had no other kind of smile in his repertoire.

I responded with polite detachment. He seemed to magnify the politeness and ignore the detachment, continuing to sit beside me, to beam upon me, and to whisper to me. I wasn't sure what he whispered, since it was so faint as to be unintelligible, and Professor Lonagan aided my discouragement of such *sotto voce* communications by frowning whenever Ferdie aimed another *sibilant communiqué*. Ferdie seemed torn between sharing whatever it was that he wanted to share and keeping in the professor's graces. For a while after the professor's reactions, Ferdie ebbed and then, too soon, flowed again.

After seminar, he went with me toward my next class. My stride kept increasing, and he struggled along, each day getting farther behind me, and I knew that we must resemble Mutt and Jeff, he short and plump and perspiring and antic, and I – well – tall and slender and perspiring and antic; he the pursuer, I the pursued; he shouting at me, his words scattering in the wind before they reached my ears into shards of tattered transmission.

I was not the only person to view us as cartoonish figures; even at my velocity, I could see the disparaging smiles of people we passed, as one member of the approaching group pointed out to the others the preposterous pair racing pell-mell down the sidewalk. As I flew into my next class, I was escaping not only the bird of prey that flapped after me, I was escaping the judgment of those observers of me and my tracker – trying to because some of my fellow studiers of the similarities between *The Stranger* and *Carrie* had observed the vaudeville outside and giggled and gawked at me as I tried to sit with dignity in my chair.

I was losing my poise, my decorum, my pride, my position, and it simply would not stand. Something had to be done.

"Something has to be done. We have to talk."

We were sitting at a table in the student union, drinking what was purportedly coffee. He was absent from his class in Peruvian Lit; I was missing a discussion on the existential implications of *Valley of the Dolls*.

I watched half a dozen emotions flit across Ferdie's face. Most seemed to be allied to hope.

"Oh?" he said. "Oh. Oh!"

I wanted to be as tactful as possible.

"No," I said. "Ferdie, this has to stop."

"What has to stop?" he asked, although the timbre of his voice indicated that he full well knew about what I was speaking.

"This chasing me. I'm – flattered, I suppose, by your interest. But we have to face facts, Ferdie. I'm not – well, I'm not ..."

"You're not what?" he inquired.

"Ferdie," I protested. "We're just so – different."

I began to feel as if I were in one of the lesser films of the 1940s, speaking dialog written by some second-rate screenwriter who had barely passed high-school composition.

"You're presuming that I – and I may – a bit. All right, I understand what you mean."

"You do? Good."

His words were fine; our conversation was getting somewhere. The slight sneer on his face was not fine; where was our conversation getting?

"Good, good, good," he said, alarming me with his tinge of hysteria. "You're bright and sophisticated and charming, witty and winsome and beguiling, while I'm short and overweight and dim and annoying and clinging, et cetera, et cetera." The last words screeched in pitch and volume, and people at tables around us stared.

"Ferdie," I said softly, trying to forestall some sort of explosion.

"Oh, we're not going to have a scene. But I want to ask you a few things. At the Halloween party, I saw you waving at Trent and Carlton and Henry."

"They're my fraternity brothers at Alpha Theta Tau."

"How many waved back at you?"

"None," I said. "They were engaged."

"Yeah. I watched Trent say something to that droop who was dripping – I mean that drip who was drooping – all over him and point to you, and they both laughed – well, he laughed, and she simpered. Carlton put his hands across his eyes after you went by and shook his head and then went back to his presentation. Henry got even more hyper, as if he was afraid that you were going to talk to him, and that's why he nearly winged his date."

"That," I said with as much dignity as I could muster, "cannot be true."

"That," he said with mockery oozing from his spacious pores, "is undeniably true. Your fraternity is basically an athletic frat, right?"

"Yes, but ..."

"And it has to maintain a certain academic standard, right?"

"Right, but ..."

"And most of the apes in that frat have the IQ of mayonnaise, correct?"

"Possibly, but ..."

19

"So it needs people like you to bring up the scholarship level. Several members tolerate you because that's what you do. But how often have you been invited to their parties, their trips to athletic events, their bull sessions? How many of even the 'scholars' pal around with you?"

"Well, I ..."

"I understand how low down the totem pole I am in my frat house. They could give me a crown for being neediest of the needy, nerdiest of the nerds. I don't kid myself. But you should declare self deception as your college major."

"You don't ..."

"I'm afraid I do. I've talked to people, Gavin. I've even heard ..." he eyed me meaningfully and fishily, "... that your real name is not Gavin but Arvin."

I shuddered and drew myself up. "That is an arrant lie. As for the rest – you may tell me all of these things, Ferrrdie," I responded, grinding out the r of his name, "but I know ..."

"You know so little – Arvin – even who you are." The statement sounded more in sorrow than anger.

Then he grabbed my arm.

"Look, Gavin, look," he said, and he wrenched me around so that we were facing a decorative mirror on a wall. "We're alike, you and I. Different, but alike. Or can you see us? I've noticed you squint at things in the distance because you're too vain to wear eyeglasses. Can you see that far? Can you see?"

He let go of me and stood and left the table. I watched his fuzzy reflection retreat, becoming finally just a barely discernible dot of movement and disappearing into the indistinct background.

I needed to talk to Professor Lonagan.

Since Ferdie had begun stalking me, my concentration and nerves had begun to suffer, my progress in the doctor's class had diminished. I had to keep up my grades in my major subject to ameliorate the atrocious grades I was getting in courses for which I had no aptitude, general college requirements like sciences and history and other annoyances.

My focus was not helped by the *tête à tête* with Ferdie in the student union. I was bothered by his comments, though they were patently untrue.

I thought about the times I had been part of social occasions with frat brothers, but that didn't require much consideration, because aside from functions to which every frat member was invited, there weren't that many.

As for the few confessional conversations or light-hearted exchanges – and no *bons mots* shared with a roommate, since I occupied a single bedroom – there were tutorial questions as a resident intellectual – but – Ferdie had a point.

It didn't help that I had to keep Trent from discovering how delectable I found his broad shoulders or Carlton how much I admired the sturdy legs that were too incompletely revealed in his long basketball shorts or how Henry's trenchantly tight tush caused a quivering at the midpoint of my body or the other parts of other house companions, sometimes seen *au naturel*, that were so devastating to me – it wasn't easy to communicate with someone when you were doing your best not to reveal the lust beating in your heart and elsewhere – even considering that, was it possible that Ferdie had another point?

And should we ponder my sex life? I was somewhere between virginal and experienced.

Oh, dear. That didn't take very long.

I took pride in being unique, including a wardrobe that was designed – too much? – to be completely unlike anyone else's – I particularly liked scarves. Were a few – several – looks that I thought were admiration really disdain or derision or any of a number of "d" words that I didn't want to consider?

Shit, I reflected.

I must reconnoiter the situation – at some other time because right now I had to consult with Professor Lonagan and find out what I could do to correct the spiral down, which I was corkscrewing rapidly in his class.

# # # # #

I was late – his office hours ended ten minutes ago. But I hurriedly ascended the stairs to his office, and out of breath, I knocked on his closed door.

No answer.

But there was movement shadowed in the pebbled glass, and there was sound – someone must be in the office.

I turned the conveniently unlocked doorknob, and I pushed the door open and was greeted by a pair of tighty-whiteys – almost literally just by the tighty-whiteys because their wearer was bent over, and all I saw was a pair of legs supporting a pair of shorts and an ass. The legs were chunkier than I preferred, and the stomach that I could see had a hint of love handles, and those were not usually to my taste. But the ass sheathed in white was a nice heart shape, and it was a nice size, and it was nice to contemplate, and I did, and then I heard a laconic cough, if a cough might be described as laconic, and this one might, short and not very loud, enigmatic but somehow replete with meaning. I looked up, and there was Professor Lonagan.

He wasn't dressed as usual. In fact, he wasn't dressed at all.

If fact, he was quite utterly, quite starkly, quite completely … nude.

Four things drew my attention. First, he was nude. Second, he was not wearing his glasses, and he peered at me and said, his voice deeper even than usual, "Gavin?"

Third, his cock was rigid, and fourth, it was a very lengthy cock.

Maybe I thought so because of the shock of seeing him in the state in which I was seeing him. I stared at his cock. No. It really was very lengthy. And it was rigid.

I was going to say something – I hoped that intelligible words would emerge from my mouth within a reasonable period of time – and just as I was going to say – something – the semi-clad, bent-over underwear model turned and raised up and grinned and said, "Gavin!" and of course, it was Ferdie.

This must be a *Circle of Hell* that Dante never dreamed of.

I tried to find a place to look that wasn't Professor Lonagan's lean, unclothed body, especially his lean, unclothed, rigid cock, and I had the horrible feeling that that my eyes were rolling in my head like pinwheels and, of course, alighting on Ferdie's crotch.

That crotch was encased in the tighty-whiteys, which had, just to the right of the fly, a dime-sized hole through which I could see Ferdie's skin, a viewing that caused me to feel a battery of emotions, one of which seemed to be a lustful influence on my own treacherous dick.

22

And as Professor Lonagan looked younger and much better without glasses and clothes, Ferdie looked much better without glasses and most of his clothes.

"I'm sure you're shocked to find us in this situation and don't know how to handle it," said Ferdie.

I glanced at the professor, and even though he possibly was so near-sighted that he couldn't clearly see me, he evidently saw enough, and his eyes seemed to get a knowing glint, and he purred, "I think that Gavin knows how he *wants* to handle this situation. Help convince him, Ferdie."

"Hmm?" asked Ferdie, and I couldn't tell if he were being ingenuous or dis.

"Take off your shorts," said Professor Lonagan.

Obedient student that he was, Ferdie did.

His prick was half risen, and it wasn't as long as Lonagan's, but it was rounder and more fully packed and, in its way, just as enticing.

I didn't want to be enticed, but as I watched, Ferdie's filet of flesh ascended to stout stiffy, and what I wanted appeared to be of little consequence, and what I wanted was taking precedence. I could tell this by the discomfort in my pants.

"Isn't this …?" I asked.

"No," said Lonagan. "What goes on in here has no influence on what goes on out there." He gestured vaguely to the door, and I closed it before someone could pass by and spy what was going on in the office, and we three rocked the campus. "It won't have the slightest influence on the grade that you wish to discuss with me."

Was this man clairvoyant?

"I may be many things," he said, drawing himself up with dignity, a formidable accomplishment for someone nude and so undeniably aroused, "but I am not a sexual harasser."

Aroused – and arousing, damn it.

And so – double damn it – was Ferdie.

I stared at Lonagan and Ferdie, my eyes again swinging back and forth like erratic pendulae.

23

"I think," said the professor after an awkward silence, "that if we're going to get anywhere at all, Gavin" – my name rolling ponderously from somewhere deep in his voice box ... "it's time for you to make your contribution."

"Huh?" I said.

"Continue with what you want. We're all – friends here."

I was on my knees.

I don't remember how I got there, but I did, and I opened my mouth more than it was already open at the improbability of this whole situation, and I buried myself in Ferdie's midsection.

One second, I was staring at Ferdie's succulent sausage, and the next, all of it was in my mouth, and I was chewing on his pubic hair, which smelled of French vanilla. His cock tasted fresh and clean, and it was heady giving him head, for me and evidently for him; he began to hum, a sort of minimalist composition, one note with occasional variations, which wasn't as annoying as it might have been. I exercised every preposition I could think of with his prick – up and down and across and under and around – and his hum surged up a pitch, and one drop of his juice squeezed onto my taste buds, and the effect was disproportionate to the amount, for the tang impelled me to increase my speed and my area of exploration to his balls, sacs obviously chock-full of his essence, and the track beneath that led to his chubbily curvy cheeks.

I briefly thought, *What the hell am I doing?* and then I decided to just keep on doing whatever the hell it was.

I don't know how much time I had spent ingesting Ferdie before I heard Professor Lanagan say, "Onto the desk," and Ferdie obeyed, taking me with him, still grasping his cock like a vacuum cleaner, and I heard papers fluttering to the floor, as if he had swept the desk clean like a scene from a not-particularly good romantic comedy, and Ferdie sat on the desk, and I nestled between his spread legs and sucked energetically.

Hands unbuckled my belt. Logic told me that they were the professor's hands. The hands undid my pants, unzipped them, slid them to the floor, followed by the new paisley boxer shorts that I was glad I wore rather than the aerated several-years-old ones I nearly had donned. There I stood with my trousers around my feet, feeling my distended dick flapping before me and a breeze behind me on my exposed ass – I hoped that the office door had not swung open.

24

The hands explored my quivering buttocks, and two thumbs ran down my fissure as if the professor were shuffling a deck of fleshcards, separating the two halves. He anointed me with some sort of oil or lotion, chilly and invigorating. I heard the rip and snap of a condom.

Then I felt something else at my buttocks, swaying back and forth and up and down and settling at last upon my pucker. Logic told me it was a professorial prick.

He pushed in – and in – steadily, not rushing. The professor had a *very* long cock.

When he was all the way in, about a foot farther, it seemed, than anyone had ever gone, than any appliance I ever used had penetrated, I expelled a sigh into Ferdie's cock slit, and Ferdie's ass elevated an inch or so from the top of the desk, and he said, "Ahhhh."

My sentiments exactly.

I released Ferdie enough to say, "Oh, Professor Lonagan!" and he said, "Under the circumstances, perhaps you should call me 'Laurence,'" and, ever the instructor, added, "With a 'u'" and "But not in class," and then he began to fuck me.

Almost all of the way out – and then all of the way in – a leisurely extraction and an unhurried reinsertion – and again, as I continued to sample Ferdie's delights and as his buzzing went up another key – and then Professor Lonagan – Laurence – pressed in a bit more definitively, banging my button, and I exclaimed, "Larry!" and he said, "Laurence," and I said, "Oh, Professor Lonagan!" using a greater complement of exclamation points in one afternoon than I'd theretofore used in an entire day.

I grabbed myself and began stroking, and a consuming heat suffused the tip of my tingling member and traveled through my groin and into the rest of me until I could feel my blood vessels simmer.

Laurence exercised his technique of deliberate intrusions and extrusions followed by the sudden bop, the abrupt sting at the terminus of my internal plumbing, several more times, and I wondered if he was attempting to get even for my Halloween impersonation of him. If he was, the laugh was on him, for the alternation of sensations was not unpleasant – even the brief, irregularly timed pain, and just as I was thinking that, he twanged me with a particularly sharp thrust, and I gasped, and I could have sworn that I heard a sigh of satisfaction from him.

I continued to traverse Ferdie's prick. He seemed to like what I was doing, for he bounced up and down on the desk, and my head rose and fell with his movements until I was getting a crick in my neck. Perhaps my tongue roaming his ample hard-on or perhaps his springing up and down like some sort of Ferdie-in-the-box was loosening his floodgates, for a steady trickle of dick fluids was rolling down my gullet.

The professor – Lonagan – Larry – whatever – his cock slid more easily into me, and his descending dick rolled into my sensitized innards, warming, palpitating, and I could hear the catch in his breath, and my own breaths alternated with his.

Someone knocked on the office door.

I froze, but Ferdie continued bouncing and Laurence continued fucking.

"Come back later," said the professor in what I thought was a remarkably controlled tone of voice. "My office hours are in ..." – he evidently checked his watch – "... eighteen minutes."

The knocker went away.

The hand with the presumed watch dropped onto my rump, followed by his other hand, and his rhythm picked up, and his cock stopped stroking and started to regularly assault me, and each time it did, my temperature ascended a degree until I was perspiring, and my cock was perspiring, too, and I was dripping, dripping, and Ferdie was dripping, dripping, and the air around me turned a lovely shade of blue, and something lifted Ferdie a notch, and his feet flailed outward and his hum neared the dogs-only range, and then his legs closed around my neck, and I could hardly breathe and the lovely shade of blue turned somewhat alarmingly blacker but only somewhat because I was so centered on Ferdie's meaty biscuit and Laurence's accelerating cock diving deeper, and my own dick was absolutely vibrating, and I thought that if sex was usually this delightful, why the hell hadn't I done more of it?

And then we arrived at the pinnacle.

Ferdie's vocalization went up so high that it disappeared into the clouds that ringed my blue-black sky, and his grip on my neck tightened, and he streamed into my mouth, and his flood had the usual bittersweet relish and something else, as if I were consuming whipped cream with some mysterious flavorings, and it was an inundation, and I gulped it down.

Behind me, the professor had evidently been seized by some sort of lustful dance, flailing my ass with his pelvis, saying, "Oh – oh," and then banging up against me, and I staggered into Ferdie, and he said, "Oh – oh," and fell backward onto the desk as his dick popped out of my mouth and stood stiffly between his legs as if saluting something.

And Laurence, bent so far above me that his chin was nearly resting on my back and I could feel his hot breath on my neck, came within me.

My pistoning hand brought me over the edge, and I shot and shot, and I thought distractedly that I was no doubt blasting messily on the professor's papers that Ferdie had dramatically swept from the desk, and I shot some more.

Then Larry collapsed over me, and caught off balance, I tripped on the pants and shorts down around my legs, and he and I tumbled to the floor and the sperm, and we lay there while Ferdie towered above us on the desktop, his cock fluttering like the flag of a mountain climber who has scaled the summit and planted the pennant of success.

Laurence shook me awake – I had evidently slept or more likely passed out from the effort of my ardor.

"Time to go," he said. He was already dressed, as was Ferdie, who was spinning in the swivel chair behind the desk.

I awkwardly stood and pulled up my underwear and trousers, and discovered that my orgasm had not spilled onto the papers knocked from the desktop. I stickily zipped up and was grateful for the plum-colored silk scarf I had worn to post-office hours, which would, I sincerely hoped, cover the extremely suspicious spot down my front.

Laurence steered me toward the door, and Ferdie followed.

"That was so – that was," I said, "Lar – Laurence."

He pointed to the floor, and I saw that I was one step past the doorframe into the hallway.

"That was so – Professor Lonagan."

"Yes," he replied, "it was. See you at seminar – Gavin. And then perhaps at another time."

"Certainly, Pro ..." I said.

27

I looked at him in the doorway, a light shining in his glasses that made it impossible for me to read his expression.

What I had gotten myself into? Or, more to the point, what had I allowed to get into me?

Professor Lonagan closed the door, and I started down the stairs, Ferdie bounding after me.

What had I done, and why had I done it, and was it possible that I might do it again? Was it possible that I might not do it again?

Walking up the stairs was a student, perhaps the one who had knocked on the door while the professor, Ferdie, and I were *tout l'ensemble*, and as he saw Ferdie and me, he smiled. Was he was merely greeting us? After the student had passed, I glanced back at him, and he was looking over his shoulder at us, and the smile had morphed into a smirk.

This afternoon, I had been doomed and delighted in one fell swoop.

What was to follow?

I stopped, and Ferdie ran into me, and my question was answered.

My fate was sealed.

ICY CONTACT, WARM BONDS
By Mark Apoapsis

I'd already changed into my pajamas – right there in my dorm room since Ryan wasn't home – and hoisted myself into my bunk, when I heard an unexpected sound. A sort of a clink, like something light but hard bouncing off the window. Puzzled, I sat up, careful not to bump my head on the ceiling as I'd done a few weeks ago when I was still getting used to the room. It was such a hassle getting in and out of this bed that I did it as little as I could get away with: usually twice a night, once to go down the hall to take a leak. At least I was getting smoother at it. The first week or two, I'd been so awkward that Ryan had offered to give me a boost – probably trying to being helpful, but it had only embarrassed me. Since then, I must have built up some upper body strength.

I heard another clink. This time I was sure it was something tapping against the window, which was weird because we were on the second floor. I swung down and went to the window and looked down.

Down there in the courtyard of our U-shaped building, a tall, slim man stood there looking up at me pleadingly. It was Ryan. Once I got over the momentary shock, it was obvious that he'd lost his keys and was locked out. Not just because he was down there, and apparently throwing pebbles at our window, but also because I could plainly see he didn't have his keys with him: he was standing there in his boxer shorts, a lone lamppost making his blond hair glow and casting the muscles of his hairless chest into sharp relief.

Knowing he must be freezing out there in the crisp autumn night, I hurriedly pulled a pair of jeans right over my pajamas and put on shoes without socks. I didn't waste time changing into a shirt, just threw a jacket on over my pajama top. Pausing to zip it up to my chin, I opened the door and quickly walked down the hall and downstairs, passing a few guys studying or playing board games in the common area on my way to the back door. They watched me curiously.

"Dude!" Ryan said in obvious relief when he saw me. "Thank God you don't sleep as heavy as I do."

"I was still awake."

29

"You didn't happen to bring any of my clothes down, did you, buddy?"

"Uh ... well ..." I said sheepishly. Apparently not that awake.

"That's okay, man. I guess if you lend me your jacket ..."

"I've just got my pajamas on underneath," I protested.

"So? Don't be such a ..." He stopped himself, and I could actually see him take a deep breath: his chest expanding as he inhaled, and his breath turning white as it hit the cold air. "OK, would you mind making another trip? I'll wait out here."

"Are you sure? You must be freezing."

"I'll live."

"I mean, it's an all-male dorm, and ..."

"Hurry it up, would you?" He hugged himself, shivering a little.

Five minutes later, we were both back in the dorm, and I was stripping back down to my pajamas. Having done what was necessary, I was ready to go back to bed, but as usual Ryan felt the need to discuss things.

"Sorry for being short with you," he said, taking off the shirt I'd brought down from his closet. "You were doing me a favor, and I had no right to get annoyed at you. Most guys would have thought nothing of walking through the halls at night in their pajamas, but hey, everyone's different." He unbuttoned his spare pair of jeans and pulled them down. "Just like some guys on this floor have no problem walking back to their rooms in nothing but a towel after a shower. I'd never be comfortable doing that."

Since he obviously wanted a conversation, I said what I was thinking: "You've got nothing to be ashamed of."

"Thanks, man, but it's not about being ashamed of my body. Eric sure doesn't have anything to be ashamed of either, but you never see him walking down the hall in a towel. Except for yesterday, that is, when I stole his clothes while he was in the shower. And you saw how mad that made him!"

Eric must be that big jock from down the hall, I gathered. That might explain the enraged yelling that had distracted me from my physics problem set. Also that extra bundle of clothing I'd noticed stashed in Ryan's closet when I rifled in it for something to bring down. I suspected that if I checked the labels, I'd find they were two sizes larger than the ones on hangers.

"I'm sure you've been wondering who did this to me."

I shrugged.

"That's who it was. Eric. And I totally had it coming. Anyway, my point is it's about not having anything to hide; it's all about vulnerability."

"But ..." He always slept in his boxers. He didn't even bother turning the light out before stripping. Half the time, he took his shirt and shoes off the minute he got home, and his pants as soon as he knew he was in for the night. And, of course, this very moment he was clad in just his boxers, even while explaining to me why he'd rather freeze outside than let the other guys see him like that.

He waited to see if I was going to say anything beyond that one word, then explained, "Roommates are supposed to be vulnerable to each other. We just trust each other. There's no getting around it; we sleep in the same room. And I'm a heavy sleeper. I mean, incredibly heavy. You could do anything to me, man! A little extra sleepwear isn't going to protect me from you, if you wanted to mess with me."

# # # # #

"I don't want you to have to keep letting me in every time until the office opens on Monday," Ryan said as we returned from breakfast, and I let us back into the room. "I'll go and trade Eric's clothes for mine right now. But you'll be around, won't you, just in case he and both his roommates are out?"

"Sure."

He came back empty-handed. And bare-chested, and barefoot, and bare-legged. "It's not funny, man! Those were my only other pair of shoes within two thousand miles."

"Sorry," I said, trying to choke down my laughter.

"You know, I don't think I've ever seen you laugh before. It's nice. I just wish it wasn't at my expense."

31

"Sorry," I said again. I wasn't the only one chuckling; I could hear the trail of laughter and opening doors he'd left all along the hall. Before any more heads could poke out of doors, I stood aside and let my red-faced roommate in.

# # # # #

As inconvenient as it was to have to coordinate the timing of my meals with someone else, there was something almost pleasant about eating with someone on purpose. Usually, I just took an empty seat at random; if anything, I went out of my way to avoid people who might try to engage me in conversation. Two meals in a row with Ryan wasn't bad at all. I could get used to this routine, I decided, as I followed my barefoot roommate up the carpeted stairs.

As he opened the fire door, he peered out, then said over his shoulder, "Just what I was talking about last night. Vulnerability."

A dozen of our neighbors were in the middle of a shirtless water fight. From the reactions of the men whenever a squirt touched their bare skin, I got the feeling their pistols were loaded with ice water.

I didn't really know any of the guys; they were just faces I'd passed in the hall these last few weeks. I didn't doubt that Ryan knew them all by now. I did recognize Eric, who just an hour before had taunted Ryan about his bare feet as we'd passed his lunch table on the way to the serving line. The huge jock, whose shaggy hair was as black as his abundant chest hair, was standing over two men cowering together on the floor – the stocky redhead and slimly muscular Latino who I vaguely remembered were in the room next to ours. They were huddled together as if trying to minimize the surface area of bare skin exposed to their opponent's water pistol. They were unarmed; two pistols lay on the floor out of reach, as if they'd been kicked away by Eric's huge bare foot.

Someone shot Eric in the back, and he whirled around to return fire. Ryan took advantage of this by creeping up behind him and lunging forward at the last minute to wrap his long arms around the big jock, lacing his finger together to pin those muscular arms to his side. Our next-door neighbors quickly helped each other to their feet and grabbed their own weapons. Ryan spun Eric around, and they began spraying down the pinned man's bare chest. The big jock howled.

I saw an opening and quietly slipped into my room. I find crowds overwhelming, even less rowdy ones than this. Besides, for the moment I had the only key. It was rare to have the room to myself and know no one could walk in on me, and it had been a week since I'd last had a chance to jerk off. For some reason, I felt a powerful urge to do so right then.

# # # # #

I was finished and had the door unlocked before Ryan returned and peeked off his sopping wet shirt. Twenty minutes later, there was a knock at the door. Ryan seemed to expect it.

"You going to be around? Armando and Brady are going to Eric's room with me to back me up. I don't think we'll have any trouble getting all my clothes back. He knows the three of us can kick his ass as easily as we did in that water fight." He stopped to pull on a fresh shirt then opened the door, where our neighbors were waiting for him. They were the ones I'd seen cowering at Eric's feet, and had also put shirts on.

"Good luck," I mumbled, turning back to my textbook.

But once again, his return was signaled not by the rattle of a key in the lock, but by a knock at the door.

"Who is it?" I called.

"Dude, please promise not to laugh this time."

Summoning all my self-control, I opened the door.

"Jack and Gus were there to back him up," he explained sheepishly as Brady and Armando followed him in. Brady's legs were even paler than his chest and had a few freckles. His blush went right down to his upper chest. Armando's white briefs contrasted appealingly with his light brown skin. If his face and chest were as flushed as his pale roommate's, it wasn't as obvious. Speaking of obvious, I noticed that his tight briefs didn't hide the size of his package as well as the baggy striped boxers his roommate wore, or the solid gray ones my own roommate was wearing.

# # # # #

They ordered out for pizza because Ryan's clothes wouldn't have fit either Armando or Brady, and anyway, he was down to one pair of jeans and one pair of dress slacks until he did laundry. Mine would have fit no better, and I didn't offer. I did go down to meet the delivery guy at the front door and brought their large pizza up to them. It smelled enticing; I knew I liked pizza because I'd had it many times with my family as a child and teenager. But I went back downstairs to have dinner on my own, not being rich enough to pass up a prepaid meal. I gave them the receipt, and they promised to pay me back as soon as they recovered their wallets.

Ryan liked to keep an ice chest filled with cold beer, although he went through maybe three cans a weekend and I'd always declined when he offered me one. Tonight, I came back to discover they'd gone through most of his supply to have with the pizza, judging by the empties scattered across the floor and the good spirits they were in. Such good spirits, in fact, that I had to go the library to get some studying done.

# # # # #

They were still there when I returned. And when I came back from the shower, they were just finishing the last of the beer. I stood around in my bathrobe and pajamas, hoping they'd get the hint that it was getting late.

Ryan, at least, finally noticed. "Uh, dude ... Can we ask another favor?"

"Oh. They're locked out of their room. Right?"

"I guess I could sleep on the floor, so they can have my bunk."

There wasn't much floor space that wasn't occupied by the bunk beds, two desks, chairs, and our foot lockers. I was afraid I'd trip over him in the dark when I got up to take a leak. Anyway, I knew I should help them out, even though they'd gotten themselves into this mess. Not that I was at all comfortable with the idea of sharing my narrow bunk, but I didn't see any good options. "One of them can bunk with each of us. That way no one has to take the floor."

"No way," Armando said, his speech slightly slurred. "If I gotta sleep right next to someone in a tiny bed, it's gonna be my buddy." He threw a brown arm around his roommate's freckled shoulders.

Ryan looked at me expectantly. I told him, "You're welcome to share my bunk, unless you'd rather sleep on the floor."

"It does have a carpet," Ryan said doubtfully, "but whenever I crash on someone's floor I always wake up with a sore back. So, yeah. Thanks. Thanks for putting up with all this, man."

"You get the wall. I may need to get up."

"Fine. I think I'll turn in now. It's been an exhausting day." He hoisted himself onto my bunk as easily as if he did it every night.

Armando and Brady showed no signs that they were going to turn in anytime soon. I realized I was waiting for them to lie down, so I could turn out the lights before I undressed – which would consist of removing my bathrobe, since I'd already changed into my pajamas in the shower stall. Even I knew that I was being pathologically shy: these guys had been stripped to their shorts against their will and were hiding out in my room, and here I was, hesitating to let them see me in my pajamas! Like they would care! I forced myself to remove the bathrobe and hang it up.

"He's got a really hairy chest," Brady observed drunkenly. "Almost as hairy as that guy Eric's."

My face felt hot. I should never have stopped wearing a T-shirt under my pajamas, the way I had the first week of school. But it was too hot for that in the room, and after I'd gotten more comfortable with Ryan, I'd gotten out of that habit.

Climbing onto my narrow bunk next to Ryan, I found I had a choice. I could lie precariously near the edge. I could ask Ryan to roll onto his side – he was on his back, with his eyes closed and his face relaxed. I could grab his shoulder to roll him over myself. Or I could sleep so close to him that I could feel the heat of his bare skin right through my flannel pajamas. I finally opted for the last choice.

They turned out the light soon afterward, but it took awhile for me to get to sleep. The occasional muffled laughter from the lower bunk didn't help, nor the whispers of "Dude! Cut it out!"

# # # # #

Some guys must have bigger bladders or something. After all that beer, Armando and Brady and Ryan had made one trip to the bathroom earlier that evening, trading off Ryan's robe, and they were set for the night. I'd had one soda with dinner, and I woke up in the middle of the night with a full bladder. As usual. What wasn't usual was that my roommate was in my bunk, and had snuggled even closer against me as we slept. I groggily remembered that there was a perfectly good explanation for him being there, but that didn't explain how my pajama top had gotten unbuttoned. We were lying skin to skin, facing each other, our bare chests pressed together.

35

I recoiled and pushed him onto his back, then regretted not moving more gently so as not to wake him up. One of us had unbuttoned my pajamas, and if it wasn't him or he didn't remember doing it, it would be doubly embarrassing to have him wake up just now.

But he didn't. He hadn't been exaggerating about being a heavy sleeper. For a moment, despite the pressure from my bladder, I lay there and watched his bare chest and stomach slowly rising and falling, right there within easy reach. It was an interesting feeling. He really did look vulnerable in his sleep. I'd never had someone display that much trust in me, especially so casually. On the other hand, it was awkward sharing a bed, especially since I found that my morning hard-on had arrived a few hours early. In fact, despite having jerked off once that day, I felt the urge again. There was no way I could relieve it with three other guys in the room. I actually considered using one of the shower stalls for that, after I'd finished the more pressing business; it was unlikely anyone would come in and hear me at this hour.

After buttoning up, I quietly swung myself out of bed. Glancing at the lower bunk, I saw that Brady had fallen asleep with his head pillowed on Armando's brown chest, which made me feel just a little bit less like a freak. I quietly put on my robe, eased the door open and shut, and padded down the hall to the bathroom. Standing at the urinal, I had to spend several minutes thinking pure thoughts before my erection subsided enough for me to pee.

# # # # #

I woke up to find my own head pillowed on my roommate's chest, with my lips so close to his armpit that I stirred the hairs with each breath. I watched this in sleepy fascination, feeling warm and relaxed. And even though everyone knows that a man's odor is supposed to be disgusting, to my surprise I didn't mind it at all: a musky kind of scent, almost pleasant, despite the fact that I was about as close to his armpit as it was possible to get.

Gently, I levered myself up before our guests could see us like this. Fortunately, Ryan once again didn't wake up, even when I swung out of bed. It was time for breakfast, so I gathered a fresh set of clothes and went down the hall to change in the bathroom. It was an unnecessary precaution; when I came back to drop off my robe and pajamas, the guys were all still asleep. I didn't try to wake them. One of them would have been difficult to

36

rouse, and the other two of them couldn't very well have come to breakfast half naked.

When I returned after breakfast and some errands, I found Ryan alone and fully dressed. "Where are your friends?"

"Back in their room. They didn't have to wait until Monday after all. You know George, that wiry little guy downstairs?"

I shook my head.

"Well, I remembered seeing him climbing the rope in the gym like a monkey, and got an idea. Stu from down the hall works on stage crew and had access to a supply of rope, so we lowered George down from Willie's room – you know, on the third floor? He lives directly above Armando and Brady. And their window was unlocked. Hey, thanks for putting up with the crowding."

"S'okay."

# # # # #

After getting his key replaced and buying a new pair of tennis shoes, Ryan started spending even more time out socializing and less in the room. I had the impression he was hanging out a lot with Armando and Brady, in particular. But although I saw less of him during the day, we started having long talks in the evening between getting ready for bed and actually turning in. Well, mostly I let him talk. And since he was bare-chested, sometimes even in just his boxers, it seem natural for me to start casually leaving my pajama top unbuttoned. By the next week, I was leaving it off entirely. Two shirtless roommates shooting the breeze late into the night. It felt good. It felt intimate. Ryan acted like it was no big deal, and I tried not to let on how daring it felt to me.

One night, after getting up to empty my bladder, I heard a strange sound when I turned on the lights in the bathroom. After relieving myself, I went looking for it. It was coming from around the corner, where the shower stalls were. As I rounded the corner, I was startled to get a glimpse of naked flesh through wide-open shower curtains. Embarrassed, I ducked back. But I was curious, so I cautiously took a second look. There was a naked guy in there, all right, but he wasn't showering, or even toweling off. He was kneeling, and his hands were bound above his head by thick ropes tied around the shower pipe. He was blindfolded and gagged. I had no trouble recognizing him, though. First of all, I was pretty sure there were only three guys on our floor with shoulders that broad and muscles that big. And only two of those were clean-shaven or had black hair, and since this guy was clearly not Asian, that narrowed it down to one. Besides, I'd seen that pattern of black chest hair over chiseled pecs, and that trail of hair spilling down over rippling abs, once before: during the water fight I'd witnessed. Even with his blue eyes covered, I knew it was my roommate's archenemy, Eric.

My first thought was to pretend I hadn't seen him. He'd never know I could have helped him and didn't; maybe he didn't even know he'd been spotted. Instead, I went up to him and removed the gag.

"Whoever you are, please, let me go. Or are you one of those bastards, back for more fun? Either way, don't leave me like this. I'll do anything."

I couldn't believe it. Had my roommate and his buddies actually managed to reduce the big, gloating jock to this? Or had he pissed someone else off? I didn't dare ask. I wanted to remain anonymous.

The trail of hair continued all the way down to merge with his pubes, I noted. His armpit hair was thick and black, but had an almost feathery texture. It looked softer than mine. Curious, I stroked it with my fingers.

"No, no, please. Not that again!" he said, choking back laughter. "Please! I'll do anything. I mean it. Anything." And to my amazement, he bent his head forward and nosed my robe open. His face was just about at crotch level. He began to nuzzle my bare belly. For some reason, I let him. Then his teeth found the waistband of my pajamas, and he started tugging them down. I stepped back.

"Where you going, dude?" he said. "Let me get those boxers off. I said I'd do anything if you let me go, and I meant it. You know you want it. I could feel how hard you are already."

The right thing to do would be to untie him and run away before he could get the blindfold off, not to take advantage of a helpless man. But how often in one lifetime does a guy like me find a musclebound jock kneeling naked and helpless at his feet, offering him a blow job? He was right about my having an erection just at the thought of it. He was getting hard himself, I saw. So I pulled down my pajamas before he could realize what they were; for all I knew, I might be the only man on the floor who slept in pajamas. I had stopped wearing shorts underneath by this time. I

38

stepped forward, letting my cock slap against his unshaven cheek. As soon as he felt it, he reared his head back and got his mouth around it.

And I discovered instantly why other guys talk so much about wanting a blow job. The feeling of warmth that enveloped me, the caress of his tongue, was like nothing I'd ever felt before. The physical sensation alone was incredible. The added knowledge that a big jock who could have wiped up the floor with me was submitting to me made it the most intense experience I could remember having. Next thing I knew, my right hand was around his thick sweaty neck, controlling his rhythm as he slid back and forth along my shaft, and my left hand was squeezing his huge but immobilized biceps.

In seconds, I felt a climax building. I let go of him and stepped back, shooting my load all over his chest, the thick ropes of fluid tangling with his chest hair. He moaned and slumped in his bonds, his chest expanding with each ragged breath.

I stood there a minute, carefully making no sound except my own heavy breathing: voicing even a grunt might identify me. Then I pulled my pajama bottoms back up and drew my robe closed around my bare torso.

"Dude, please. I'm begging you, man. Don't leave me here for the other guys to find, with your cum drying on my chest. Let me go."

So I worked loose the knot binding one of his wrists. As soon as I saw it coming loose, I turned and ran.

# # # # #

I couldn't get back to sleep at all that night. I lay awake worrying about what Eric would do if he figured out it was me. The guy had locked Ryan outside in nothing but his boxers just for making him walk back to his room in a towel. What would he do to punish me for making me suck my dick?

When the sky started turning light, I realized I'd soon have to get up for my early-morning class, so I decided to give up on sleep, get some coffee, and study for an hour before getting breakfast and going to class.

The next night, it caught up with me. I fell asleep at my desk, trying to concentrate on a problem set, woke up to use the bathroom – this time without any surprise sexual encounters – and fell deeply asleep as soon as I climbed into my bunk. I had no morning classes the next day, so I didn't set my alarm. It was Ryan who woke me up, by repeating my name several times in an urgent tone. He probably figured I'd freak out if he shook my bare shoulder. He was probably right.

"Dude, I hate to bother you, but I need your help."

He wouldn't explain, but once I was dressed, he led me next door and showed me. "I'm afraid to cut them loose without someone to help support them. They might swing down and crack their heads, or dislocate a shoulder or something."

"My shoulders are killing me already," Brady moaned.

"Just get us loose," Armando grunted. "We've been hanging here all night."

I'd never been in Armando and Brady's room before. They'd modified the standard floor plan our room had come with. They'd built a sturdy wooden loft, with both desks side by side underneath, and both mattresses pushed together on top, providing the equivalent of a king-sized bed, and leaving plenty of floor space. That explained how they'd had room for parties. I'd heard music through our shared wall a few times, and Ryan had sometimes attended.

Armando and Brady had been suspended spread-eagle under their loft, above their desks, their hands and feet secured to the four posts of the loft with big wads of silver duct tape. Armando was hanging face down above his roommate. They hadn't been taken by surprise in their sleep; both men were fully dressed in jeans and long-sleeve shirts, although Brady's pullover shirt had gotten pulled up, completely exposing his pale belly.

I ducked between the men's outstretched arms and grabbed Brady by the armpits, taking some of the weight off his shoulders while Ryan peeled away layers of tape from one foot. I was being forced into more physical contact with other guys this past week than my whole life – without even counting the encounter in the shower stall. In fact, I was looking right into the open neck of Armando's button-down shirt, which had enough slack in it that I could see the entire length of his compactly-muscled chest, all the way down to his navel. And I was getting a good whiff of Brady's musky scent, a not-unpleasant odor much like Ryan's yet different.

Finally, a bare foot was revealed, pink from having tape ripped off it. Once it was free, things got even more awkward as Brady's leg swung down and his weight was supported by only three limbs. Ryan franticly worked to free the other foot as I struggled to support as much of Brady's weight as I could. Then we gently lowered him down. The tape around his wrists was stuck to his sleeve, not to bare skin, so he was able to pull his arms out of his sleeves and wriggle out of his shirt, leaving it dangling from the posts when his head came free.

My back was starting to complain, so we switched places. Brady and Ryan each grabbed one of Armando's armpits while I worked to free one of his feet.

"Who did this to you?" Ryan asked.

"Who do you think? Eric and his two cronies," Brady said.

"They got us good this time," Armando admitted sheepishly, as I freed a second bare foot while keeping the first one trapped under my arm. Now only his arms were bound.

"Well, it's not like we weren't asking for it, after what we did to him," Ryan said.

As I lowered Armando's legs to the ground, I privately wondered why they'd tried to get even, if they knew things were going to keep escalating.

"Thanks, buddy. Could you also unbutton my shirt?" Armando asked me.

Hesitating, I glanced at Ryan, but he was busy massaging Brady's bare shoulders. So I unbuttoned Armando's shirt and pushed it off his shoulders to help him tug his upraised arms free. I liked the way he smelled, too. I could probably tell these three guys apart in a blindfold test now.

"I guess they'll be coming for me next," Ryan said, sounding more excited than scared.

Brady looked at me. When I nervously looked away, I noticed that Armando was also looking at me. "You might be safer crashing here with us until they're done with Ryan," Brady said.

"Yeah, our bed easily holds three people," his roommate added earnestly. Then, with a wicked grin, he began to add, "Although usually …"

"Dude!" Brady broke in. "Can't you tell he's embarrassed enough as it is?" He tried to put a hand on my shoulder, but I turned away and headed back to my room.

# # # # #

I slept in my own bunk that night, of course. I was awakened in the middle of the night by the sound of Ryan's key turning in the lock. It wasn't unusual for him to come home late from a party. Only, now that I was awake, I remembered he'd gone to bed at the same time I did. Maybe he was coming back from the bathroom, although I hadn't heard him leave.

Then the light was switched on. I opened my eyes, and in the blinding light I saw three figures entering my room. By the time my eyes had adjusted, one of them had grabbed my wrists in his meaty hands, pinning them against my blanket-covered chest, and the other two were hauling my sleeping roommate out of the lower bunk. I recognized one of those two as Eric, looking decidedly more in control of the situation than the last time I'd gotten a good look at him, and I guessed the other two thugs were his roommates. I'd seen them around on our floor.

"Man, this guy can sleep through anything," the man holding Ryan's feet said. He was a beefy guy with light brown hair and a fringe of beard on his chin.

"What do you want us to do with his roommate?" asked the big Asian guy pinning me. He forced my nearest arm above my head. My struggles only resulted in the blanket slipping down a few inches. I was acutely aware that my armpit was completely exposed, and that the humiliation Eric planned on paying Ryan back for had apparently included tickling.

"Nothing," Eric told him. "He's a noncombatant."

"We should at least tie him up," he argued. "You can't expect him to just lie here and watch the whole thing."

"Yeah," Eric's bearded roommate said, helping to spread out Ryan's limp form on the carpet. "We'd never sit by while someone ganged up on you."

"Where were you when I needed you? Uh, during the water fight, I mean."

"Wait. I've got an idea." Letting go of my still-sleeping roommate's feet, Eric's roommate got up and stepped over to the foot of my bed. He pulled the blanket up and grabbed my ankles. "I heard he made two trips to rescue Ryan the night you locked him out in his boxers, when he could have just lent him his jacket. Why do you suppose that is?"

"That's right," said the guy pinning my arms, "and have you noticed how he always wraps his robe really tight after a shower, like he doesn't even want the guys to see his chest hair?" He let go of my far wrist and began toying with the chest hair that was now peeking out over the edge of the blanket. I couldn't believe this was happening. And while I was trying to push his hand away, his roommate grabbed the cuffs of my pajama legs and started pulling them toward him. I felt the elastic waistband slide down my lower belly, stretch to pass over my hips, catch on my slightly hard cock and flip past it, then go slack as it continued unimpeded down my thighs. I felt the flannel sliding down my legs and the rough texture of the wool blanket touching my crotch and my cock. And there wasn't much I could do about it, with two much stronger guys on me and Eric crouching by my roommate watching.

"Is he naked under there?" asked the guy holding my pajamas in his fist.

To my horror, his roommate stopped playing with my chest hair and lifted the edge of the blanket to peer down the full length of my body. "Yep! He's naked."

"Good. I'll bet he won't give us any trouble."

"Gus, get back down here and help me hold Ryan for when he wakes up. Jack, see if there's any ice in that ice chest in the corner."

Gus covered my bare feet back up and returned to holding my roommate's. His Asian buddy let go of my wrist and stepped away, allowing me to pull the blanket up to my chin. He stole my towel from its hook and found some ice, which he handed to Eric, then took his place holding Ryan's wrists. I watched helplessly as my half-naked roommate was held spread-eagle on the carpet before my eyes, with his archenemy crouching at his side with ice in his hand.

Ryan could sleep through an amazing amount of noise and manhandling, but a handful of crushed ice on his bare stomach woke him up instantly. He screamed and arched his back, writhing in his captor's grasp. Eric ground the ice into his belly for a few seconds more as he whimpered helplessly. When he relented, Ryan went limp, breathing hard, his eyes wide. Then he glanced in my direction.

"Your roommate can't help you," Gus said. "I don't think he'll come down without these." He brandished my pajamas like a trophy.

43

"If he does, he just going to wind up stretched out beside you, naked," Jack said with satisfaction.

"Just leave him alone," Ryan pleaded. "He's not part of this. Do anything you want to me."

"Oh, I intend to," Eric said, selecting a fresh shard of ice and holding it threateningly just above my roommate's nipple.

# # # # #

When they left an hour later, Ryan lay on the floor for a full minute, getting his breathing under control, before he finally pulled his boxers back up.

"I can't believe he actually put ice on your balls. That must have ..."

"Dude! Do me a favor. Don't tell anyone. OK?"

"And then, when he ran it up and down the underside of your ..."

"Especially not that part!" he said, sitting up and retrieving my pajamas. "People will think I was enjoying it."

"Were you?" I asked, as he stood up.

"Swear you won't say anything," he demanded, holding my pajamas just out of reach.

Promise not to talk to other people? That must seem to a big sacrifice to someone like him. "Don't worry, I can keep a secret."

"Even Armando and Brady. All they need to know is that we're going to pay those guys back but good."

# # # # #

The next afternoon, Eric came home from classes and found the lights off in his room and the shades drawn. Usually his roommates would be home at this hour. While he was groping for the light switch, Ryan jumped on his back, and Armando and Brady each grabbed an arm. I threw my shoulders into his knees from behind, and he collapsed under Ryan's weight.

"You guys are so dead!" Eric said. "My buddies will be home any minute. Let me go, and I'll make them go easy on you."

44

Wordlessly, I hit the lights, and let him see that his roommates were in no position to help him.

Jack and Gus were trussed up side by side on the floor with silver duct tape. We'd stripped them both to their boxers and wound more tape several times around their chests, binding them together. Heavy-duty ropes were tied around Jack's right wrist and Gus's left wrist and secured to the head and foot of the upper bunk, leaving their outer arms outstretched. Jack's left arm and Gus's right were taped to each other with more duct tape, so were their left and right legs. Their outer legs were taped to the carpet at their ankles and shins, leaving their crotches exposed, so they'd feel that much more vulnerable. They weren't going anywhere. More tape across their mouths had prevented them from warning their buddy of the ambush.

"You're a dead man, Ryan! Getting back at me is one thing, but hurting my roommates ..."

"Don't worry," Ryan said, "we haven't hurt them. Although you're going to."

"No way! I'd never hurt those guys. Do your worst, but you can't make me."

"You'll hurt them after we leave," Armando explained. "Unless we stay and watch. See, Gus here has a fair amount of chest hair, almost as much as you. Well, he's not going to have quite as much when you get done ripping off all this tape. And once you've ripped that off, you've still got to do his legs."

"And now you're going to do the same to me?"

"Worse," Ryan said. "We taped them up, so we have our hands free to work on you while they watch."

Eric struggled, but all he could do was kick the air, since Armando and Brady were leaning on his wrists and Ryan was kneeling on his chest, probably grinding the buttons of his shirt into his skin with his knees.

"Get his shoes off before he kicks someone," Ryan told me over his shoulder. So I carefully approached from the side and grabbed an ankle, unlacing and tugging off one of the huge shoes.

"Let's take off his belt," Brady suggested, "and tie it around his ankles."

We stretched him out where his helpless roommates would have a good view. Then I opened the ice chest we'd brought over and handed Ryan a big sliver of ice wrapped in the T-shirt we'd taken off Gus.

"Tell us where you stashed our clothes and keys," he said, holding the ice shard against the big man's throat while Armando and Brady pinned his wrists.

"Never! Do your worst."

I unbuttoned Eric's shirt, and Ryan traced an icy line from the hollow of the helpless jock's throat down the length of his sternum. By the time he reached the belly, the big man was actually whimpering.

We taped his forearms to each other, above his head, so we could all work on him at once. Ryan peeled the white athletic socks off his big feet and slid thin chips of ice between his toes, while Armando and Brady took turns probing his belly button with a rounded, melting shard.

"They're in the hamper in the corner!" he finally cried. "In a plastic bag at the bottom."

After Armando and Brady had dug through the whole hamper and scattered its contents on the floor, Eric snickered, "I hope you liked searching through my sweaty gym clothes."

I had a wicked idea and worked up enough courage to lean close to my roommate and whisper it in his ear. Ryan casually put his hand on my shoulder as he listened, like it was the most natural gesture in the world.

"Great idea!" he said, squeezing my shoulder. "Guys, pick out his two sweatiest T-shirts and rub them in his roommates' faces."

"No, come on! Leave my roommates out of this. Whatever you want to do, do it to me."

"OK. Deal. So, have they ever seen you stark naked?" Ryan asked him tauntingly, fingering the button on his jeans.

"Sure."

"They have?" Ryan was unprepared for that. "Well, but I'll bet they've never seen it hard."

"No ..." Eric groaned. I couldn't tell if that was an answer, or a plea.

"What? Really?" Armando said, while Brady said, "They haven't?"

They soon would. Ryan was probably thinking we'd have to slowly tease an erection from the jock with our hands. But once we got his pants around his knees, it was clear he already had a raging hard-on, even before we pulled his boxers clear of it.

"Look at that. We'll have to get some ice on that, to bring down the swelling."

Eric moaned and writhed in our grasp.

Ryan knelt at his side, leaned down almost nose to nose, and took Eric's face in his hands. "Tell us where you hid our clothes."

"Lower right drawer of the middle desk," he said, defeated. "Your keys are in the top drawer."

This proved to be true. "Now, with that load off our minds, we can finish paying him back at our leisure," Ryan said.

"Noooo!"

Ten minutes later, as Armando and Brady inched ice cubes up his hairy inner thighs, closer and closer to his balls, while I combed his armpit hair with a broken ice cube and Ryan teased chest hair away to expose a nipple, Eric finally cried out, "No more! Please! Anything but that!"

"Anything?" asked Armando tauntingly.

"Come here," Eric said. Armando crawled forward and let him whisper something in his ear. He looked shocked, then broke into a grin.

"All of us? You're on. Except for one part: You have to do it right here, in front of your roommates."

# # # # #

Armando's was the first uncircumcised penis I'd ever seen. At least, the first one I'd ever gotten a good look at. And I had no qualms about looking at it: Armando's obviously wanted us all to witness Eric, now kneeling completely naked and bound hand and foot with duct tape, take his still-soft cock in his mouth. I was rock-hard myself, just from the sight of our vanquished foe kneeling submissively at my ally's feet – naked, because I had started the stripping process when I removed his shoes and unbuttoned his shirt, and had later helped to remove the last of his clothes; and helpless because I had helped tape his ankles and wrists. Actually, I'd had an erection continuously since we'd first gotten Jack and Gus stripped and at our mercy, but now it was almost painful, trapped there in my jeans, and I almost wished I'd been bold enough to volunteer to be first in line. It didn't help that the soft sounds both men were making brought back the recent memory of my own first experience, or that my own remembered pleasure was now reflected in Armando's face.

I learned something when Eric briefly released Armando's cock to lap at his balls: an erect cock looks about the same whether it's circumcised or not.

When he finally climaxed, Armando did what had never occurred to me to do: he ejaculated right into Eric's mouth. I could tell when it happened by the way Armando moaned and by the way the big jock began sucking more frantically. I put my hand on Ryan's shoulder and whispered a lewd suggestion, and he told Eric, "Be sure it all gets into your mouth. If you miss one drop, we're rubbing it into Gus's chest hair."

Brady stepped up to his roommate's side as he was shooting the last of his load, and put his arm around his shoulders. "And be sure to swallow real good, too. It's my turn next, and I don't want my buddy's cum all over my dick."

"Wouldn't be the first time," Armando snickered.

"Dude!" Brady protested.

Brady's circumcised cock was completely flaccid when he first took it out, but it swelled quickly as Eric's tongue teased it. A moment after the big man took his cock into his mouth, Brady said softly, "Whoa. He's way better at this than any chick we ever got to do this for us."

After watching his roommate climax into the jock's mouth, and then inspecting his buddy's shaft to satisfy himself that Eric had licked it completely clean, Armando turned to me and Ryan. "Which of you wants to be next?"

"I don't know if I'm really into this, guys," Ryan said uncertainly.

"What are you suggesting?" Armando demanded. "That we're 'really' into this in a way that you're not?"

"You don't have to be into it," Brady said, still catching his breath. "The point isn't to enjoy it. The point is to humiliate him."

"OK. When you put it that way ..."

But after five minutes of apparently skillful licking and sucking that should have brought any cock to full attention, my roommate's organ was still soft. It was the first time I'd seen it soft, come to think of it; the one other time I'd seen it, it had been erect by the time they'd taken his boxers off and had still been half-erect when he finally pulled them up.

"Guys? This really isn't doing anything for me." He stepped back and pulled his pants up.

"Oh, no you don't! He agreed to do all of us, and he's not getting off that easy." They pinned Ryan's arms behind his back and yanked his pants down again. To my surprise, his cock was finally getting hard now, even before Eric's tongue touched it again. He struggled in his buddies' arms, breathing hard, but it was over in seconds. He moaned and went limp as he spent himself, letting his buddies hold him up while the kneeling jock sucked him dry.

"That goes for you, too," Brady told me. "Do we need to hold you too?"

"No," I said, stepping up and unzipping my fly. Better that than have them pull down my pants.

"Wow, he's already hard. Look at the size of that. Bigger than any of us!"

My face feeling as hot as my cock, I hid it in Eric's mouth as quickly as I could, and made him take it all at once, so that his nose was buried in my pubes. After a couple of seconds, he pulled off and stared up at me in amazement. "You!?!"

"What's he mean?" Ryan asked.

"Shut up and get to work," I told Eric, surprising everyone, including myself.

The big jock grinned up at me. "Yes, sir."

I kneaded his meaty shoulders in a steady rhythm, and he sucked me in obedience to the rhythm I set. I'd been hard for so long that I would probably have exploded in his mouth immediately, but I was inhibited by all these guys watching. I'd never even dared masturbate with someone in earshot before, and here my roommate and his buddies – our buddies, I realized with a certain warm satisfaction – were watching closely, not to mention Eric's own gagged and bound, half-naked roommates. It took many long minutes of agonizing pleasure for my muscular sex slave to build me up toward a climax.

Sure, we spent half of the next weekend lying in a closet in one big naked human bundle of duct tape, with Ryan's nose in my armpit and mine stuck between Armando and Brady's pressed-together crotches. But it was totally worth it. And we're already planning something big to pay those three jocks back.

DONG PONG
By R. W. Clinger

Jase and I were not playing a normal game of Beer Pong at Zeta Psi. In fact, I was blown away by the game's odd rules. Of course, the ping pong table was set up with plastic cups formed into a triangle on either end. Both bare-chested teams had a single plastic ball each and ...

Rule 1: You miss a cup, you have to lick a frat guy's nipple and armpit.

Rule 2: You miss two cups, a frat guy loses his pants and you have to lick his navel and take a whiff of his V-patch of curly pubes.

Rule 3: You miss three cups, you have to suck a frat guy's cock and balls.

Rule 4: You miss four cups, you have to lick a frat guy's ass.

Rule 5: You miss five cups, you end up in a closet with a guy of your choice, and you get an ass-ram.

Rule 6: Everyone drinks. Anyone who plays cannot have an empty hand. If a player is caught without a drink in his hand, they end up in the closet with a guy of their choice, and a condom in hand for a rough ass-pounding.

"Pretty Boy, it's your turn," brutish Ginger pushed his elbow into my bare side and about knocked me over. Cheap beer spilled out of my plastic Dixie cup and rolled down and over my plane of chiseled and smooth chest, into my jeans and cotton Aussiebums.

To my surprise, an inebriated Melvin "Ginger" Reinholt (adorable red-colored hair, piercing Mediterranean-green eyes, body of plated steel, tall as a New York City skyscraper) reached two fingers against my chest, collected the few drops of beer, stuffed the fingers into his mouth, and said in a rather drunken manner, "Chest-yum."

Okay. That was interesting, and weird. Zeta Psi was a straight fraternity with a slew of guys who just happened to like the opposite sex. What the fuck was going on? Was it the start-off season of Gay Days, which I didn't know about? Was it some kind of gag they were all playing on me, even if they didn't know I was the only queer among them? Whatever. I could work out the details later. For now, I had to take my turn and play some pong.

"Hit it, Pretty Boy!" the group of bare-chested hotties chanted around me as I geometrically calculated my aim for my ball to land in one of the plastic cups.

Pretty Boy. How did I get that nickname among my nicely built brothers? Each of them considered me a model of sorts because of my blond hair, boyishly pale face, purple-blue eyes, and medium-sized chest on my five-eleven frame. I was Pretty Boy, all the way, without a doubt.

My eyes reviewed the college dudes watching my every move: muscled guys with tattoos, jocks with firm nipples, twinks with pale-colored skin and sexy-weak looking frames, two bears, an Italian guy with Mafia good looks, two Sioux Indians with New Moon bods, a tasty Cuban, and three chiseled Jamaicans. All of them coaxed me to bounce a ping pong ball into a cup and score for my team of eight young men.

"Do it!" Ginger yelled beside me.

"Come on, Pretty Boy!" Jase called out on the opposite side of the table, cheering me on in hopes that I would score a point for our team.

The tension rose to a nail-biting moment. Carefully, I released the ping pong ball from my right index finger and thumb with a little force. The ball bounced once off the table, rimmed one of the Dixie cups … circled its lip … and rolled onto the table, and eventually fell to the floor.

I was a lousy player at Beer Pong. The worst. And now, I knew I was in trouble. Which guy would I have to lick?

Ginger was beautifully blitzed beside me. Within a few seconds, he leashed his hulking arm around my center, manipulated his firm nipple to my lips, and informed, "Pay your dues and lick it, pal."

And so it was done. I extended my tongue and licked his pointed nipple, which caused a semi-erection in my jeans that I had to conceal in front of the straight frat guys. Ginger's nipple tasted sweet and sweaty, which I sort of liked.

"The pit now!" One of the Sioux Indians yelled from across the room. "Lick his pit; Pretty Boy!"

Ginger lifted his masculine-scented arm of sweat and grime. I had to stand on my toes a bit to reach his pit, managed a strong whiff, and extended my tongue. Lips and nose and chin met the fabric of his underarm and bathed in its strong man-rank and dampness.

In truth, I could have shot a load of cream into my jeans by that intoxicating smell, and fell under Ginger's armpit spell and overwhelming frat boy-smell. I wanted my face buried against his hairy underarm for the rest of my college career, infatuated with the wrestler's stench.

"He loves it! Look at him fucking go!" someone roared, which prompted me to unfortunately back away from Ginger's succulent pit and allow our game to proceed.

The frat brats were athletes by nature. They were young men who knew how to play Beer Pong with top-notch skill, which included Jase and Ginger. Even when those dudes were totally inebriated, every single damn one of them could land their ball into a plastic cup.

Approximately ten minutes after my nipple and armpit snack, Ginger banged his elbow into my toned gut and informed, "It's your turn again, Pretty Boy."

Seconds later, I calculated my ping pong ball toss, gently released it forward, watched it bounce off two cups, and …

"That's two misses!" some dude on the other team hollered at the top of his lungs, obviously thrilled at my loss. "Pretty Boy is going to be a fucking licker!"

As my destiny was called out for the room to hear, I prepared myself to lick one of my brothers' navels and V-area of pubic tangles; the appropriate definition of a licker among our group. Helplessly, I prayed not to sport a boner and become excited by such a risqué event, since I was not out to the fraternity. But, selfishly, I wanted nothing more than to feed my hunger and devour all of those tasty frat brats, one by one.

To my surprise, Jase stepped around the ping pong table, casually moved up to me, began to unbuckle his Levi's, and announced for all to hear, "I'll do it."

Hoots and hollers of utter enthusiasm echoed off the basement's walls. The young men became crazy-wild because a straight guy nicknamed Pretty Boy had to sniff some dude-navel and triangular man-hair between a frat guy's toned legs.

As Jase released his uncut hose of six floppy inches, I desirably studied him from head to toe: twenty years old, five-ten frame, 179 pounds of frat boy muscle, soft-brown eyes, Irish-sloped nose, a dimple in his left cheek, rose-red lips, broad shoulders, tangles of brown hair between his pecs, more tangles of brown hair beneath his puckered navel, no underwear, thick thighs, hairless balls like pendulums. Jase was beautiful, in every aspect of the word. He was my personal friend, one of the best, and I was going to taste him for the very first time.

As I fell to my knees, prepared to take a lick of his sexy-hot navel, he winked at me and started putting on a show for the rest of the fraternity. He warned, "Don't bite me, fucker ... I will knock your face off."

The testosterone-filled brothers woofed and yelled with excelled gratification. Some did high fives while others merely raised their beer-filled plastic cups to toast that desirable moment of my face meeting Jase's skin.

When my lips parted and my tongue stretched out of my mouth, I instantly grew granite-firm behind my denim. Pre-bubbles of ooze leaked out of my shaft and decorated the area between my chiseled thighs as my tongue greeted my friend's fuzzy navel. Elation was discovered and offered unlimited waves of guy-with-guy pleasure. The boner inside my jeans wanted nothing less than to be stroked or sucked by one of the frat brats, ready to explode its pent-up juice.

More hoots and hollers of man-joy flooded the basement. Screeching whistles from rowdy scholars echoed in all of our ears. One of the brothers yelled, "Whiff his patch!" while someone else roared, "Eat him up!"

And so it was done, fulfilling my deed in that ruthless game of what I would end up calling Dong Pong instead of Beer Pong. I ran my face down and along Jase's firm abs and discreetly flicked my tongue in and out, which none of the frats saw. Powerlessly, I absorbed his savory sweat and stink and sweetness, taking all of his masculine niceness into my system. My lips and chin dragged against the soft springs of hair that made up his treasure trail and fell relentlessly into his tangles of V-bristles above his still-limp rod. Pleasantly, I inhaled Jase's desirable aroma in full, and became weak and dizzy, almost falling to the cement floor.

To no avail, I caught my balance by clutching Jase's bare hips with my palms. Fingers dug into his flesh, and my face compressed itself against his succulent body. Truth was my chin grazed the base of his deflated cock, which unconditionally caused more sap to leak out of my denim-covered tool.

"Fucking yeah!" a meathead on the other team howled.

"Whiffer at work!" one of the Sioux Indians shouted.

And Ginger, who was somewhere behind me, possibly eyeing up my bulbous ass to heedlessly fuck, or something gay because of his high alcohol consumption, yelled, "That's what I'm talking about!"

Of course, my licking and sniffing seized. The game had to continue. Proudly, I pulled away from Jase, who rustled my blond hair with a palm, winked at me again, and quietly said down to me, "Nice work, Pretty Boy. You almost made me hard."

Honestly, I never intended to be such a bad Beer Pong player. I did not purposely throw my first three turns. The beer helped me miss my third turn and …

"You fucking suck at this game, Pretty Boy!" a jock behind me bellowed.

"You toss like a girl!" someone else yapped.

Ginger announced to all the frat brats, "Pretty Boy has to suck some balls and cock!"

"Let him choose who he wants to suck off!" Jase called out, which no one argued with.

After meticulously calculating and scanning the bare-chested and drunk circle of fiery-hot young men, I chose Rossi Tangelo out of the lot, the steamy-hot Italian Mafia dude from the opposing team. Rossi just happened to be my type, a guy I wanted to fall in love with, fuck every day, and keep against my bare skin forever. I pointed to his hulking and hairy chest, took in his onyx-black eyes, ink-colored crew cut, five o'clock shadow, erect nipples, ab-covered torso, tapered waist, and said, "I choose Rossi."

Rossi was twenty-one years old, a junior who would be graduating from our college the following year. His six-one frame moved through the young men and stopped in front of me, ready for my mouth. He demanded from me, "Get on your knees and open your face, Pretty Boy. I've got some meat to share with your throat."

55

As the fraternity boys yelped in agreement, overzealous for my feeding, I dropped to my knees again, cordially opened my mouth like a little bird ready to eat, and waited patiently for my Rossi-meal.

Above me, Rossi unleashed his flesh-beast. He released the belt buckle on his Diesels, unbuttoned the denim, and ...

Seven inches of uncut tube fell out of his jeans; I was in love at first sight. His pick was the most desired and manly thing I had ever seen on the planet: veined and decorated with just the perfect amount of manscaped bush, urine-scented with a hint of one or two dried droplets of spicy spew from his morning jackoff session. Half-hidden under his limp shaft was his sack of balls: hairy and a little wrinkled, drooping down to his knees like a porn star's.

Irreversibly, I licked my lips, which some of the brothers saw but didn't really care to react to since they were beer-blitzed. I took the initiative and pulled down Rossi's Diesels to his knees, moved my face to his limp cock, and lapped at its mushroom-shaped head with my tongue. Then, I slipped the tip of his tool between my lips, felt it grow semi-hard within my mouth, and started moving my face to and fro, blowing him.

Granted, the rules of the game stated that I was only to suck his cock once, not provide a hearty blowjob and possible goo-release for the guy. Truth was I couldn't help it. I wanted all of Rossi's inflated cock inside my body, down the back of my narrow throat, and his hairy balls to slap against my chin. Hell, I wouldn't have minded at all if he shot his creamy sap into my mouth, finding an orgasm and blowing his wad; that was how much I liked the Mafia frat man.

Of course, I didn't want to be showy in front of my brothers. Although I wanted to tug, caress, or manhandle the junior's sack of balls, I didn't. Pretty Boy me was still in my closet and planned not to exit such comforting confines any time soon. Instead, beerless for the first time, I kept my arms at my sides and fingertips pressed into the basement's cement floor.

Because I liked to play games fairly, I quickly pulled my lips off of his floppy dog, titled my head down a few inches, and licked his balls with an extended tongue.

Rossi moaned with delight, happy to have me on my knees. Once my suck and lick were finished, filling my obligation, he informed me, "I don't think you're done yet, Pretty Boy."

The frats guffawed in unison, disbelieving what had just transpired.

I met my eyes with the goon's, sneered happily, and knew what he was talking about. In fact, I licked my lips, and mouthed silently, "Do it ... Fuck my face."

Had the brothers of my fraternity not been blitzed on their cheap beer, that mouth-gig with Rossi wouldn't have continued. All the guys in the basement were loaded though, intoxicated to their limits, and seemed to watch us like a racy, reality show on television.

With Rossi's hands planted on my shoulders, he directed his flaccid meat into my mouth. He thumped my face, jostling his hips forward and backward. Three humps ensued, a groan of pleasure escaped him, and then he grumbled, "Suck my rod ... Make me blast my load."

The frat boys were out of control, wide-eyed and bedazzled by what they were witnessing between Rossi and me. Yelps and hearty laughs ricocheted off the walls. Cell phones were in use, videotaping our frat show. All were snickered on their beers, happy and wild. Two yelled out my name. A third called out, "Plow him, Rossi! ... Cum on his face, dude!" And Ginger confessed, "That's fucking hot!"

Rossi's lumber turned into ten hard inches in my mouth and throat. Seven inches of droopy dick grew unremittingly into eight ... nine ... and finally ten metal-hard inches. One of his palms found the back of my head for balance. Rossi croaked with joy, "Suck it, man ... Take it all."

I gagged and choked beneath him. His hip motion was erratic and tremulous, but fully desired. All of his stern inches slid down the back of my throat, pulled out, and slid down again.

The frat dudes cheered us on. More cameras took video. One guy even yelled out, "Shoot your boys into him, Rossi!"

Consciously, I knew Rossi was going to fire his load. When his breathing intensified and his last movement became unstoppable, I realized he couldn't keep his creamy freight inside his junk any longer. Plus, the look on his face – wide eyes, flushed cheeks, trembling lips – told me that he was almost ready to combust.

I was not about to gargle his sticky boys and pulled away from his firm knob, promptly turned my head to the right and ...

Rossi held the base of his stick with his left hand and churned a load on my face. Italian sap glazed my cheek and neck, missing my mouth and lips by a mere few millimeters. A grunt escaped his beautiful mouth, two grunts ... and he said down to me, "You look good wearing my goo, Pretty Boy."

The frat brothers whooped with laughter. Some patted me on my back and congratulated me on my blowjob. Others patted Rossi on his back and exclaimed, "Damn, you rock!" Some just looked at the two of us in astonishment, disbelieving what we had just accomplished. Honestly, we were heroes of some sort, leaders in our pack of horny and young men, dudes who weren't afraid of giving or receiving blowjobs with other dudes.

Ginger poured beer on my face and wiped Rossi's gluey boys away with his balled up T-shirt. In doing so, someone in the far reaches of the basement yelled at an ear-splitting decibel, "Let the game continue!"

And, so it was done.

I admit that I threw the next round. Secretly, I had a craving to tackle one of the Sioux Indian's asses. Cougar was his name, and he had the most luscious puckering bottom out of all the two thousand students who attended our private college. Cougar was absolutely delicious from head to toe, a twin of Jacob in Stephenie Myer's *Twilight* saga. The man was to die for regarding all the right sexual reasons, and mine for the taking at that most opportune time.

When I threw the fourth round, faking disappointment, Ginger called out, "Pretty Boy, pick an ass to lick! ... Any ass!"

I made all of the frat brothers turn around to show off their amazing asses. Some wiggled in play while others bent over in fun. One jock decided to unzip his jeans and push his Nike shorts and C-IN2 boxer-briefs down to his ankles, showing off his bald balls and tight rump, which I was half-tempted to pick for my personal pleasure. Another brother decided to spank himself in a sexual manner, teasing me. Two frats stood beside each other and brushed hips together, bobbing up and down like manic fools.

Truthfully, I only had a hunger for Cougar's bottom, which I had viewed a number of times in the house: creamy-brown in hue, tight and bulbous, smackable and hairless. It was the best looking ass out of the lot, which only caused my animal-like hunger to increase by the passing seconds.

"Cougar!" I exclaimed and pointed at the sexy Sioux.

The Native American stepped out of the group, drunkenly skipped up to me, almost touched his lips to my lips, and said, "The dick must lick."

I nodded my head in a challenge and chanted, "Bring it on."

The crowd went crazy; inebriated lunatics with plastic beer cups in their shaky hands. Whooping and screaming dudes of a different caliber, cheered us on.

"Let me bend over then."

"I'm ready any time you are, Cougar."

As if on cue, the Jacob look-alike undid his jeans, dropped them to the cement floor with his Rufskin briefs, stepped out of the combo, and bent over for my pleasure (and his), grasping his narrow ankles.

Of course I was skilled in swabbing a dude's ass with my straying tongue; it's why gay guys usually dated me. Carefully, I used both palms and pulled his ass cheeks apart and stared into his pink-tight center. I moved one fingertip to his compact hole, brushed it against that hairless opening, and then provided a lick to his bottom once ... twice ... three times, sending Cougar into a state of moaning pleasure.

"Fuck me," accidentally rolled out of his mouth as I caused him to bounce up and down a little, enjoying his lick-ride. Groans escaped his front hole as I lathered his back hole two more times with my tongue-spit. As he swayed to and fro in front of me, his smooth and dark-skinned sack of native balls swung into my chin numerous times. That was a total turn-on for me and caused yet another bubble of juice to leak into my briefs, moistening my erect goods.

"Deeper!" Cougar yelled at the top of his voice, overwhelmed by my tongue-bath. Again, he bolted into my face, spellbound by my lick-fest.

Frankly, I was quite sure I could have made him spray a load of his seed all over the basement floor without either of us manipulating his rod; that is how excelled I was at ass-labor. Although Rossi received a healthy and unexpected blowjob from me and squirted his release onto my pretty boy face, that didn't mean I was going to get Cougar off, too. Beer Pong had its rules, which we all had to follow to the best of our abilities. As far I was concerned about the man bent over in front of me, I licked his rump (exactly what I wanted from him) and had paid my dues according the game's rules.

When Cougar finally stood and spun around, he leaned into me and whispered, "You can finish me off sometime later, pal."

I laughed, sucked up his good looks, and replied, "Any time you want. It will be my pleasure."

In a matter of seconds, the frat boys were back at the game, taking turns and tossing ping pong balls into the plastic cups, productive at play. Ginger made his shot. Jase made his shot. Rossi made his shot. And Cougar made his shot. It was my turn to see if I could bounce a ping pong ball into one of the Dixie cups. So far, I sucked at Beer Pong to the nth degree; shame on me. Of course, my expectations were not at all high regarding a score; I definitely had a better chance at scoring with Connor Behling, the straightest of the bunch.

I was drunk. No, I was loaded, almost in a blackout state from drinking way too much. As I stood next to Ginger, ready to toss the ping pong ball for the final time, I saw over thirty Dixie cups moving left and right on the table. Hell, I had to at least nail one of them, right?

Wrong! I missed all the cups on my try. The ping pong ball bounced over three of the cups and eventually took flight to the floor. Fuck!

"Damn," Ginger said, patting my back with concern.

Rossi yelled, "Pick a guy to take in the closet and let him nail you!"

I didn't even have to think about the assortment of men. Secretly, I had always wanted to be nailed by Connor Behling, since he was hardcore straight and didn't seem to have a single ounce of queer in his body. So, I pointed at him, and called out his name. Seconds later, before I even knew it, we stripped out of our clothes in front of all the brothers and were in a basement closet, sucking face.

A single bulb hung overhead in the five square feet of closet littered with sports equipment: footballs, shoulder pads, hand weights, hockey skates, bowling balls, and a ski mask. I studied Connor: twenty years old, black hair, cerulean-colored eyes, cleft in the center of his chin, rugged jawline, slender lips, meaty shoulders on a six-one frame, 210 pounds of nicely sculpted meat, and a wanker that was already hard and upright at nine inches, and almost two inches wide.

"I have a condom and lube," Connor said, obviously holding both while he entered the closet with me.

"Put it on and get to work," I instructed, glowing from ear to ear, proving that even the straightest guy in the house found me attractive and wanted my ass.

As he rolled the plastic down and over his stick and lubed it up, he said, "Plant your palms against a wall, Pretty Boy. I want my payment for your loss."

I listened like a good boy, found the left wall inside the closet, straightened my arms and placed my palms against the bare cement.

Connor didn't waste any time at all. He spanked my ass with his right palm and steered one inch of his pick into the tight crevice of my bottom. Two of his inches about caused me to faint. Three inches of his wide shaft just about ripped my insides apart. Four ... five ... and six inches glided into my man-chute, reaching my intestines and beyond. Seven and eight inches of his rammer caused my upright body to waver to the left and right. And, the final inch felt as if it were going split me into two Pretty Boy halves, poking into my insides like a lamp post or telephone pole.

"Ride it. I know you're a power bottom," Connor said.

Some guys could see right through me, I guess. I did as I was told and found the moment with Connor enlightening. I backed vigorously and heatedly into his nine-inch dick, pulled away, pushed my weight onto his pole again, pulled away and ...

"Fuck yeah," Connor moaned as his dick seemed to like my ride.

I was pleasuring the both of us. Together we brutally moved to and fro, discovering friction between us. When I backed my bottom into his stern and sweaty middle, his cock rushed into my rump. On fire, we groaned and moaned at the same pitch. Noises flooded the closet with our man-inside-man action.

Outside the closet, the frat brats laughed and seemed amazed at our connection. I heard Ginger say, "Connor is really fucking him."

Jase admitted, "I wished Pretty Boy would have picked me."

Rossi confessed, "They sound hot ... I'd like to be in on that gig."

Our action was almost over, though; every good moment eventually comes to an end. I moaned one last time as euphoria shifted throughout my core. Without even touching my rod, spew shot out of its mass and iced the floor. Four arcs were released and splashed the cement, leaving me spent, windblown and bliss-filled.

Connor sprayed his load right after I blew mine. Over my right shoulder, I watched him quickly pull out of my tight hub, lose the plastic from his slab of meat, and jack his tool a few times with his left palm and fingers and ...

"Shooting," he grunted, globing his thick and sticky churn onto the plane of my sweaty back, where it affixed to and stung my flesh.

Following our candid fuck, he pulled me up to his chest, collapsed his lips against the top of my spine, pulled off and away, and shared, "That was the best ass I've ever had. I might just stick with guys from here on out."

My response was rather forward but truthful, "You can bang me any day, pal. Your cock felt super cozy up my ass."

Connor was amused with my comment, spun me around, connected my queer lips with his straight ones, and blew me away by shoving his tongue into my mouth while grabbing the still-erect pole between my perspiration-covered legs.

The next day was quiet in the Zeta Psi frat house. Dudes milked their hangovers after our ultimate game of Beer Pong. Bodies were strewn everywhere: some entangled together and completely naked; others with brief-covered cocks next to a brother's lips. I, too, had a hangover, but nothing like most of the frat brats.

Jase found me in the buff and took advantage of my skin, which I loved. The guy let me pound him for the next two hours. I was totally unstoppable with my thumps.

To my surprise, that wasn't the end of my sexual escapades with the frats. In fact, I learned that it was just the beginning.

Following that weekend, Ginger wanted a blowjob from me in the shower, which I granted, but only if he blew me off, too; the handsome dude kindly accepted.

Rossi asked if he could nail me with his ten inches against his bedroom wall; surely I couldn't pass that opportunity up and didn't.

Cougar begged me to fuck him over his bed, so he could finish coming after I licked his ass at our weekend Beer Pong game; something I was glad to help him out with.

Connor climbed into my bed one night, pulled my briefs off and dropped them to the floor. Before I knew what was happening, I was spooned by the straight guy, kissed along my neck and shoulders, and ... he jacked me off. Following my release, he wanted to know if I would do the same thing to him. I informed him in a rather frisky manner, "Heck yeah ... but I'd rather use my mouth. What do you say?" Connor didn't object and peeled his own briefs off of his succulent skin.

And, by the end of that first week I almost did something naughty to every brother in the house, playing a new game among horny, fraternity dudes; a naked game I simply liked to call Dong Pong – no clothes required, of course.

SHIRTS VERSUS SKINS
By HL Champa

"Ready for the basketball game, Matt?"

"I think we'll do just fine, Dan. You remember what happened last year, don't you? The question is are you Deltas ready to get your asses kicked?"

"You seem pretty confident. Care to make it interesting, Matt?"

I blew a stream of cigarette smoke directly into Dan's face. I couldn't believe he was using such a horrible clichéd line. Right next to him stood Tyler, the biggest asshole in all of Delta house. I hated him, and Dan had gone down in my estimation for spending so much time with such a fool. Dan and I had hooked up freshman year. He sucked cock like a dream, and I would be lying if I said I didn't want another chance with him. But, the Deltas were our rivals, and with the intramural finals coming up, Dan was trying to bait me into doing something stupid. Like making a ridiculous bet for money I didn't have or letting Dan humiliate me in front of my Tau Kappa Epsilon frat brothers.

I was confident we were going to win the game. We had beaten Delta house in basketball every year, even before I'd pledged. Our team was better than ever. There was no way we were going to let them win this year. Dan had no reason to be confident, and Tyler was one of the worst players I had ever seen. But for some reason, they had cornered me outside Myer Hall and were acting all cocky about the game the next day. And, it was really pissing me off.

"What did you have in mind, Dan? Mom didn't send you any money this week, so you need to take mine?"

Dan just laughed, and like a good little bitch, Tyler joined right in. I had heard they were fucking, but of course, being Deltas they kept it mostly quiet. Everyone knew, but very few people talked about it. The closet of that frat house must be huge. It was hard to imagine them as boyfriends, but as they stood in front of me, hands on hips, I could see that they had started acting just like each other. Dan finally spoke, after his usual dramatic pause.

65

"I don't want your money Matt. I was thinking of something a little more personal."

He took a step towards me, in a vain attempt to be seductive. Grabbing the cigarette from between my fingers, he took a long drag before handing it back to me. Tyler stayed behind, looking around with an air of superiority that was based on absolutely nothing. I let Dan put his hand around my shoulder, but I tried not to react when I felt my stomach flip over at his touch. He was cute, despite his annoying qualities, and if I looked hard enough, I could still see that shy boy I hooked up with back when we first came to school. I decided to cut to the chase and end this conversation once and for all.

"So, you want to fuck me, is that it, Dan?

"Come on; don't tell me you haven't thought about it since we hooked up all those years ago. Besides, we never got the chance to finish what we started."

He spoke like it had been twenty years, instead of just two. Always so damned dramatic. I thought of lying, but I didn't see the point.

"Maybe once or twice. But, I've managed to go on, somehow. Besides, what about Tyler? You sure he would agree to that?"

"Tyler and I have an understanding, Matt."

"Of course you do, Dan. Why am I not surprised?"

"So, do we have a deal, Matt? Come on a little friendly wager between old friends. Besides, if you lose, you still win."

"You think a lot of yourself don't you, Dan?"

"I think I can afford to, Matt. You're memory is pretty good, isn't it?"

I was shaking my head and fully ready to say no to his stupid idea, when my anger and frustration got a hold of my brain, and I spoke before truly thinking.

"Listen, Dan. If you and your pathetic teammates manage to win the game, I'll take both you and Tyler on."

"What did you say Matt?"

"You heard me. If you guys win, I'll give you what you want, and I'll even let your boyfriend join in."

My last words caught Tyler's attention, and he slid next to Dan, whose mouth had fallen open in shock. I waited a moment before walking away, but neither of them spoke. I heard Dan call after me, his voice high and loud.

"It's a bet!"

# # # # #

I stood at the free throw line, the basketball felt heavy and solid in my hands. Sweat was dripping off my nose as I looked up at the rim, which seemed a mile away after playing the second overtime period. It all came down to this. The game was in my hands, literally. All I had to do was make my second free throw and the TKE streak would remain intact. Dan and Tyler were both staring at me from opposite sides of the key, hoping with the rest of their team for me to fail. My brothers were waiting for me to secure victory, so we could all go and get wasted. We were already long overdue for a drink, especially me. I knew I could make the shot with little trouble; making free throws was the one thing I could always do. I was ten for ten for the whole game, having just made the first of my two shots. But, Dan's words rang out in my head, and my thoughts turned back to the bet I had foolishly agreed to the day before.

I stole a look at Tyler, who was smirking at Dan, before both sets of eyes turned back to me. My team began calling out to me, trying to encourage me, but all I could hear was Dan's voice yelling about our bet. Shaking my head, trying to clear it out, I dribbled the ball a few times and lined up my shot one more time. As the ball left my hands, I was sure it was going in. But, at the last moment, it sailed right and hit off the rim with an inglorious thud. The ball hit the wood floor, and the Deltas started to celebrate in earnest, the inevitable taunting filled my ears as I headed out of the gym to collect my things. The rest of my brothers were quick to disown me, leaving me behind as they nearly ran out the door towards the waiting kegs. I felt a hand fall on each of my shoulders and didn't bother to look to see who it was, as I already knew.

"So, Matt. I guess we'll see you later tonight at our place. Let's say eleven. Tyler and I are really looking forward to collecting on our bet. By the way, nice shot."

# # # # #

I thought about backing out, but I knew I couldn't. Before I left home, I threw back a couple of shots of liquid courage, just to settle my nerves and make my feet move on the sidewalks that led me to Dan's place. Knocking on the door to the apartment, I thanked my lucky stars that he and Tyler didn't live within the confines of the Delta house anymore. At least it spared me the walk of shame after they were done with me. I consoled myself with the thought that there were worse ways to spend a night. Hell, it might even turn out to be a good time. Those thoughts quickly disappeared as Tyler's smarmy face met mine as the door pulled open. His smile brought fear back to my body, and I felt the sweat starting to form on my back. Dan appeared beside him, his arm draped loosely over Tyler's shoulder. Tyler spoke first, his voice doing little to ease my mind.

"We didn't think you were going to show up. You're late."

Dan dug his elbow into Tyler's ribs and cut his annoying diatribe off. I was thankful for his intervention, but I still didn't feel any more comfortable. Dan grabbed my hand and dragged me inside their messy place. He pulled me to the living room and pushed me towards the couch.

"Sit down, Matt. I'll get us all some drinks."

Dan went to the kitchen, and Tyler plunked down next to me, just a little too close for my taste. I waited for him to jump me right then, but he just sat there staring at me with lecherous eyes. Dan reappeared with three shot glasses and one bottle of vodka. My head was entirely too clear for what was about to happen, and I welcomed the thought of more alcohol in my system. Dan poured, and I grabbed my shot and downed it before the other two even got the glasses to their lips. After they drank, I expected someone to say something, but we all sat there in silence. Finally, I couldn't take it anymore, and I grabbed the bottle and drank straight from it before breaking my silence.

"So, are we going to do this, or what?"

Dan and Tyler laughed in unison, and Dan dropped a hand to my knee. I looked down at it, and noticed my stomach had the same reaction as it did outside Myer Hall when he touched me. I shifted in my seat on the couch, Tyler inching closer as I tried to stay focused on Dan.

"You got somewhere to be, Matt? Because you seem to be in a rush. You just got here. We have all night, you know."

"Look, Dan. I'm just here to make good on a bet. Nothing more."

68

"We know. But, what's the hurry? You know, it might just be fun, if you relax a little."

Dan moved his hand higher, my breath catching in my throat as he leaned over to me and breathed in my ear. His teeth closed on my lobe, biting gently before pulling away again. My eyes met Tyler's, but he just slouched down on the couch, content to watch his boyfriend get me all worked up. I turned to look at Dan, just in time for him to kiss me hard, his tongue wasting no time plunging into my mouth. His taste took me back to that late night, freshman year. But, he was no longer that shy boy, and he held all the cards tonight. Dan bit my lower lip, making me cry out, and I heard Tyler laugh at my pain. When he pulled away, Dan was smirking, looking extremely satisfied with himself. His voice sounded harder than I had ever heard it when he spoke.

"Take your clothes off, Matt."

Dan pushed me off the couch, so I was standing in front of both of them. I had never been timid about being naked in front of anyone before, but the way Dan and Tyler looked at me made me feel self-conscious and nervous. Pulling my shirt over my head, Tyler spoke up before I could go any further.

"God, you're right Dan. He is hot. For a TKE boy."

"Oh, don't worry, Tyler. It gets better. Wait until you see his cock."

Dan's words made me blush, and I hadn't blushed in years. My hands hesitated on my belt buckle, but I bit the bullet and shucked off my jeans along with my boxers in one motion. Tyler drew in a breath and again opened his annoying mouth.

"You're right, Dan. It is a nice cock."

After I stripped, Dan again made me sweat, taking his sweet fucking time getting off the couch. He stood in front of me, his eyes taking a long swipe up and down my body before he said another word.

"Get on your knees, Matt. It's time to make good on that smart-ass bet of yours."

I kept my eyes on his as I lowered to the floor, breaking my glance only long enough to notice the bulge in Dan's pants. I held my breath as he opened his pants and took out his hardening cock, holding it right in front of my face.

"Suck it, Matt. We want to see you take me all the way down your throat."

I leaned forward, letting Dan's dick rub against my face before I wrapped my lips around the tip. Dan took my head in his hands, and pushed himself deeper into my throat. I almost choked as he forced himself into my mouth, but he relented when I grabbed his thighs and pushed him away just a bit. I relaxed after that, letting Dan have his way, my own cock rising as he fucked my mouth.

"Not so smug now, are you, Matt?"

The voice wasn't Dan's. It was Tyler's. The couch creaked as he stood up, moving right next to Dan. Out of the corner of my eye, I saw his cock in his hand, stroking as he watched me suck Dan's dick. He didn't stay idle long, pulling me away from Dan and shoving his own cock into my mouth. Tyler was bigger than Dan, but I had no trouble sucking him deep into my gullet. I expected to be disgusted by Tyler, but sucking him off only made me hotter, and I couldn't stop myself from wrapping my fist around my cock and jerking.

"Stop it, Matt. No one told you to jerk yourself off."

Dan was once again calling the shots, his voice threatening enough to make me listen.

"That's a good boy, Matt. Now, bring that smart mouth back over here."

I did as I was told; the power they were wielding over me turning me on more than I ever thought it would. I'd made the bet as a joke, but it was serious now. Dan was gentler the second time around, but I didn't get too comfortable before Tyler got impatient and yanked me back his way. As I moved back and forth between their two cocks, I could hear Dan and Tyler kissing and stripping each other of the rest of their clothes. Suddenly, my mouth was empty, and I looked up at them from the floor, not knowing what to expect from them next.

"Get up, Matt. Get on your knees, on the couch."

Instead of Tyler's demand pissing me off, it made me crazy, and I dutifully made my way to their sofa, pressing my knees into the center cushion. Tyler sat down next to me and pulled my face back onto his cock, and I groaned as I felt his hand grab the back of my neck. Dan moved behind me, his hands tracing over my body as I slowed my pace on Tyler's cock. The next moment, Dan began moving his tongue up the back of my leg, making me squirm under his touch. His big hands moved up my inner thighs, pausing just below my prick. For a moment, he did nothing, and I waited, tense and anxious for his next move.

Tyler was pushing his cock into my mouth at a nice, slow pace when I felt Dan's tongue sweep from my balls to my puckered ass. His mouth was hot on my skin, and his fingers parted my cheeks, exposing me to his deep tongue strokes. After a few, torturous minutes, he stopped teasing me, and dipped his tongue into my asshole. Dan dug his fingers into my hips, holding me still while he rimmed me between plunging thrusts of his tongue. I tried to pull away from Tyler, unable to concentrate, but he kept me in place, and full of his cock. I felt Dan run his fingers down my crack, and push one inside of me. Taking one of my balls into his mouth, he began fucking my ass with his thick digit. I rocked back and forth between the two of them, trying not to give one too much attention.

"That's it, Matt. Suck that cock nice and deep. I want you to choke on my cum."

Tyler's taunts only egged me on, making me more desperate by the minute. Dan's face and hands suddenly moved away from my ass. I swiveled my hips in the air, trying in vain to find him again. I felt the couch move and heard Dan's footsteps moving quickly around the apartment. Dan returned to the couch quickly, his hands cupping my ass cheeks, and for a moment, I stopped everything I was doing, releasing Tyler from between my lips. Dan's fingers were back inside me, lubing my ass with the liquid he had gone to retrieve. Without any fanfare, Dan entered me, slower than I could bear. I was rubbing my face against Tyler's thigh, moaning quietly between clenched teeth.

To my surprise, Tyler's hands ran through my hair, calming me while Dan moved his cock inside me. I bit gently into Tyler's thigh, riding high between the pleasure and pain of Dan's cock stretching me out. Once I opened up, I felt him slide all the way inside me, his pelvis resting against me for long seconds before pulling back again. Dan's voice broke me from my private world and brought me back to the here and now.

"Keep sucking him, Matt; I want to watch you take that cock in your mouth."

Tyler tightened his grip on me and pulled me back down onto his waiting dick, which hadn't softened a bit. I opened my mouth obediently and sucked him, as Dan slammed his cock into me, pushing me forward.

71

My eyes were closed, as the pleasure of the two of them inside me overwhelmed me. Dan increased his pace, and I felt his fingers reach under me, finding my cock hard and waiting for attention. He wrapped his fist around me and started to jerk me, gently at first, but with each thrust of his cock into my ass, his hand worked me harder.

"God, I'm so glad you missed that shot, Matt. I've been wanting to fuck you for so long. And, when I'm done, Tyler's going to take his turn, pounding you senseless."

Dan's words boiled my blood, and my muffled cries around Tyler's cock grew more fervent as I sucked him as hard as I could. I pushed back against Dan, trying to bring us all closer to the edge. Dan twisted his wrist and ran his thumb over my weeping slit, and just as the pain and pleasure crested inside me, Tyler started to come into my mouth, his hands holding my head in place as his hips came up to meet my mouth. I didn't think twice, just swallowed, tasting his salty sweet cum as it ran down my throat. He released my head, his hands resting limply on my back as his moaning stopped. Tyler was spent, and I released his cock as I turned to look at Dan.

We nearly came together, my ass contracting around him as he sped up and pounded into me. His fingers, now wet with my cum, moved over my cock until I had to push him away when it all became too much. With just a few more thrusts, Dan fell onto me, collapsing for a few minutes until his strength returned.

We sat, exhausted and sweaty, slowly moving away from each other, but still touching. Tyler and Dan leaned over me and kissed, but I could barely keep my eyes open. Dan noticed my fatigue and laughed, bringing me back to life with a tug of my hair.

"I'll let you rest up for now, Matt. But, I told you, we're not quite done with you yet. You still owe Delta Rho some restitution."

"Don't worry, Dan. I'm definitely good for it. After all, a bet's a bet."

WHITE ELEPHANT
By Rob Rosen

It was initiation night, my junior year. I made sure to scarf down a big dinner, knowing I'd need some cushioning in my belly, something to soak up all the impending tequila. And beer. And probably some bourbon, if memory served correctly. Not that it was ever all that easy to remember initiation night, mind you. First couple of hours are generally crisp and in focus, then, well everything tends to get a bit hazy after that, singed around the edges. That night was no different. Uh, okay, in fact it turned out different as fuck. Though, to be fair, we could only blame the massive quantities of booze.

Mostly.

I arrived back at the house right on time, stopping on the edge of the lawn, staring down at our house at the bottom of the hill, my room dark on the second floor. The house was lit up, though, gleaming white columns glowing against a backdrop of nighttime sky. Our flag was flying high, barely fluttering, the evening almost breezeless, hot and sticky. I smiled, the sound of fraternity chanting reaching my ears as I headed down, all baritone, tinged with testosterone. This was always a night to look forward to, when pledges joined the ranks, the fold increased. A night of rituals, of celebration, and, of course, drunken debauchery. My head swam at the thought, butterflies released from my belly in a happy swarm.

Eighty brothers ringed fifteen pledges, beer cans held up high, the chanting at a crescendoed pitch. I joined the circle, a Budweiser passed my way. Pledges stared outward, nervous looking, and rightly so. The hazing was more mental than physical, but still, it would be a night of torture for them. Brotherhood had to be earned, which is what made it so memorable. And worth celebrating.

Hours later, we were all as one, no more pledges, wide grins on everyone's faces, hard alcohol replacing beer. Revelers walked the row, brothers from other frats going from their houses to ours and back again. It was a blur of college good cheer, of dudes looking to get laid, girls stumbling from one house to the next, music blaring from open windows. It was a good night to be young. And unsupervised.

Then again, isn't it always?

Still, youth doesn't come with a whole lot of wisdom. Or common sense when tequila, and beer, and bourbon join the fray. Meaning, the emptier my cup got, the more likely it was to be refilled. Over and over and over again. Until, I found myself stumbling up the stairs, the house spinning, looking for a witch to land on. Or a bed. Which is what I plopped down on a short while later, clothes tossed off, garbage pail at the ready, just in case.

And that's where I found myself sometime in the middle of the night, the clock blazing 4:26. I squinted at it and scratched my head. The room was merely rocking now, the spinning, thankfully, at an end. Still, the clock didn't look right. "Huh," I groaned. "That's not my clock."

It was then, in the silence of the night, I heard the shuffling next to me. I wasn't, it seemed, alone. I jumped when an arm bumped me. He jumped, too, when he realized I was in his bed. "What the fuck?" he yelped, jumping up, his back going vertical. "Get out, dude!"

I rolled off and fell on the fall, landing with a dull thud. "Oops, wrong bed," I managed, those butterflies in my belly now long dead, turning like so much spoiled milk. "Too much booze," I explained.

He looked over and down. "Glenn, that you?"

I looked up. It was Steve, who had the room next to mine. Not too ironically, I'd had a crush on him since freshman year. Guy was stunning, with a capital S. "Sorry, dude. My bad. I'll just, uh, I'll just go to my room."

He laughed and flopped back down. "Some night, huh?" he said, with a heavy sigh. "No more tequila for me. Ever."

I stood and grabbed my clothes. "Until next weekend," I chided.

Again he laughed. "Night, dude." He rolled over, and I let myself out.

The house was now dead silent and stinking of beer, a faint aroma of fresh puke someplace nearby, cans everywhere, boxes of pizza discarded yards from overflowing garbage cans. I grimaced. Without pledges, we'd all have to clean. Then I opened my door, my ears greeted to the sounds of moans, one male, one female. I quickly closed the door. "Fuckin-A," I cursed. "Someone found a spare bed. Namely mine." And I wasn't about to throw them out. A scene was the last thing my throbbing head needed.

I tried downstairs, the living room looking like a cyclone had hit it, every spare couch occupied by brothers who didn't live in the house, more asleep on the carpet. "No room at the inn," I grumbled, heading back upstairs, staring at the lifeless hallway, holding my nose, figuring out my options.

Sighing, I clicked open Steve's door again. "Dude," I whispered.

"What?" he whispered back.

"Someone stole my bed and all the couches are taken. Can I crash here?" It was more a plea than a question. By then, I was desperate to be prone.

He flipped over and covered his eyes from the light of the hallway. Stifling a laugh, he waved me in. "You owe me one," he said as I walked inside and shut the door behind me. Then he slid over, making room for me. I paused. I thought it would be me and the floor, not me and Steve, pleasant and yet terrifying though the thought may have been. Still, beggars couldn't be choosers. In other words, I dumped my clothes back on the floor and hopped in.

It was a twin-sized bed, so we were very much side by side. "Thanks," I said.

"Don't mention it," he replied. "Seriously. Don't. To anyone."

I looked over at him, the light of the moon casting his handsome face in a warm, silver glow. "As if, dude." Then I rolled over, as did he, back to back. Which is exactly when I realized he was sleeping commando, when my hand accidentally brushed his exposed rump, my fingers brushing the soft fuzzy down of him.

"Hey," he barked, flipping over again.

"Sorry," I barked back. "You're naked." I turned, his face now an inch from mine.

He managed a mesmerizing smile. "Dude, it's my bed. My rules. And I don't like sleeping in my drawers." His eyes locked with mine, the blue of his shining like a beacon, despite the near darkness of the room.

I pushed my growing stiffy between my legs. Quite literally, he had me between a rock and a hard place. "Hope your rules don't apply to guests," I squeaked out, my voice nearly catching in my throat as my heart went thump in my chest.

He chuckled, the sound washing over me like the ocean on a hot summer's day at the beach. My cock broke free of my legs, stretching at the thin fabric of my boxers. "Up to you," he replied. "Just don't go poking me anyplace you shouldn't." His eyes stayed open, as did mine. The silence was nearly deafening. "What?" he asked.

"What, what?" I replied. "Shut your eyes already."

He smirked. "Now I can't sleep. And it's hotter than hell in here. Too much body heat, too small a bed." Suddenly, he pushed down the blanket. I fixed my eyes straight ahead, desperate to look down, terrified to, as well. "Better," he added.

"Better," I agreed. "Though I'm wide the fuck awake and still drunk. You?"

That laugh of his returned. "I should've stopped about three beers ago." He burped. "Four."

"Four," I agreed, rolling back over on my back. The close proximity to his face was making me uneasy. Not to mention horny as all hell. I put my hands behind my head and stared at the ceiling. Then he turned over and did the same. And my eyes went from the ceiling down the naked length of his chiseled body, his mid-section at full-mast. Mine, too. Go figure.

"Your dick is hard, dude," he whispered.

"So is yours."

Silence. More silence. Save for my heart now pounding in my ears. Then he laughed again. "Know that saying, dude, about the white elephant in the room?"

I echoed his laughter, mine wracked with nerves. "Yup. What about it?"

He smacked his prick, sending it flinging from side to side. "White elephant."

With a gulp, I released mine out of the flap, the glistening head springing straight up. "White elephants, dude. Plural."

He reached his hand over and grabbed mine. I reached over and grabbed his. It was as easy as that. I gave his a stroke. It pulsed in my grip. "Can I ask you a weird question, dude?" he asked.

I nodded. "Uh, you're holding my dick. What could be weirder than that?"

"You have a point," he replied, rolling over, my prick still in his mitt. I rolled over, too, his still in mine. "But, uh, I was just wondering." He paused, those stunning eyes of his drilling down into me. "You, uh, you ever make it with another dude before?"

I paused, as well. Uncharted waters. Rocky boat. "Uh, yeah. You?"

He smiled, head inching closer to mine. "Couple of times in high school. But living in a fraternity house sort of makes it, well, impossible. Too much at stake."

"Unless you're already naked and hard with another brother," I amended, sliding in even closer, adding, "Suddenly, I'm not so drunk, dude."

Closer still. "Me neither." His lips brushed mine, a spark jumping the gap until the gap was closed completely, our mouths pressed up so tight it was impossible to tell where he ended and I began. He groaned and released my cock, wrapping his arms around my back instead, pulling me in to him. He came back up for air, his forehead against my forehead. "You ever think about doing this before, Glenn? With me, I mean?"

I nodded and smiled. "I, uh, I sometimes see you going into the shower, and I pretend I need one, too." I laughed, picturing the image. "Then I wait for you to turn around, and I bend down to soap up my feet; only, I'm really getting face to ass with you." I kissed him again, gently, softly, perfectly. "It's a, it's a real nice ass, dude. Honestly, it was near impossible to stand there and not bend in an inch further for a taste."

He clapped his hands, suddenly pushing away from me, on all fours before I knew it, a small reading light flicked on. "Initiation night, dude," he said, spreading his cheeks apart for me. "Initiate me."

I hopped off the bed and slid out of my boxers, cock so stiff it hurt, then I jumped in behind him on all fours, face to glorious ass, this time with nothing stopping me. "That's what brothers are for," I purred, leaning in, the smell of him, musk and sweat and soap, wafting up my nose, causing my dick to bounce.

"We'll have to write that into the bylaws," he said, his ass moving in reverse, hole on my mouth now, my tongue swirling around the soft halo of hair before diving in, lapping at his ring and then shoving my way

77

inside. He bucked and moaned, pushing his cock between his hairy thighs. Like a kid in a candy store, I gorged myself on both, alternating between sucking on the fat head and his puckered, tight hole. He moaned again, louder. "I always wondered what your mouth would feel like around my dick, dude."

"Now you know, dude," I replied, downing him in one fell swoop, precum hitting the back of my throat like a bullet as a happy gagging tear streamed down my face. The moan turned to groan as I sucked him off and glided a finger deep inside his hole. It grabbed a hold of me like a vice, his body quaking as I wriggled it around, feeling the smooth, muscled interior of him.

"Fuuuck," he exhaled, the sound travelling down the length of his body and right on through to mine.

I popped his prick out of my mouth. "You wanna?"

Fast as lightning, he was on his back again, that stunning white elephant of his pointing up at me, heavy balls dangling way down low. "Rubber and lube are in the jar behind you, Glenn."

I smiled and reached around, rolling the rubber down the length of my shaft before greasing the both of us up, a finger slid up inside his ass, then two, his hole sucking me in like a Hoover. Three years in the making, I stared down at him, hungry, eager to be inside. He groaned again, pumping his prick, waiting.

Of course, I didn't make him wait too long.

I lifted up his legs, pulling them wide, bent at the knee, until his feet rested on my shoulders, my cock butting up against his hole. He stared up at me and smiled, chest rising and falling as I gently eased my way inside. He sucked in his breath, his eyelids fluttering, his ring gripping me tight, then he exhaled and released, allowing me to continue. In I slid, farther, deeper, every nerve ending in my body suddenly on fire. "Ever think you'd get fucked by another brother?" I rasped, half-way in, then all the way, my balls banging up against his perfect, little ass.

He moaned, the pace quickened on his fifth limb of a cock. "Only in my dreams, dude," he replied.

I pinched his thigh. He winced. "Nope, not dreaming, dude."

He sighed and rammed his ass into my crotch, sending my cock into overdrive. I slid it out and rammed it on in, out, in, slowly at first, but them picking up steam, both our balls rising. His eyes stayed locked on mine and mine on his, the sun rising along the horizon now, casting our fucking in a warm orange glow, illuminating the sweat that pooled between his pecs.

"Make me come, dude," he rasped, eyes sparkling like sapphires, mouth in a pant.

I smiled and nodded. "My pleasure, dude," I replied, letting him have it with both guns, pummeling his ass, both of our moans in sync now, his pumping mirroring my pounding.

"Close," I growled.

"Closer," he growled right on back.

His body quaked, the bed shaking, bouncing, as his cock erupted, thick streams of spunk spewing up and out, drenching his chest, his belly, coating that deep tan of his in a murky white. His hole locked on tight to my dick, which shot a split second later, my knees buckling as I filled his ass up with ounce after steaming hot ounce of cum, both of us fighting to catch our breaths as we milked every last drop of cum from our steely dicks.

I pulled out and collapsed on top of him, his arms quickly encircling me. He laughed, fingers running through my back sweat. "If they only knew, dude."

I returned his laugh in full. "Uh, better if they didn't."

He nodded. "Yeah, probably not such a good idea."

We fell asleep like that, me on top of him, bodies united, glued together with sweat and cum. Brother to brother, as it were. When the sun was up much higher, and the room hot as hell, we both got up, our dried loads still sticking to us. "Shower?" I suggested.

"Then coffee," he added, grabbing us each a towel. "A double. Head is pounding, dude."

I laughed, checking to make sure the coast was clear down the hallway. "Thank goodness it's not just me; I thought someone was hammering at my skull."

"No more booze," he said, soon enough, hanging his towel up outside the large shower stall we all shared.

"For tonight, anyway," I joked, with a smile, also hanging up my towel, both of us standing there, naked, him eyeing me, me eyeing him.

Then we parted the shower curtain. We weren't alone. Our brother, Jack, was in there, head beneath a spray of water, looking as haggard as the two of us did. We joined him, the two of us facing him from the other side. Jack was a god among men, so that pounding in my heart made a beeline for my cock, which I'd learned, somehow, to keep limp. No easy feat, mind you. Still, when he turned, I grabbed for the soap, bent over, and started cleaning my calves. Steve did the same, both of our faces just a few inches from Jack's awesome butt.

Steve turned my way and smiled, mouthing, Yum!

Not as nice as yours, I mouthed back.

He shrugged and nodded. Yup. Then he stood and pointed at his dangling dick, then at my still bent over ass.

Yup, I mouthed back, smiling big and bright and wide, that headache of mine almost completely vanished. Then I pointed at my prick, winking all the while. White elephant, dude. White fucking elephant.

"DEAR VALORIE"
By Derrick Della Giorgia

Nicholas removed the carton from his lap in slow motion and placed it on the floor next to his Blackberry. He never looked again at that last slice of cheddar cheese and black olives pizza. His blue eyes locked on the last scenes of Resident Evil: Afterlife.

"I'll eat that." Benjamin's scarred hand and the bandages wrapped around his wrist searched for the leftovers. It wasn't unusual for the captain of the rugby team to be hurt, in a cast or covered with bruises. More surprising, the fact he'd decided to spend a Friday night watching a movie with his best friend's gay twin.

"Fucking amazing!" Nicholas commented right before the titles.

"Good one, Samuel!" Benjamin finished his Budweiser and burped. He didn't know the twin watching the movie with him was straight Nicholas. He actually thought he was spending the night with Nicholas' gay brother Samuel. He'd already confessed to himself that he had fantasies about fucking Samuel, but that wasn't the reason why he was there. He didn't feel like partying with the rest of the frat dudes this weekend. Everybody has those kinds of thoughts. It was okay. Everything was under control. Samuel couldn't read his mind, and he would never notice his hard-on if he kept that pizza box perfectly balanced on his crossed legs.

"Let's watch another one!" Nicholas on all fours switched DVDs and returned to his spot. He'd studied his plan to perfection. He'd furiously refused to believe Troy's accusations, according to whom Benjamin was waiting for the right occasion to fuck Samuel. Convinced that was only Troy's envy speaking, he expected to tease the big captain all night without success. A couple of movies and as much beer as it might require, he could swear Benjamin would never make a pass at him, or Samuel – as he believed. Troy was only looking for revenge. The poor kid was the joke of the dorm; now for his mild lisp, now for the pallor of his skin, constantly for being rejected by all the chicks. Rumor had it that he was so horny that in order to fall asleep he had to jerk off watching porn every single night.

"Sure man, I've got nothing else to do." A second can of beer was in his bruised hand when he allowed himself to turn around for a split second and look at the twin. Those light blue shorts he was wearing were damn sexy. He couldn't believe he was thinking about it. The more he fought the idea, the more the image of Samuel sucking his cock grew stronger. To feel a little safer, he drank and burped more, as if that guttural sound he was able to produce could enhance his masculinity. He liked tits, he liked pussy. There was no reason to doubt that. As a matter of fact, he had pounded what was her name twice in a row less than 24 hours earlier. She told him, he was a real man. *What the fuck is it with me then?* He tortured himself.

"How's your wrist going?" Nicholas asked, nonchalantly. Psychologically, that would create a moment of intimacy between the two. He didn't really know how to proceed. *How do you lure a guy into your pants? Sweetness? Bluntness? Pure vulgarity?* He wished he could ask Samuel what to do. But it was bad enough he was wearing his clothes, watching movies in his room, even pretending he was him. This time he'd definitely broken their trust, he thought as he stretched his back and laid his arms on the couch behind them. He made sure his hand swiftly rubbed Benjamin's back. Inexplicably, he noticed his heart had taken a faster pace. *Shit, I don't wanna do this. I should leave right now. Fuck Troy!* The growing rage annoyed the hell out of him. Where was the problem? Was he scared to find out Benjamin was gay or bisexual or whatever he was? Was it the guilt of doing this to Samuel? Or to his best friend? It was the most embarrassing feeling he'd ever experienced. Yet, he couldn't decipher where it came from.

"It's fine." Benjamin confirmed his wrist was not a big deal but didn't even flinch. He'd decided not to acknowledge the contact. He knew Samuel was making a pass at him. For Christ's sake, he was a gay guy sitting next to the rugby team captain, one of the hottest guys in the campus. The temptation so imponderable that Samuel was probably dying to jump at him and get at work between his legs. Oh, he would suck really well, too. It is common knowledge gay guys know how to take it in their mouths. The nameless chick was good, too, last night, but good for a woman. According to some friends of his, there was no comparison!

Neither one was watching the second movie. If asked, they wouldn't have known what the title was. Nicholas checked his Blackberry: Ten-thirty. Troy was waiting for an answer two rooms down. If Benjamin was gay, Troy could finally ruin his reputation, most likely get him kicked out of the fraternity and the rugby team. Not to mention the colossal impact that that would have on the available girls. If he wasn't, Nicholas would have saved his best friend, and White-Glow – as Troy was referred to in the fraternity – was dead. No way would he survive this one.

"Gimme that, I'll throw it away." Nickolas gestured for Benjamin to pass him the pizza box. Without that, it'd be easier to get closer. Maybe rub legs, touch him. The twin kept repeating to himself that he needed to move on. But some questions popped back up in his brain. Was this the only alternative he had to find out, or what he'd actually like to do? Wasn't it simpler at this point to directly ask Benjamin whether he'd ever had same sex fantasies? Or if he'd ever dreamed of fucking Samuel, as Troy was so certain. He guessed it wasn't. After all those times they'd been naked in front of each other, the innumerable secrets, the most intimate talking, after getting over Samuel's coming out, it was just not easier! He needed to do it. Somehow, he wanted to do it! But it didn't have anything to do with Valorie. As he saw things, this was another thing. He would definitely tell her. Of course, he would tell his girlfriend! Worst thing that could happen, she would punish him with the same coin. He knew he'd text her right away.

"Alright ..." Unwillingly, Benjamin released his protection. He couldn't think of any excuse not to. He could only quickly rearrange his legs to cover his real intentions. That hard-on had not gone anywhere in the meantime. Nor had his fantasies. How painful would it be to push Samuel's head down on him with his broken wrist? What would it take for the homosexual twin to understand? Would he tell his brother? The fantasies were contaminated with those question marks, but not for that the desire diminished.

Samuel would have never done it, but what the hell. "How would you like it if I sucked your cock?" The words escaped Nicholas' mouth, perfectly. Before he was finished, he felt dizzy, angry, guilty, anxious, sick. All at once. But if he had to pick, disturbingly excited would best describe his state of mind. Excited and ready, no matter what.

Benjamin froze. In a paranoid attack, many ways of interpreting that question invaded his mind. Samuel had seen his hard-on, and he was teasing him. Some chick had asked him to test him. Someone in the team had noticed he sometimes liked to look for a little too long at his mates while they showered. Nicholas had asked him. How could they know his fantasies? Or – lastly – did Samuel truly want to suck his cock?

Somebody died in the unknown movie. Inspired by the violent scene, Benjamin grabbed the twin's head and pushed it into his pants. Then he closed his eyelids with all the strength he had. Had there been a way, he'd have neutralized his hearing, too. The captain's massive body was trying to protect his own vulnerable soul. All he wanted right now was to be sucked by Samuel.

"You fucking asshole!" Nicholas' face had banged against the hard bulge, and he was furious. He was furious Troy was right. He was furious his friend had lied to him. He was furious because he was hoping that Benjamin's indifference to his proposal would have relieved him from his confusion. He punched Benjamin in the face and looked for his Blackberry. "Come see the FAG!" As he told Troy he realized his lips had been so close to ...

"Whoa!" Benjamin stood up. He looked disoriented.

"It's me shit brain, it's Nicholas. Troy was right. You do like cock!" He immediately regretted calling Troy. It was clear to him now. The only reason he was pissed was that now there was absolutely nothing to stop him from doing what he longed to do.

"What? What the fuck?" The captain had been unmasked, and he didn't like it. He kicked the trash bin where the pizza boxes had been buried, then the couch. Violence, again, equaled masculinity. His last resort.

But Nicholas decided otherwise and threw himself at the rugby player's feet, both his hands on the secret erection. They couldn't really tell who was slapping who and why. Until one couldn't speak anymore, and the other quit talking. Nicholas impatiently forced the whole cock down his throat and gagged. It wasn't the dream blow job a gay guy would have performed – as Benjamin had thought – but he didn't give up. The whole act was just naïvely rough and uncontrolled. So much so that the real man – as the captain had just been baptized – collapsed on the couch, his dick bouncing in the air.

When White-Glow Troy opened the door with one hand while holding a joint in the other, the violence age was over. And as soon as the smoke cloud he'd puffed out cleared, he found himself in front of two naked guys fucking like it was Mykonos. Handfuls of ass, stretching lips, holes twitching to the rhythm of friendly spasms.

"Look at you, scum!" Troy approached the fused couple and bent to reach their ears. "Everybody's a FAG!" He was so stoned, he couldn't keep serious.

"Shut the fuck up weirdo!" The captain was back. After sliding out of Nicholas' asshole, Benjamin kicked the door closed and hit Troy in the head. "You were right, weren't you, Whaaahite Glow?" He was out of his mind. Halfway between orgasm and madness. Willing to reach extreme pleasure as soon as possible, desirous to hit the boiling desert and bathe in the melting snow.

"It's okay." Nicholas joined them by the TV set and tried to calm things down. Now he was scared this would turn into disaster. He waited, and on both sides of his ass the red prints of Benjamin's wide hands started to hurt.

Troy scrutinized both of them, standing with their juices going and hungry for more. Neither hard-on had come down. The room smelled like cock on underwear worn more than one day. He couldn't help but laugh. A long painful endless laugh at the end of which he slowly approached the couch and sat down in disbelief. It was his way out of masturbation. Why hadn't he thought of that before? Was man-to-man sex cool now just because the rugby team captain had adopted it? Was that what he wanted? The cannabis made those considerations dilute. At the end of the tunnel, he had no answer, but his hand felt his flesh growing in between his legs. As in an enchanted coma, his fingers unbuttoned the jeans, dragged the boxers down over knees and ankles, went back to crotch. "Fuck the hell out of me! Tear me apart! I wanna part with my asshole!" He recited, assuming a dog-style position that for some reason had always intrigued him for the total abandonment to the other person's likes. His lisp had disappeared.

Benjamin and Nicholas stared at the back of Troy's thighs in that position. For once, the pallor of his skin caused an effect that wasn't associated to a nickname or an insult. His body was hairless and unexpectedly inviting, free of the inhibitory brakes they were both still fighting against. The young frat boys looked at each other, discovering one was the mirror image of the other. Ass in tension, hips gently jutting out: all senses concentrated on the full erection. Their brains anticipating and multiplying the ways what came next would bring a new angle into their life, a new flavor into their underwear. The straight twin was the first one to surrender to the liquid changes in his right hand, and walked towards the target. The captain followed, almost shyly. What was there to say?

They unanimously decided to adopt a simple scheme. Benjamin pumped Troy from behind while Nicholas fucked his mouth. They didn't know they were the only people in the dorm, so they didn't scream enough. But the three of them obtained what they were looking for. Troy came on Samuel's cushions what seemed to him fifty times before Benjamin was satisfied. Nicholas seasoned Troy's mouth, and they messaged one another's cum-wet bodies.

As promised, Nicholas told everything to Valorie in a long email: "Dear Valorie …"

ORAL EXAMS
By Landon Dixon

I woke up with a start. Where the hell was I?

I looked over at the naked brother sleeping next to me. Oh yeah, I thought with a warm, satisfied smile, the frat house. The guy in bed next to me was Ozzie Jones, a full-fledged member of the fraternity I was desperately trying to join.

It was Ozzie's bed. I was as naked as he was. We'd hit it off at a party, split half a keg, and then Ozzie had split my black ass right down the middle with his chocolate stirstick, with my enthusiastic encouragement; mentoring a pledge in the most manly manner.

I stretched my limbs like a panther, gazing at Ozzie. He was lying on his side, facing me, the cutest sleepy-time expression on his hot chocolate face. His dong was at rest, as well, flopped down over his right thigh, four inches of licorice delight even unerect.

It was just past 9:00 am. The sun was burning against the wispy curtains of the frat house bedroom. Morning, I knew from my liberal education, was the time when men were most full of testosterone, dicks most inflatable. It was time to build me some wood.

I reached over and ran my fingers along Ozzie's left thigh, lightly stroking the smooth, ebony skin. He smacked his plush lips, washed them with the tip of his bright pink tongue, sighing contentedly. Like me.

I traced my fingers down to his pube-pebbled balls, circled, stroked the hefty, hanging pair. Ozzie groaned, a twitch running through the length of his night-shaded cock. I tickled his nuts with the tips of my fingers, making them tighten, making that snake between his loins engorge all on its own.

Exams were coming up. Ozzie had crammed me the night before. Now it was time for me to take my orals, put in some good word-of-mouth on my chances of moving from pledge to full fraternity brother. I slithered lower down on the bed, got waist-level with the bro, stuck out my gleaming pink tongue and tapped the slit of his hood with it.

Ozzie stiffened. So did his dick. But his eyes didn't open, just his mouth in a murmur of unconscious appreciation, as I swirled my wet tongue around and around his cap. The purple-black knob soon shone with my spit, swelled with my tongue-lashing, mushrooming out at me on the end of the guy's fast-rising dong.

I let his cockhead flow right into my mouth on its own engorging velocity. Then I sealed my puffy lips around it and sucked, tugging on the meaty cock-cap.

Ozzie grunted, clutched his pillow, shunted his hips back and forth, fucking my mouth in his wet dream sleep. Only this was no dream. This was hot reality, a dreamboat's dick in my mouth. His mamba glided in and out, swollen veined shaft brushing my lips, sliding along my tongue, expanding ever greater.

I set my lips and tongue tighter. Ozzie pumped his hips harder. He bumped the back of my throat with his beefy hood, the brother's cock surged out to its full eight delicious dark inches or so, helped greatly along by my sucking mouth.

I cupped his balls, squeezed them, spurring him forward. He thrust quicker, deeper, hips sliding on the satin sheets, dong pistoning my mouth, filling me full. My cheeks ballooned and throat bulged with meat. I huffed hot, humid air out of my gaping nostrils and against Ozzie's groin, sucking as urgently as he was pumping my face.

He never saw it coming because his eyes were still closed. But he felt it, right down to his manhandled sack. And I felt it, and tasted it, and reveled in it. His dusky nuts seized cum-tight and his cock pronged cum-hard. He jerked, spurting.

Hot, salty semen sprayed my throat, Ozzie's cock jumping in my mouth with every burst. I kept on sucking, swallowing now, as well, drinking the guy's orgasm in big, hungry gulps. His lean, lithe body shuddered repeatedly, as he poured out the results of my oral exam.

"Okay, Lex," Clarence said from the cracked-open door, "you've passed that part of the initiation."

Ozzie's eyes popped open, liquid brown and slightly glazed. He stared down at me sucking the last of his juice out of his dick, milking his balls with my fingers. And a huge grin broke brilliant white over his handsome, happy face.

Clarence and the two other brothers barged into the bedroom. I popped Ozzie out of my mouth and squeezed his slippery shaft, licked up the last drop of jizz out of his slit with relish. Just before the guys dragged me out of the bed and into the center of the room, put me on my knees.

"Part two of the orals," Clarence stated. "And this one's gonna be a little harder to swallow."

I licked my lips and grinned. As Clarence and the two other tall, dark and handsome frat bros popped open their pants and pulled out their cocks. "We're gonna see if you can handle a full, course load," Clarence grunted, stroking his brown stretch of beef.

The other two guys were Denell and Barron. Denell was the star center of the university basketball team. He had mocha-colored skin and long, lanky features and long dreadlocks, a smooth, slender dick that just wouldn't quit, as I witnessed his hand. He pulled that hose out nine inches or more, fisted one foot away from my shining face.

Barron was broad in the shoulders and heavily-muscled all over, pitch-dark as the Nubian prince Ozzie lying watching in bed. The man sported a shaved head and a tapered goatee, two gold earrings. His cock was wrist-thick and heavy-looking, gorgingly turgid in his tugging hand. I waggled my tongue at it.

Clarence grimaced, stroking slow and sure on his flesh-hose, aiming the bloated nozzle my way. He was the leader of the pack of dicks, a studious stud with black-rimmed glasses and a mowed-down fro, an intense, seriously sexy face and trim, lean body. His cock sprouted from his loins rubber ink-black as Ozzie's, just as long and lethal-looking.

Heavy-breathing filled the heated air, along with the sweet, cloying scent of sperm on the boil, the phwacking of hands stretching foreskins. I sat on my heels and gripped my thighs and bent my head forward, like a hunting dog pointing, eagerly watching, anxiously awaiting. I wasn't allowed to stroke or lick or suck, just get hosed, the three-man bukkake testing my ability to deal with men under pressure.

Denell grunted, and jerked, his knees buckling. His slender right hand was a blur on his slim dong, his left twisting his nuts. I held my breath. Sperm leapt out of his slit, splashed my forehead.

I raised my head and threw my mouth wide-open. And the next gush hit the back of my throat, on-target. I gagged, recovered, gulped. Another

89

spurt, sailing into my mouth and splattering my tongue. And another and another and another.

The giant bent almost in two, jacking his dong with abandon. I swallowed equally recklessly, my Adam's apple bobbing to beat the hand.

Clarence cried, "Outcoming!"

I whipped my head around to his iron-hard rod, as he put the finishing burnishes on it, then blew molten. A huge gout of semen shot directly into my mouth, followed instantaneously by a second, a third, a fourth, a fifth. I didn't have time to swallow, the blasts coming too fast and furious.

Clarence quivered like he'd been plugged into the wall socket, reflexively jacking, on empty. I showed him the pool of jizz in my mouth. His eyes almost bugged out his lenses, as I closed my mouth and took one huge gulp, coating my throat and esophagus and stomach lining with his steaming load.

Barron pumped his noir fireplug of a dick in a frenzy. I thrust my face at the pointing and primed hood. He went off, jetting into my eyes, against my nose. It was like being hit full-blast by a firehose.

The guy absolutely creamed my face, washing every inch of my physiognomy except for my mouth, leaving me dripping with cum. I used my hands now, scooping the sperm off my cheeks and chin and into my mouth. It took four or five finger-passes, but I got most of the massive spurtage into my mouth.

Then I smiled at the stunned, gasping brothers, rinsing the rubbery jism around in my mouth, swishing from side to side. Then swallowing, just as thoroughly and wholeheartedly as I'd taken Ozzie's original load.

They allowed me a couple of hours to recover. I needed no time, though; 'they' needed the time. And when we all finally gathered down in the rec room of the frat house, their ranks had been bolstered by two other brothers and five other pledges.

This was the final oral exam. Six pledges were left, to suck six cocks. The first three to get their brothers to blow were full-fledged in the fraternity.

We formed a line, six pledges facing six brothers, on our knees. I'd gotten Tre, and not by accident, I suspected. I'd passed the other two orals with flying colors and jizz, and now I was really being put to the test. The bulge in Tre's pants was mind-blowing, mouth-stretching to the extreme, without doubt.

Clarence raised his arm. "Ready, set ... blow!"

Buttons popped and zippers rasped. I didn't have to dig around in Tre's shorts to pull out his cock, like some of the other pledges had to. The guy wasn't wearing any underwear, and his mahogany log fell out of his pants like a tree falling in the darkened forest.

It was enormous. I'd never seen a dick so large firsthand before. And my first hand could barely fit around it. My fingers strained to encompass its tremendous girth. I looked up at Tre, struggling to clasp and heft his meat. He grinned down at me, arms crossed, blunt face beaming confidence.

I finally gripped his blood sausage with both hands and tugged. Got nowhere. The thing just hung there, huge and unresponsive.

Frantic slurping filled the electric air. I glanced over at my competitors. Most of them had already latched their supple lips onto bulbed hoods and bloated shafts and were sucking with a vengeance, the bros already trembling under the wet-vaccing pressure.

I clutched Tre's cock, staring at the one-eyed, mammoth hood staring impassively back at me. The shaft of the brother's dong was just as wide as the cap, the whole thing a turgid slab of blackened beef with the unstiffened texture of molasses. I sucked air into my lungs, slapped my tongue against the gargantuan tip of the monster.

He – and it – didn't budge an inch. I twirled my tongue around hood, spit-painted shaft, and got as much as a rise as you get from unleavened black bread. I popped my jaw muscles and took chewy hood right into my mouth, pulled with my lips, pumping shaft with my two hands.

The reaction was the same – none.

I pushed my head forward with a mounting sense of desperation, a mouth gone wide as its ever gone. I managed to consume maybe three inches of cable, and sucked. And got not even a throb of recognition for my efforts.

Tre's cock didn't stiffen, didn't engorge one single millimeter in my tugging mouth and hands.

Meanwhile, up and down the cock line the other kneeling boys were racing towards the jizznish line. The dicks they were sucking and throating, jacking, were at rigid attention, pulsating with mounting pleasure even to the naked eye. The ominous sound of brothers grunting and groaning could be heard above the heady slurping and thwacking.

Tre's dong was a no-blow zone, even 'my' exemplary oral skills failing to penetrate its thick skin.

This was a real test of my sexual wits. I flailed around for a plan of action. I grasped Tre's balls, twiddled them, thinking, thinking, thinking.

Tre moaned and quivered. I batted my eyes, clearing my mind.

I cupped, squeezed Tre's sack, sensually massaged the man's nuts. And he bucked like Black Beauty at a rodeo, his dong poling straight out into my face. I'd found the guy's sweet spot!

I'm not a tea-bagger by nature. Why settle for the ballsy hors d'oeuvres when you can consume the full-course meal above? I say. But now I went low-down and dirty, shoving my face in between Tre's quivering legs and lapping at his hanging pouch.

"Fuck!" he gasped, jumping.

His shaven balls were as bloated beyond belief as his cock. They were a real mouthful, but a doable mouthful. I licked the wrinkles until they etched even deeper with tightness, then sucked the heavy sack right into my mouth and held it there.

Tre stared wildly down at me, his package disappeared in my face. His cock jutted out a dark country mile above me, the veins beating with red-hot, rushing blood. As I sucked on his sack as a whole, his balls one by one.

Men were moaning up and down the line. Only two minutes – an erotic eternity – had passed, and the dick-slick enthusiasm of the pledges was taking a toll on the brothers. Spray-off was just around the corner.

I reached up and took hold of Tre's peetrunk, pulled it aside, so he could see my shining eyes, my lips working his testes and scrotum. My hands and mouth were filled with genitalia. I was filled with confidence. Because Tre's balls were full of bubbling sperm.

I juggled his nuts on the end of my tongue, cranking his cock. He jerked, jumped up onto his toes, yowling at the ceiling.

Everyone was watching us. I gave them a sight to behold. I had King Dong by the balls, and I sucked full-bore on his nuts, letting go of his pipe. And his cock exploded up above me, hands and mouth-free.

"Motherfucker!" Tre roared, blasting jizz out of his cannon.

He rocketed rope after rope of sizzling sperm, shooting almost clear across the room. You could've heard a prick drop above the big guy's mewling. I was making my bro blow with just my mouth clamped on his balls, controlling his super-spurts with each squeeze of my lips.

I'd discovered the secret to the man's sexcess, and I was milking it for all it was worth.

And showman and cocksman that I am, I just couldn't resist finishing off tres Tre with a bang. As he shuddered his fifth or sixth burst of delight, I popped my mouth off his sack and grabbed his balls with my hand, yanked them down. Cutting off his ecstatic flow.

He gaped at me, his body vibrating like a live wire, cock doing the same, the awesome appendage straining desperately to return to firing, but lacking the ammunition. "Welcome to the fraternity, Brother Lex!" Tre screamed.

That's what I'd been longing to hear. I loosened the deathgrip on his nuts, let the juice fly again.

I scored top of the pledge class on my oral exams.

HALLOWEEN HARD-ON
By Logan Zachary

The Beta House stood at the end of the cul de sac. All the lights were on and the music throbbed from deep within the center of the fraternity. Smiling jack-o'-lanterns lined the street and led up the walkway to the front door.

The Beta Boys were hosting the annual Halloween bash, and the night promised to be exciting.

Jack looked into his closet and tried to decide what his costume would be this year. He wanted something easy and quick. He didn't want to carry a prop, wear a mask, wig or make-up. His football player's body clad only in a pair of white boxer shorts filled the doorway.

"Jack, are you coming out of the closet?" his roommate Travis asked.

"Don't you wish?" Jack smiled at him.

"Honey, I share a room with you. I know."

Jack bent over, making the white cotton hug his ass as he picked up a pair of socks. He spun and tossed the smelly pair at Travis and hit him in the face.

"What are you going to wear as your costume?" Travis moved into the room, still staring at Jack's butt.

"You're looking at it." Jack slapped his tight end.

"What are you supposed to be?" Travis flopped down on his bed.

"A man who needs to wash his clothes."

"That would win first place for sure."

"Fuck you." Jack pulled out a red flannel shirt and tried to pull out the wrinkles.

"Anytime you want, you know that. You look great in whatever you wear or don't wear."

"What do you want?" Jack balled up his shirt and tossed it back into the pile.

"Nothing, I just wanted to let you know that they have a Haunted House in that old house behind our frat."

"The one they're remodeling?"

"Yes." Travis rolled onto his stomach on the bed.

"I hate haunted houses."

"Are you chicken?" Travis rested his chin on his hand as he watched Jack, his muscles rippling under the cotton.

"I'm just not into that kind of thing." Jack reached into his boxers and scratched his hairy ass. He turned back into the closet and pulled out his bib overalls. He held them in front of himself.

"Hot."

"I'm going as a farmer this year." Jack started to step into the bibs.

"Wait." Travis held his hand up.

"What?"

"You can't wear your boxers." Travis shook his head.

"Commando?" Jack asked.

"Commando." Travis spun around and sat on the edge of the bed closest to Jack.

Jack started to pull them off when he saw Travis lean forward. "You show me yours, and I'll …" He pulled the waistband down and flashed him his thick blond hairy bush. The thick base of his cock crested just before he pulled them back up.

"Please, oh please." Travis clapped his hands.

"Strip for me, and I'll strip for you." Jack turned his back, pulled off his boxers and stepped into his bibs. He flexed his hairy ass at Travis. He spread his muscular cheeks and slapped each one. Bending over, he pulled his bibs up and hooked one strap, but left the other one dangle.

Travis grabbed his crotch and rubbed. "You are such a cock tease."

"What are you going as?" Jack walked over to Travis on the bed, his bulging groin at eye level.

"I'm working tonight, so no party for me." Travis looked at his watch and pushed up, his eyes even closer to Jack's cock. He inhaled deeply and licked his lips. "Someday."

The party raged on, and Jack was bored. He walked through the house and out the back door. He stood in the cold night, letting the breeze cool his bare chest. Dry leaves rustled as they blew across the yard. He looked at the path that ran to the old neighbor's house. The Haunted House. No one at the party had spoken about it, but Jack hadn't paid any attention to much of their conversations.

He finished his beer and set the empty bottle on the back step. He peered across the backyard and saw nothing. Shouldn't there be more action going on across the backyard? A scream, a laugh, anything? Was there even a Haunted House going on?

Inside the frat house, the party and music raged on.

Jack walked through the backyard and into the house that was under construction. How scary had the guys made this place? He knew that the remodelers had just started the rehab of the old place last week, but what could they have done in a few days? Maybe that's why it was safe to use as a haunted house, no risk or worry of damage.

He walked up the back stairs into the kitchen, a sink dripped and stained with splashes of brown and rust. Was that supposed to be blood? Or just dirt from years of neglect?

The dining room was empty, the windows boarded up, and wall paper peeled back from the walls. Part of the dry wall came away with it, exposing rows of laths that looked like ribs.

A noise came from the other room, and Jack paused before pushing the swinging door open. A couch without cushions, a large armchair with stuffing sticking out, and fireplace crammed with debris and wood filled the space.

A shuffling startled him, and as he turned around to see what it was, a cloaked figure grabbed him and lifted him off the floor. His two-hundred-pound frame rose easily and slammed into the wall. Another cloaked figure appeared with a nail gun in hand.

"Oh Shit!"

The nail gun touched his bib overall's pant leg and fired. Rapidly, the gun worked up the side of his leg and stopped at his waist. It paused for a second and moved to the other side. Quickly, his other pant leg was nailed to the wall. The cloaked figure moved to stand in front of him and looked up. He brought the gun to his shoulder strap and fired ten nails to secure him.

Jack leaned forward and more nails shot out and into his bib overalls, holding him fast to the wall. "Hey! What the hell?"

A few more nails pinned his hips to the wall, as his feet dangled in mid-air.

"All right, trick or treat, very funny, but enough is enough. Let me down." Jack waved his arms around and tried to free himself.

One of the cloaked figures reached inside and pulled out a large pair of shears. The light caught the silver, and it flashed at him.

"What are you going to do with that?"

The man moved closer and spilled the blades into Jack's fly.

Snip.

The scissors cut the denim.

A cool breeze entered his bibs and flowed over his cock and balls. Jack pulled back as the blades cut again.

Snip.

The bib's opening widened, and the man switched directions. He cut down, parallel to the fly and continued down to the inseam.

Jack felt his hairy balls rise up as he felt the cold metal blade of the scissors pass underneath and curve, starting up along the other side. A patch opened up as the swatch of denim fell to the floor. He felt his cock stir and start to swell.

The other figure took out a flashlight and aimed at his groin. "Look at that, he's starting to get a Halloween hard-on."

The piece of denim fell to the floor as all of Jack's glory was displayed.

Two more hooded figures entered the living room. "Looks like we have a cheerleader. Two big furry pom poms are being shaken at us."

"We should take care of that." The man with the shears snapped his fingers and one of the hooded men left, only to return with a basin with water, shaving cream and a straight edge razor.

"You've got to be kidding," Jack said. He pulled on his bibs, which refused to budge from the wall.

"I'm sure you feel like the fly caught in the spider's web." The man approached with the shears and set the cold metal blades against his dangling hairy balls.

Jack's cock bounced and swelled to full length. He felt the blade move and a gentle tug on his hair.

Snip.

"I'm sure the razor will do a cleaner job."

Jack felt a warm wash cloth wrap around his balls and wet them thoroughly. The can of shave cream shot a handful of foam and with a few swipes, his testicles were lathered up.

All four hooded figures moved closer to watch the one with the razor kneel down for a better view. The one with the flashlight aimed the beam to his ball sac.

"Hold very still. The razor is sharp. We wouldn't want an unfortunate accident to occur."

Jack closed his eyes as he felt the rasp of the sharp blade stroke along one of his balls.

The shaver pulled his dangling skin tight and took another swipe.

Warm wet foam ran down his leg, and he hoped it wasn't blood.

"Beautiful."

Jack could feel their stare on his package. His cock danced with each stroke.

"He's starting to ooze. You must be doing a great job."

Jack felt a warm breath exhale over his tender skin. "What else did they have in store for him?" he wondered.

The skilled hands moved to his other testicle and pulled the skin tight. Rasp, rasp, rasp, and the sharp blade did its work.

The warm wash cloth wiped him clean of hair and shaving cream, the smell of sweat and minty Foamy entered his nose, and he felt more precum flow out of his cock.

"So what should we do to him next?" A tool box was opened, and he searched for the right tool. He pulled out two small clamps and handed them to one of the men.

The man walked over to his chest and rubbed the cold metal over his exposed nipple and watched as it rose. He opened the clamp and pinched his nipple. He set it and let the tool hang from his erect tip. He took the other one and reached under the bibs and stimulated the other nipple.

Jack willed his body not to respond, but his flesh rose up into a sharp point.

The metal closed on his nipple. The pinch hurt and made him feel his heartbeat. He flicked the clamp and made it jiggle. The pressure sent warm waves through Jack's body.

"Why are you doing this to me?" Jack asked.

A large butt plug emerged from the toolbox, and one man grabbed it. He picked up the bottle of lube and smeared the sex toy with the clear fluid. "Wanna plug that hole in your pants?" He laughed at his bad joke and stepped between his legs. He slipped the plug into the bibs opening and moved it between Jack's butt cheeks.

Jack squirmed as the latex toy slipped between his cheeks and sought his tight hole. He clenched his butt tight, but the man found his pucker.

"Relax, it won't hurt as much. Besides, we have all night." He took Jack's cock into his mouth and swallowed him whole.

The surprise relaxed his ass, and the tip entered him slightly.

The plug twisted and slipped in deeper. It pushed in and pulled out, only to be twisted and re-inserted. The tongue that worked over his cock pulled more precum out of the thick shaft.

The leader tapped him on the shoulder. "Before you go too far," he pulled his hand out from the robe and looked at his watch. "It's almost midnight; we should get ready." He picked up the shears and looked up at Jack. "Would you like to be released?" He snipped the scissors once.

"You're going to cut my bibs?"

The figure slipped the blades into the hole and ran the cold metal along his cock.

"I see your point. They're trashed already." Jack nodded.

He started cutting up from the cuff to his inseam. One leg fell free of the denim. He cut the bib part off and started down the second leg. One last snip, and Jack dropped to the floor.

Jack looked at the door and wondered if he should make a break for it or just join in. If he ran, they would chase and probably catch him, besides he was buck ass naked except for his shoes.

The cloaked figure read his mind. "I'll drag your sorry ass back here, personally. Or we could move this Halloween party back to the frat house, but then there may be many more trick or treaters wanting that sweet ass."

Two of the cloaked figures grabbed his arms and dragged him to the sofa. They bent him over the back.

Jack felt his ass cheeks spread and someone explore the lubed opening. The clamps on his nipples fell off as his chest rubbed across the back of the couch.

A finger circled Jack's hole, seeking entry. It darted in and out, seeing if the butt plug had relaxed him.

Jack felt his erection press against the crushed velvet and his smooth balls swung back and forth.

The figure behind him dropped to his knees and licked down his crack. It teased his opening and entered as it could. Slowly the mouth worked lower to his tender, newly shaved flesh and pulled one orb into his mouth. He swallowed it whole and milked it with his tongue.

Jack spread is legs wider as the pleasure increased.

The fourth man stepped in front of him and reached up under his cloak. He fished out his hard-on and brought it to Jack's full lips.

Jack wet them in anticipation.

The figure rubbed his dick across his mouth and left a streak of precum along the way.

Jack licked the sweet fluid away and grazed the tip of the offered cock. He cleaned the pearl from the tip.

The man between his legs switched balls and sucked on the other one, drawing it in as far as he could.

Jack felt his cock ooze precum out of the shaft and soak into the couch. The man sucking on his balls milked more out of him, and he felt both balls enter the hot, wet mouth. He was going to shoot very soon if this continued.

The man on the floor let his balls slide out of his mouth, and he stood up. He pulled up his cloak and worked his cock out. He slipped on a condom and lubed up Jack's ass and his dick. He pressed forward and reached around to grab Jack's cock.

Jack's ass relaxed, and the dick entered him with one smooth stroke. He felt the guy pump into him a few times, and then his whole body shuddered, and he stopped.

The hand wrapped around his cock squeezed tight and just held him as his climax filled the rubber.

"You came already?" a man scolded. "It's midnight. It's time."

All the hands released Jack, and he stood up slowly. He felt the lube run down his leg. He turned around, pressed his back to the couch, and watched as the men surrounded him.

The four robed men formed a semi circle around Jack and bowed to him.

Jack looked from one to the next. He watched as the men pulled their hoods back. Brendan, the Frat's president, Clayton, the vice President, and Robert, the treasurer smiled up at him, and then Travis!

"Travis, you set me up. You're such an asshole," Jack said.

"I wanted to make your Halloween special. Boys, let's do it." He pulled his robe open, and it slipped down his body to pool around his feet. Travis wore a leather studded jock strap and a leather harness across his broad chest. His hairy chest and pierced nipples showed through the straps and metal loops.

Clayton wore a white jock pulled tight over his huge dick. His ebony skin shone in the dark. Smooth and pumped with muscles, his frame would make a bodybuilder proud.

Robert was a bear, hairy and hulking. Black square cut boxers covered his ass and tried to hold his huge bulge in, a wet spot soaked through the fabric after his orgasm.

Brendan was the model frat boy, perfect in every way, golden brown skin, perfect teeth, blue eyes, blond highlighted hair, and a chiseled body off a runway in New York. He wore white Calvins. The spread of fine chest hair covered his pecs and trailed down to a perfect set of abs. Any porn video studio would snatch him up in an instant.

Jack savored the nearly naked men who stared at him. "Trick or treat." He smiled despite himself. "Am I meant to be the virgin sacrifice at midnight?"

Brendan pulled out a thick blanket and spread it on the floor. He leaned over and started the wood in the fireplace on fire. Flames lapped up the wood and smoke rose up the chimney. Shadows danced around the room and warmth filled the damp space.

Jack tried to cover his erection, but knew everyone had seen him and it did little to make it go down. The contact of his hands only made it more sensitive and hard, precum oozed out of the fat head and worked down his thick shaft.

Travis stepped in front of him and said, "Happy Halloween." He gave Jack a kiss, which deepened. Tongues tasted as desire grew. Travis wrapped his arms around Jack and pulled him close. He felt Jack's cock slide up his torso and rest against his navel. He rubbed his butt and squeezed his cheeks.

Jack felt the heat flow from Travis' body into his.

The fire added warmth to the room, and the three other men joined them. Brendan licked one of Jack's ears, as Clayton dropped to his knees and spread the cheeks Travis massaged. He buried his face between the fleshy orbs and licked.

Jack pushed back on his face and relaxed his ass.

Robert dropped down between his legs and found Jack's smooth balls. He licked the sensitive skin and sucked the low hanging sac into his mouth. He rolled it with his tongue and pulled on it.

Jack marveled at the unexpected feeling of the newly shaved balls. Every nerve fiber tingled.

Travis guided Jack to the center of the blanket and helped him to lie down. He pulled the leather jock from his cock and let the monster swing free. "You started well on this; I hope you could finish."

Clayton worked between his legs. "I hope they loosened you up." He pulled off his white jock, and Jack gasped when he saw the length and girth of his dick. "You're really going to enjoy this. I know I will."

Brendan handed a condom to Clayton and placed the bottle of lube close. He found a pillow and placed it under Jack's hips as Clayton picked up his ass. He brought Jack's legs along side of his neck as Brendan slipped the pillow under his hips.

Travis knelt over Jack's face and guided his cock to his mouth. He rubbed the wet tip over his lips and waited for it to open.

Jack settled his ass on the pillow and felt Clayton move between his legs. He took a deep breath before Travis pushed his cock deeper into his mouth.

Clayton's dick found his opening and pressed forward. His fat mushroom head tried to enter, but stalled.

Brendan knelt and grabbed Jack's cock and stroked it. Jack's ass opened and swallowed Clayton's dick. He started humping and moving forward, plowing in deeper and deeper.

Jack rolled with the rhythm of Clayton and Travis, bouncing off one dick and onto the other. The speed increased as did the depth and intensity. Brendan worked his cock in time with the others.

Robert moved closer, and Jack reached out and grabbed his dick. He rubbed it through his boxers and felt the dampness on the pouch.

Brendan pulled off his Calvins and unrolled a rubber on Jack's dick. He lubed it and carefully moved over his throbbing member. Slowly, he lowered himself on Jack and descended. He guided Jack's dick inside and rode him.

Jack ping ponged as Brendan rode him. The four men moved in tandem. Robert's dick came out of his shorts. His dick filled Jack's hand as he settled back and worked it over his arousal.

The fire cracked and sparked across the room. The heat and smoke mingled in the room and cast dancing shadows around the room. Jack savored the taste, the smell, the feelings and closed his eyes to hold them all in. He felt his balls start to rise up, and his whole body started to tingle. He pulled harder on Travis' dick; he pressed down on Clayton's cock, and drilled into Brendan. His hand increased his speed on Robert.

Jack rode the wave of pleasure and increased his pace. He felt his shaved balls rise up along side of his shaft, and he shot into his condom.

Brendan's ass milked as another orgasm gushed out.

Jack's ass clamped down on Clayton's cock as it emptied. His mouth held Travis' dick and swallowed the cream. White, thick heat flowed down his throat and added to all the firing nerve endings of his body. His whole body convulsed as the waves of pleasure and orgasm soared through all of the men.

Robert felt the tension on his cock and shot his load again. He threw his head back and felt every hair on his body stand on end.

The men collapsed into a heap on the floor and lay there panting. One by one, the men rose and slowly collected themselves.

Jack lay in the center of the room and watched as the men dressed. He pushed up onto his elbows and enjoyed the views.

Travis looked down at him and asked, "Well? What are you waiting for?"

"It's not like I have any clothes to wear." Jack pointed to the shredded bibs.

Travis started to pull his cloak off.

"I don't want to wear something with your dick tracks."

"You had my cock down your throat, but you won't wear my clothes."

Jack sat up and crossed his legs.

"Did you want me to run back to the house and get you something to wear?"

Jack shook his head. "I don't trust you guys to come back."

"You can walk back naked. I'd follow close behind."

"Not an option." Jack stood up and waited.

Travis picked up the shears and quickly cut two holes in the white blanket. He threw it over Jack's head and said, "You can be a ghost."

Jack felt the warm cloth cover his naked body, and he headed back to the frat house. He followed the four as they walked across the yard, up the back stairs and into the kitchen.

"I'll run upstairs and find something else to wear." Jack walked into the living room and started toward the stairs.

Travis stepped on the tail of the blanket.

"Hey, you're on my blanket."

Travis grabbed the cloth and held tight.

The room was full of partiers, drinking, talking, and dancing.

"Travis, let go." Jack pulled on the blanket, and it shifted on his body. He pulled his head out and wrapped the edge around himself. His bare shoulder felt the warmth of the room, as he tried to keep his legs, ass, and quickly arousing dick covered.

Travis pulled the blanket with all of his might. The material slipped from Jack's hands, and he fell down onto the floor, naked.

The crowd surged forward and stared down at Jack's naked body.

"Hey, everybody," Travis shouted and pointed at Jack, "Here's your trick or treat."

And they all had a Happy Halloween orgy.

THE TEST
By T.A. Meeker

"Ethan!" my dad yelled from downstairs. "It's already seven o'clock!"

Dad has always been an early-riser, but not me. I was still dragging my feet around the room, packing everything I thought I might need. I hadn't even gotten dressed yet.

"Ethan!" More bite to his voice this time. "You hear me?"

"Yes, Dad! I'll be right there!" I ran my hands down my bare chest to see if I was dry from my morning shower. Close enough. I grabbed the bottle of Jergen's lotion from the night stand next to my bed.

I like putting lotion on in front of the mirror, mostly because I think I'm a good looking guy. I just turned eighteen last month, and because I've been a farm boy all my life, I had already developed a decent muscular cut. I have blond hair, cut short. I don't grow much hair on my body. None on my chest, and I shave my pubes.

I stood in front of the full-length mirror attached to the back of my bedroom door, slathering gobs of lotion over my shoulders and down my arms. It had a great almond scent. I slid my thumb under the elastic band of my underwear and eased the white briefs to the floor.

My cock flopped out and swung like the pendulum on a clock. I squeezed more lotion into my hands and smeared it down my belly and over my balls. My cock started to stiffen. I posed from side to side, checking myself out. Nice! I rubbed lotion down the length of the shaft once and stopped, wishing I had more time.

I finished my lotion routine and quickly got dressed. Dad was getting pissed. Good thing I had already packed some stuff the night before.

When I went downstairs, I smelled fresh-brewed coffee. Dad was waiting in the kitchen with a cup in his hand. He jingled his car keys in his other hand.

"These are the last two," I said, carrying my black suitcases.

"Hurry up. Go put 'em in the car. Let's go!"

There was no arguing with Dad. He had always been tough. He had been too tough with mom, and that's probably why she had left him.

Dad expected me to follow in his footsteps, asking me to be tough, play football, and join the wrestling team. Problem was I wasn't interested in those things. Of course, I couldn't let him know that. I had to keep pictures of Taylor Swift and Carrie Underwood taped to my walls, even though I was more interested in Eminem, but not so much his music.

This was going to be my freshman year at the University of Iowa. I was nervous, and Dad lectured me all the way there. More expectations. Punishments if I embarrassed him. No monetary support if I couldn't keep at least a B average. His rants went on and on, which didn't ease my nerves.

He parked in the lot in front of my dorm, and I unloaded my own bags. Struggling, I managed to drag them toward the building. Of course, Dad didn't help. He had just waved and drove off.

Luckily, when I reached the dorm and stood looking up the stairwell, three guys approached me and asked to help carry my bags.

"What floor you on?" the tallest one asked. His two friends grabbed all my bags.

"I'm in 403," I said.

"Hey! That's our floor, too." He turned toward his friends and smirked. "Come on, we'll show you where you're at."

The two guys with my bags started up the stairwell. Why did the guy smirk at his friends? I hoped he didn't think I was weak. I had to be strong, build a good reputation. That's what Dad had said. I held my hand out to shake with the tall guy. "My name's Ethan."

When the guy shook my hand, I made sure to return a firm grip. No mistakes. This guy looked a little older than I and was probably in his junior or senior year. His two friends looked a little younger.

"I'm Cody," he replied.

This guy was gorgeous. He had dark hair, almost black. His eyes were light, maybe green or crystal blue. And he was well-built. The arms of his short-sleeved T-shirt stretched tightly around his biceps as if the material were spandex rather than cotton. I knew there had to be a six-pack hiding under there. *Don't stare! Had I looked too long? Be more careful*, I told myself.

When I looked up at him, Cody had his eyebrows furrowed.

"Are you coming?" he asked.

"Yeah." Just about.

When Cody and I reached room 403, his two friends had already taken my bags inside. They were laughing with another guy in the room.

Cody pointed at the guy sitting on the lower bunk of my new bed. "That's your roommate, Logan. He's hardly ever here."

I smiled, and Logan nodded at me. So far, college was proving to be somewhat intimidating. All these guys looked ripped. What happened to the scrawny, dorky, brainiacs with horn-rimmed glasses?

Logan slipped on his shoes and a baseball cap. He nodded at me once again as he left the room, shutting the door on his way out.

"Before you get too comfortable," Cody said, "we have to make sure you can stay on this floor."

"What do you mean?" I was confused. The college had assigned me to this room.

Cody's friends gathered around him. "We've done a great job at weeding-out people that don't fit in on this floor."

Now I was worried. My heart hammered. Did he suspect something was weird with me? *Be tough. Don't back down.*

"I paid to be in this dorm!"

Cody laughed and his friends smiled. "I appreciate that, and you can stay in this building. But, we have a short series of test you have to pass if you want to stay on this floor."

One of Cody's friends stepped forward and said, "It's three tests actually. Spaced out over three days. The more tests you pass, the better your status will be in our group. You have to pass at least one test to our satisfaction in order to stay on this floor."

The other friend stepped forward to add his bit. "Otherwise, you can move down to third floor with all the pussies."

"Your first test will be tomorrow," Cody said. Then he motioned toward the door, and he and his friends left me alone in my room.

I really didn't care if I passed their stupid tests, but if Dad found out I got moved to the pussy floor, there'd be hell to pay. These guys were pretty jock-looking. Hanging out with them might help build a strong reputation. I'd have to at least see what their tests were about. Besides, I only had to pass one.

Cody and my roommate showed up the next evening.

"Test time, Ethan," Cody said. "This is the physical strength test."

Logan pulled the desk chair to the middle of the room and sat down.

"All you have to do is 100 consecutive push-ups," Cody said.

"That's easy." I could do this.

"With me sitting on your back." Cody grinned. "And Logan there is going to keep count."

Cody probably weighed 195 pounds and was about 6'2". I was strong, but there was no way I was going to be able to do this. Not 100. I had to try, so I grabbed my collar and peeled my shirt over my head.

Cody came closer and gave my biceps a gentle squeeze. "So, these are the guns, huh?"

His hands felt great. Much softer than I would have imagined. He was wearing a pair of white Russell Athletic nylon mesh shorts, which clearly displayed his bulging package. I could even see the edge of the glans pressing against the thin fabric. I had to force my eyes away.

I got into position on the floor. Mike straddled my back and sat down like he was going to ride a horse. With his legs spread, I could feel his warm packaged resting on my bare back. His balls felt like a sock full of hot rice. I don't think he was wearing underwear. Uncontrollably, my cock grew.

Logan counted my push-ups out loud. I managed ten good ones and almost got the eleventh, but it was too much. I dropped to the floor under Cody's weight. My cock was smashed between my belly and the tile floor.

When Cody stood up, I noticed that he had a slight erection. Although, it could have been my hopeful imagination.

"How'd he do?" Cody asked Logan.

"Only ten."

"That's all?" Cody shook his head. "I'm afraid that's not going to cut it."

"The test is impossible," I said. "I bet you couldn't do it either."

"But I'm not the one taking the tests, am I?" Cody snatched my shirt off the floor and tossed it to me. "Don't worry, you still have two test left."

The next day, Logan woke up early. He said he was going out of town with some friends to a rave in Chicago. He said not to expect him back that night.

It sucked that he didn't invite me, but I wasn't really into the rave scene. Logan probably wasn't either. I suspected he only went for the drugs. Nevertheless, I was alone all day, dreading what impossible test would be next.

Cody showed up around eight o'clock that night. He wore a black T-shirt with a faded logo, tan cargo shorts, and black Nike sandals. He had a digital camera in his hand.

"No judges or witnesses today?" I asked.

Cody raised the camera. "This is all the proof we'll need."

"I'm not doing anything illegal."

"No, no. We wouldn't expect you to. In fact, this test is easy and fun." Cody smiled. "You'll pass this one. Most everyone does."

"Let's get it over with. What is it?"

"Okay. This test is to prove your self-confidence." Cody came over to me and wrapped his arm around my shoulders. "You're going to grab your towel and your bar of soap, go take a shower, and come back to your room."

"That's it?" I asked. "What's the catch? Why the camera?"

"I'm going to take a picture of you going down the hall to prove you did it." With that, Cody took his arm off my shoulder and snapped a close-up of my face, the flash burning my retinas.

I pushed his camera arm away from my face and grabbed my towel from the ladder on the bunk bed.

"I'll be waiting in the hall," Cody said and left the room.

The showers were at the very end of the hall, some thirty rooms away. They were community showers, but each one had a stall door for privacy. We weren't in a coed building anyway. What I didn't understand was how this test was going to prove my self-confidence ... until I left the room. Then I found out.

Students filled the hall, and Cody was waiting with his camera a few doors down. One of his friends had joined him. When Cody saw me, he put his hand up like a stop sign, shaking his head.

"No, Ethan," he said, leading me back into my room. His friend came in also, and shut the door behind us. "I said towel and soap. I didn't say anything about all this other stuff."

"What other stuff?"

"Your clothes!" Cody and his friend grinned. "You're going to walk down the hall nude, with your towel wrapped around your shoulders."

My face went pale. I couldn't do this. I wasn't ashamed of my body. I knew I looked good. I wasn't afraid about the size of my cock; I carried about eight inches. What I couldn't do was show everyone that I shaved my pubes. Besides, my dick would instantly get hard if I walked naked in front of Cody. How could I explain those things? I'd be sent to the pussy floor for sure.

Cody said he and his friend were going to go wait in the hall again, but I stopped them.

"I'm not doing it," I said. "Fail me if you want, but I'm not doing it."

Cody raised his eyebrows. "Are you sure?"

"Positive."

A moment of silence passed. "Okay ..." He kind of sang the word. "Then, you've only got one test left."

"That's fine."

Cody sized me up, from head to toe. "We're going to do your last test now, tough guy." He stood facing me. He was so close, I could feel his warm breath, and our noses almost touched.

His friend walked around and stopped behind me. I thought they were getting ready to kick my ass.

112

"This last test is confidential," Cody said. "If you disclose anything about this test, me and my buddy Matt ..." – he pointed behind me – "... are going to make sure moving to third floor will be the least of your problems."

"I'm not going to tell anybody about your stupid tests."

"Good." Cody looked into my eyes. "One last thing ... we're not forcing you to take this test. You can give up anytime you want, but you'll be moving to third floor. Now take off your shirt."

I obeyed, yanking my shirt over my head. Matt grabbed my bare arms from behind. My shirt fell to the floor. "Hey!"

Cody went to the door and locked it. He turned back toward me and peeled his own shirt off.

"I'm not fighting you," I said, staring at his body. His smooth tanned skin was stretched over his chiseled chest and washboard abs. There was that six-pack I knew he had. He obviously spent a lot of time in the college's fitness center. He also had a beautiful muscular V-shape at the bottom of his stomach that disappeared into his cargo shorts. My cock started to grow. Matt pulled my arms back tighter.

"We're not going to fight," Cody said. "This test is going to prove your sexuality." He stepped closer to me.

His cologne smelled sweet, like CK. And those arms and shoulders, so well-defined. My cock was now standing straight up, the tip trying to escape the waist of my jersey shorts.

Cody unbuttoned his shorts and slid the zipper down. He didn't take his shorts off, but they slid down a little, revealing the rest of the beautiful V. He wasn't wearing underwear. His pubic hair was dark and trimmed short. He was very well-groomed. I could just barely see the base of his cock. My heart raced. I wished he'd let his shorts go, so I could see it all. But, I didn't know what this test was about. It was probably a trick to see if I'd go for it, to see if I was a homo.

"What the hell are you doing?" I asked. My face was flushed.

"Shut up!" Matt yelled, pulling my arms back.

Cody reached forward and grabbed the legs of my shorts, yanking them down, taking my briefs with them. My shaved cock and balls bounced free in his face. I was hard as an iron pipe and a speck of precum glistened at the tip.

He took a step back and said, "Looks like this one's excited." We met eyes. "Very excited."

Matt pushed down on my arms. "Get on your knees!"

"You can't be serious," I said.

Cody nodded. "You heard him. Get on your knees."

When I didn't move, Matt forced me down. My knees hit the floor, and Matt sat down behind me, still holding my arms. Cody stepped closer and let his shorts fall.

His dick was thick and hard, pointing straight forward, at my face. The tip of his manhood came to a slight point and the slit was gently parted. I could smell his warm skin. He grabbed his throbbing meat by the base and slapped his rod against my wet lips.

If this was the test, and I was supposed to refuse, then I was going to fail! I had to have him, taste him, swallow him. I parted my lips and allowed the head of his cock to slip into my mouth.

He pulled it back out. A strand of saliva connected my lips to him. "If you come before me, you fail the test."

Matt let my arms go, but his hands were still on me. They found their way down my sides and across my stomach. Matt's left hand cupped my balls, his right hand stroked the length of my cock. He was using my precum as lubricant.

Now that my arms were free, I wrapped them around Cody's waist and pushed my nose into his package. His balls smelled like soap. I'd have to do a good job, and fast, because I was ready to explode when I first saw Cody's completely nude body.

I ran my tongue along the underside of his balls all the way to the tip of his perfect shaft, where I teased his piss slit. This thing was probably a good nine inches, definitely bigger than mine. I shoved it into my mouth and down my throat, pumping and twisting my head in a steady rhythm. I massaged his ass cheeks, pulling them apart, and probing the edge of his hole with my finger.

Cody's knees were wobbling, and he moaned. His left hand landed behind my head, rumpling my hair, forcing his cock deeper into my throat.

I choked a couple of times, but I didn't want him to stop. But, suddenly, he did. Matt stopped stroking me, just in time. I looked at my cock. It was red with a vein raging down the side. I needed to get off.

Matt went over to the desk chair, dropped his pants, and sat down. Matt was across the room, but directly in front of me. He was staring at me and had started stroking his cock.

Cody took Matt's spot behind me, and pushed me onto my hands and knees. His hands were on my ass, pulling my cheeks apart.

At first, I thought it was his dick pressing against my entrance, but it was his tongue! He was licking my crack like a dog licking peanut butter off a Polish sausage. I was coated with spit. He even jammed his tongue inside a few times. I thought I was going to come. This incredibly hot guy had his tongue in my ass. I was dripping precum all over the tile floor in long streams.

I was aching for more, and Cody gave it to me. He was on his knees behind me. I felt his monster crawl into my crack, making a wet slapping noise as the tip slid through the slippery mess his mouth left behind. He ran it up and down between my cheeks before he allowed it to ease its way inside.

Across the room, Matt was biting his lower lip, watching us. He jackhammered faster when he heard my moan of pleasure-pain as Cody entered me. I squeezed my eyes shut. It was so good.

Cody burrowed himself deeper as I relaxed and loosened up. I wanted his full length, and he gave it to me. I didn't have a choice. He started breathing harder and faster, and to my surprise, he grabbed my cock. I was dripping wet, but he closed his fist around me like a vise. He leaned forward over my back. I felt his sweaty chest and stomach pressing against me. It was so hot. His strong hand continued to stroke me, sliding over the tip of my cock to collect more lubricant.

That was it. I couldn't hold back any longer. My dick spasmed in his hand as it pumped and pumped ribbons of thick hot cum onto the floor. It became so sloppy in his hand; he had to know what happened. He pulled his hand off my cock. I thought he was going to stop and tell me I failed the test. But, he was shaking. He grabbed my waist with both hands and plunged himself deep inside. I felt his monster throbbing, pulsing his load of cum inside me. His hands slipped up to my stomach. There was cum everywhere. He pulled out, then rolled onto his back, pulling me with him.

I was on my back on top of him, his hands rubbing our mess into my chest and stomach.

Matt had finished and was cleaning himself up with my towel when Cody looked out from under me and asked him, "So, do you think he passed?"

Matt nodded his head, smiled, and mouthed the words, "Oh yeah." He wiped his hands.

"Yeah," Cody said, "I think so, too. In fact, I think you passed with a higher score than anyone else on this floor." He held me in his arms.

In the days that passed, my new friends told me that I was going to be the new test initiator when Cody graduated next year. Maybe college wasn't going to be so intimidating after all.

GITCHA!
By Landon Dixon

I pumped Rodney's cock, through his gitch. He groaned, pumping me back, his big, black hand gliding up and down my hard-on in my tight, white underwear, the heat of his palm, the grip of his fingers, the slide of the cotton, making me moan into the guy's face inches away.

We were stretched out on the bed side by side, completely naked except for our underwear, stroking each other like two close frat brothers should stroke one another. Ours was a liberal fraternity, open to anyone regardless of orientation, and Rodney and I had gotten to know each other intimately on the first day of the fall term.

His plush lips found mine, planted a wet kiss, his tongue surging into my mouth and up against my tongue; as we jacked each other's erections, pumping hard and hot and tight, pulling with passion through the thin material of our briefs.

"Thanks for inviting me up to your room," he breathed in my face.

"Thanks for 'coming' up," I murmured back, staring into the guy's amber eyes, tugging his throbbing gitch snake even harder.

The late-afternoon sun streamed golden in through the open window, putting a nice, warm glow on everything, a sensual sheen on Rodney's licorice black body; two guys lovingly and heatedly pulling dick, frat brothers forever. I stuck out my tongue and painted Rodney's lips with it, making his mouth shine with my saliva. He groaned, and looped his free arm around my neck on the pillow, pulling me closer. We kissed, Frenched, our hands moving faster and faster on our pulsating pricks, the pace and passion building and building.

I gripped his back, rubbed his back, kissed his long neck, bit into the velvety skin. He pumped his hips, his cock thrusting in my shunting palm. He grasped me even tighter, tugged even harder. The tension thickened, the room and our cocks torrid with it. We gasped into each other's faces, pulling gitch-clad dick with reckless, relentless purpose.

It was a race now, to see who could get the other off first.

We stared at one another, the single-sized bed creaking with our straining bodies and deft, stroking hands. Laughter drifted up from downstairs, far away, our hot breath steaming together in gasps.

"Oh, Jesus! Yes!" Rodney cried. His eyelids fluttered, his body shooting out straight, cock steeling in my pumping hand.

"Fuck!" I rasped, my balls boiling, prick surging. Rodney's clutching, fast-shifting hand was pulling me over the edge, into paradise.

We jerked together, bucking against one another. I felt the guy's dong spasm in my hand, shoot sperm into his underwear in powerful bursts, my own dick doing the same in his tugging hand. I shimmered with pure sexual electricity, my head spinning, cock spraying.

It went on forever, the pair of us locked, cocked together, blowing sweet, savage ecstasy, soiling our briefs with utter joy. And then it was over, way too soon, both of us shivering and shuddering, drizzling the last of our jizz out of our clenched and drained cocks.

"Should we leave our 'loaded' gitch for the new pledges to launder?" Rodney asked me. As we basked in the warm afterglow of our spent lust.

I kissed the guy, squeezing his softening dick with affection. "Yeah, let's …" Then I had a better idea – involving sperm-loaded underwear. "Let's do a gitch raid," I said. "Tonight. On that he-man fraternity with all the jocks."

Rodney looked at me, licking his dark lips with his bright pink tongue. "Huh?"

I let go of his cock, grabbed onto his shoulder. "Yeah, it's perfect. There's a football game tonight. Their house will be empty."

"What's a 'gitch' raid?"

"Like a panty raid, except we take men's underwear. And … leave a pair of loaded briefs behind – as our calling card." I was loving the idea. "So the muscle-heads know it wasn't the sisters from any of the sororities on campus who were going through their intimates."

Rodney's eyes gleamed. "Yeah, man, that sounds like a plan."

Hell, it was a plan. I kissed the guy on the lips, gripped his cock through his gitch and rubbed it around in the cooling load I'd pulled out of him.

# # # # #

We set out at 9:30 pm, just the two of us. A small, well-motivated, loving squad was required for such a delicate, precision mission as this. Besides, I wasn't a hundred percent sure just who else shared our bent in the fraternity.

It was dark, the campus all but deserted – everyone out at the football stadium on the western outskirts. The air was still warm, Rodney and I sweating, as we ran around to the back of the huge, three-story former mansion on fraternity row that was home to the jock boys.

The house was dark, too. Rodney and I quietly unfolded the extension ladder we'd been lugging and positioned it up against the side of the white-washed wall, under the sill of a third story window. I turned to the guy, said, "You first."

He stared at me, the whites of his eyes showing bright. We were both dressed in black, sans underwear beneath our sweatpants for quick draw and firing. "Um ... you know, Mike ... I, uh, don't know if this is such a great idea, after all."

"What!?" I hissed, the ladder shaking in our hands on either side. "It's a great idea! Just needs some guts to carry it off. Now get your sweet ass up those rungs – pronto!"

Rodney still hesitated. "Uh, yeah. Those guys are pretty big, you know. And they aren't exactly gay friendly. Maybe we should just ..."

He let go of the ladder and took off running.

"Son of a mother!" I muttered, watching my frat brother scoot around the corner of the house.

I looked up the ladder, at that third story window beckoning. A couple of minutes ticked by, frozen in time.

"It's a one-man job anyway," I finally grunted, resolutely gripping the trembling ladder on either side and going up the rungs solo. In cock-burglar mode.

The window was sticky but not locked. Like we'd figured. I pushed it open with a squeak and a groan (the window made some noise, too). Then I held my breath, listening to the pounding of my heart and the blood pumping in my ears. I didn't hear a thing coming from the interior of the darkened bedroom – no snoring, no grunting, no heavy footsteps of some beefy frat boy stomping over to the window to fling me and my ladder thirty feet down. I climbed over the sill, into the room.

I thumped to the floor, jumped up, every nerve tense, body wired, sweat streaking my face and pits. I flicked on my miniature flashlight and beamed it around the room. The bed was empty. There was a dresser up against the far wall. I made for it, a grin on my kisser.

The top drawer slid open with only a slight scrape. I shone the light down. Jack-pot!

This guy was loaded with underwear, a collection of briefs, boxers, and bikinis the likes I hadn't seen since last weekend – when I'd gone on one of my fishing expeditions through the men's section at a downtown department store. I started stuffing the gitch into the top of my turtleneck.

I was soon full, the drawer empty, my body reveling in the feel of the stranger's underwear against my damp skin. It was time for me to unload.

I'd left a tiger-striped pair of bikini briefs behind for my dirty purpose. And now I whipped out my cock, wrapped the exotically-patterned, shiny-surfaced gitch around my dick and started stroking. I'd gotten semi-erect just feeling frat boy's underwear in my hands and against my chest, and now I sproinged out fully-erect, feeling it against my cock.

I pumped quick and tight, letting the soft, sensuous material stroke me. What I'd never bothered mentioning to Rodney was that my raging men's underwear fetish was the real reason behind my idea for the gitch raid. Frat prankery and gay payback to homophobes were just secondary considerations, spin-off benefits.

I was feeling fine, jacking smooth. When hands suddenly seized my arms on either side, spun me around. And flashlight beams spotlighted my face.

"Frotting our underwear, huh, frat boy?" someone growled from the opposite wall – the wall the window was set in. The wall I hadn't bothered exploring with my own flashlight when I'd climbed into the room.

I was busted cold, hot and panting. A beam of light focused on my bare erection, the pair of striped underwear strewn on the floor. The evidence was all against me.

The punishment was swift in coming.

"You're going to suck us off. Then we're going to fuck you in the ass," the voice commanded.

The flashlight glare was taken off my startled face. My arms were released. And in the dim light, I saw the six guys standing against the wall. They were all completely naked – except for the gitch swaddling their loins, the gitch swaddling their heads. They were wearing white briefs over their faces like cotton football helmets, the leg openings serving as eyeholes.

My cock jumped higher, bobbing in the air. I vaguely realized that I could've run – out the bedroom door and down the stairs to freedom. The way was clear, the two guys who'd been gripping my arms now lined up along the wall with their brothers. Their buff, sexily-clad brothers.

I could've run. But looking at those almost bare bodies – slim and sleek, built and beefy, black and white – and feeling the pull of my prick without any hand at all on it, I knew for sure I was going to stick around, and take what was coming to me. It only seemed right.

I crossed the room on shaky legs, sank down onto trembling knees. The masked men formed a circle around me. I gripped a thinly-clothed dick with one hand, another with my other hand, stuck out my tongue and licked the rigid outline of cock in the pair of underwear directly in front of me. The men grunted softly, breathing harder. Their cocks swelled in my tugging hands, inflated under my stroking tongue.

It was a meat market, the stiffened lengths of beef cotton-packaged that special way I love. I shifted around on my knees, my head spinning and prick throbbing out in front of me, palming hard cocks, licking pulsating prongs. My hands were drenched in sweat, and my mouth drooled happiness, pulling on and lapping at the hardened dongs that threatened to explode right out of their bulging confines as I bathed and buffed them.

I went round and round. The room spun along with my head. Men openly groaned and thrust into my hands, up against my mouth. The humid air hung down heavy with spicy sweat, the tangy scent of precum. Underwear got soaked with my spit, clinging even closer to those horny outlines that filled my clutching and pumping hands, swelled up and along my dragging tongue.

"Time to get fucked – up the ass!" the voice stated.

I reeled backwards on my bare haunches and was pulled erect. Someone lifted my feet one at a time, stripped off my sweats, while someone else slipped that tiger-striped pair of gitch onto my legs, pulled it up to my wobbly knees. Then I was led over to the foot of the bed and draped over the wooden railing.

Lube slapped up against my bare ass, making me jump. It felt cool and slick, compared to my heated, heaving body. I bit my lip, as fingers scrubbed in between my butt cheeks, swirled around my manhole. I'd taken it up the behind plenty of times before in my young sex life, but never from six men together at once.

Still, I thrust out my taut little bottom defiantly, my ass and prick and the rest of me up to the challenge. Jock cock. Bring it on!

The first dick banged against my pucker, splitting my quivering cheeks and plowing my resisting ring and plunging my gripping anus. The guy went in full-bore, full speed, right down to the balls. Leaving me gasping, bloated with lust.

He grasped my hips and pumped his, driving his dong back and forth in my chute. I clung to the bedspread, rocked, getting thumped and chuffed bum and soul.

He pulled out. Another cock speared in, shunting me hard.

Like good frat brothers, these guys believed in sharing, not hogging; in this case, hole, for too very long. I was slammed down to the bowels and sawed to and fro, one after another after another after another. I could feel different sizes, different lengths and thicknesses, different textures, all of them banging me hard and fast. I was stuffed and stoked, my wanton ass gaping empty only for a moment, before being filled and fucked again. It was total bliss, raw and reaming.

"Okay, guys, let's give him what he came here to give us!"

The men grunted in agreement. Hands grabbed onto my waist and hard-on thundered up my alley. The guy pounded into my chute, flinging me back and forth. I moaned, feeling a hot spurt of cum sear my anus even more.

But then the cock was out, the guy groaning. And I felt the forgotten pair of underwear between my legs jerk, sag. The guy was jacking off into the gitch, unloading his steaming load into the bikini briefs I'd been caught red-cocked with.

Another guy rammed my ass, pumped me hard and heavy. Then yanked out and sprayed – into the underwear.

Man after man repeated the process. I almost cried out for blessed relief, for one guy to really cream my screaming anus. They'd fucked me raw, but where was the payoff? My ass ached for a white-hot coating, my own flapping cock straining for jerk-off. The gitch got filled but good.

It had to be the last guy, I guess, who pulled out and added to my burden, then suddenly pulled the spermed underwear right up my thighs and onto my groin. I shot vertical, warm semen enveloping my raging cock and boiling balls. I'd never felt anything like it before. It was weird, wild, liquid nasty wonderful. I jerked, jolted by all-out ecstasy, my own cock spurting into the mess of man-juice all on its own.

I bucked over and over, barely keeping my feet. I spouted sperm like never before, adding more heat and heaviness to that overflowing pair of bikini briefs.

I left like that – gitch pasted to my chest with sweat, gitch squished to my loins with men's satiated lust.

# # # # #

The frat house was quiet when I arrived back. Rodney showed up about ten minutes after I'd returned to my bedroom. "You should've stayed, man!" I blurted, barely able to contain my excitement.

The guy was still wearing his black turtleneck and sweats. And now he started stripping them off, revealing his smooth, slender, charcoal body. "Yeah?"

"Fuck, yeah!" I yelped, letting it out. "It … was … awesome! They caught me in the middle of …"

I stopped my exuberant recital, as Rodney slipped his tight, white briefs off his groin and long legs – and slipped the pair of gitch over his head. "Go on," he said, his twinkling amber eyes looking out at me from the leg openings.

I stared at the guy, at the underwear on his head, his hardening cock down below. "Son of a mother!" I muttered.

"Hey, don't fill your drawers, bro," he laughed. He pointed at his snake rising up into the air. "Come and gitch it!"

PICKUP ON AISLE SIX
By Jim McDonough

The glass of the ice cream case fogged as David tried to decide which flavor he was going to buy this week. Did he want chocolate or did he want something with nuts? He got even more exasperated as he caught a glimpse of his own reflection in the fogged glass. How had it all come to this?

A half-hour earlier, he had been at the bar with his friends Jose and Alec like every other Friday night. David had been bored out of his mind. They never did anything different. Every Friday night, the three friends went out to dinner in Nob Hill and then stopped at the bar for drinks. Every Friday night, they bitched about their classes, sucked down cocktail after cocktail and stared at the same guys who populated the bar every week.

For the past several weeks, David had been making excuses and leaving early, telling his friends that he was tired. He couldn't take it anymore. Something had to give. He didn't want to hurt his friends feelings, but David was totally over the bar scene. There had to be a better way to meet somebody other than hanging around and listening to music he didn't like or worse yet, trying the whole online thing.

On his way home, David stopped at the grocery store to pick up a few things, but mostly to satisfy his craving for ice cream. Inevitably, he would find himself staring at Ben & Jerry, just like he stared at the guys who frequented the bar. When he would get home, he would find comfort sitting in front of the TV polishing off an entire pint in one sitting. It was a good thing he hadn't given up on going to the gym and working out every afternoon.

"The chocolate is always a good choice," said a voice from behind.

David turned around and smiled. It was Ray Hernandez from his American lit class. He had seen Ray earlier at Pulse with a couple of guys from his fraternity.

"I went with chocolate last week. I'm thinking I need a change."

"Well there is chocolate chip. You'd still have some chocolate, but it's not too overwhelming. And besides it is my favorite."

"Your favorite?" asked David.

"Yeah, we could split a pint. You really shouldn't eat a whole pint." Ray poked David in the stomach. "Getting a little soft."

David blushed and his cock stirred at Ray's touch.

"Hey, I am not."

"Just joking, dude."

David wondered why Ray was toying with him. On a good day, he could only hope to be ignored by a guy like Ray. What was going on?

"I wasn't kidding about splitting the pint, though. Get the chocolate chip, and we can hang out."

"You serious?"

"Yeah. Pulse was a total bore, and I don't feel like going back to the frat house."

David wondered why a guy like Ray could be leaving the bar by himself. He was easily one of the hottest guys in the sophomore class at UNM. The T-shirt he wore clung to his torso like a second skin, and the jeans he was wearing hung off him, showing just a hint of asscrack. When Ray brushed his hand through his deep, dark hair and smiled. David practically came in his pants

"You live near here?" asked Ray. "Most of the guys at the frat house are out studying for some big Calculus test on Monday."

"I'm just down the street, off Carlisle."

"Cool. We'll pay for the ice cream, and I'll follow you home."

"Okay," said David.

Five minutes after they left the grocery store, Ray pulled in behind David in his driveway and followed him inside.

"Nice place," said Ray. "You live alone?"

"Thanks. Yeah, I live alone. My dad bought this place as an investment right before I started at UNM."

"Lucky you. Living at the house can get a little annoying sometimes."

"It can't be that bad," said David.

"That's what you think. I'll invite you over sometime, and you can let me know what you think. I've got no privacy at all, and there's always a party going on. You've got a real sweet set up here."

"Thanks again," said David. "Why don't you make yourself comfortable, and I'll get some bowls for the ice-cream. Don't want it to melt."

"Sure thing." Ray plopped down on the couch and grabbed the remote. "You have cable?"

"Yeah. See if anything's on. I'll be right back with the ice cream."

David wandered into his kitchen, not believing that Ray was sitting out in his living room. Wait until he told he told Jose and Alec.

David grabbed a couple of bowls and began to scoop the ice cream. He then grabbed some spoons and was about to head back out into the living room when he was startled by Ray standing in the doorway to the kitchen.

"All those channels and nothing to watch," said Ray.

"Yeah, I suppose." David handed Ray the bowl of ice cream. "Guess we can just hang out."

Ray set the bowl of ice cream on the counter and then wrapped his arm around David's waist and nuzzled his neck.

"I can think of something else we can do."

David almost dropped his bowel. "What the hell?"

"Give it to me," said Ray.

David handed the bowl to Ray and Ray dug into the ice cream and offered the spoonful up to David. David gobbled it up while Ray ate a spoonful himself.

"It's pretty good," said David.

"Told you." Ray smiled and David began melting just as fast as the ice cream.

Ray fed David another spoon and then stepped closer. He grabbed David's ass and then kissed him, slipping his tongue into his mouth.

Ray's tongue swirled around David's mouth along with the remaining ice cream and chocolate chips. His cock strained inside his jeans.

David pulled back and took the spoon from Ray. "Your turn." He fed Ray a spoonful of ice cream and returned the kiss.

"Damn, this is hot. You're hot," said Ray.

David blushed. "No I'm not."

"Cut it out. You are, too. Every week when I see you at the bar, I want to talk to you, but you are always with your friends."

"You know Alec and Jose. Don't you?"

"Don't think so. Anyway the three of you are always together like Siamese triplets or something, and you sometimes seem a little unapproachable."

"I'm sorry." David blushed. "I never realized that."

Ray leaned against the kitchen counter and grabbed the other bowl of ice cream, which was starting to melt. He ate a couple of spoonfuls as David attacked his bowl. He offered Ray another spoonful.

"What about in class?" asked David. "You never say more than hello in class."

Ray gulped. "I know. I can be kind of shy, and I'm not really out to many people at school. The guys at the house know, and they're mostly cool about it, but I don't make a point of advertising it."

"Oh."

"Does that bother you?"

"No, not really."

"Well, I'm glad I ran into you at the grocery store tonight." Ray dug his finger into the bowl and offered up a dollop of ice cream to David. David took Ray's finger into his mouth and licked off the ice cream, while staring into Ray's dark brown eyes.

"Don't seem that shy to me," said David. "Come on."

David grabbed Ray's hand and led him to his bedroom at the back of the house.

David and Ray stood at the foot of David's bed, both hesitant to make a move. After standing and staring at each other for a few moments, Ray stripped off his shirt, exposing his hairless, well-defined torso. There was just a hint of dark hair trailing from his belly button and disappearing into the waistband of his underwear.

Following suit, David shucked his T-shirt and dropped it on the floor. He and Ray stood silently as if in a trance. David then reached out and pulled Ray to him. David kissed Ray tentatively at first, but the kiss became more intense.

Ray slipped his hand into the back of David's pants. He rubbed the palm of his hand over David's ass as David groaned.

"Feels so good," said Ray.

Ray pressed his lips to David's and locked his arms around him, pulling David tightly to him. David still tasted hints of the chocolate chip ice cream as he kissed Ray. David ran his fingers through Ray's dark hair and kissed him harder.

David motioned to Ray, and they both climbed onto David's bed. They both rolled around the bed several times, locked in an embrace.

Ray let out a loud laugh as he and David wrestled on the bed. Ray eventually was able to pin David's shoulders to the mattress and then repositioned himself on top of him.

· They both paused to catch their breath. Ray sat on top of David, just staring into his eyes.

"I've wanted to do this forever," said Ray. He rolled off David and lay next to him, wrapping his arm around him and snuggling close.

"God, me, too," said David. He was never going to admit to just how many times he had jacked off thinking about Ray. He still couldn't believe they were in his bed together.

Ray reached over and unbuttoned David's jeans and unzipped his zipper, He then began tugging them off before depositing them on the floor. David laughed, and Ray kissed him again. David pulled Ray closer and kissed his harder. As Ray hugged David tight, he realized just how comfortable his naked body felt pressed against his.

The two were quickly caught up in the pleasure they were giving each other – the sensations of lips against skin, tongues dancing in each other's mouths.

David kissed Ray's shoulder and closed his eyes and let out a deep breath. He flicked his tongue across Ray's nipples and then continued tonguing his way down his taut belly.

David teased and taunted Ray with his tongue until he reached his belly. He glanced up at Ray, and Ray nodded as David unbuttoned Ray's jeans. David quickly pulled Ray's jeans and underwear down and off and then deposited them on the growing pile of clothing next to the bed.

Ray's thick uncut cock was dribbling precum. David positioned himself between Ray's legs and took him into his mouth. Ray sighed as David began to suck him.

"Oh, David. Don't stop."

David kept sucking Ray's dick without letting up. Ray was wrapped up in the pleasure David was giving him. His body tensed, his cock was throbbing. He had never felt like this before. What had always been a fantasy was now a reality. David was sucking Ray's dick.

As David continued, he reached down and grasped his own dick in his right hand and began to slowly jack off. His own cock was slick with dribbling precum. David tightened the grasp on his dick and smeared his juice over his shaft and cockhead, getting himself good and slick.

David continued sucking Ray's cock and began playing with his foreskin, sliding it up and down his shaft while he licked and sucked at his cockhead.

David got up and knelt between Ray's legs. He wrapped his fist around Ray's swollen cock. Ray lay on the bed in silence, observing David's every more. David cupped Ray's balls in his other hand and squeezed them gently, rolling them around in his hand. Then, David squeezed Ray's cock a little harder, and a large clear drop of precum dripped out and down his shaft. Ray watched intently as his juice drizzled down his cock. David quickly leaned over and licked it up like he was eating melting ice cream and didn't stop there. Ray was dripping like a leaky faucet.

Ray shifted on the bed, and David began exploring Ray's body with his tongue. He began licking Ray's balls while Ray emitted soft and frequent groans. He then licked further between Ray's legs.

"Roll over," said David.

Ray rolled over, and David immediately dove in between the cheeks of Ray's ass. He taunted Ray with his tongue, circling around his hole. Ray groaned in pleasure as David continued eating his ass.

"Fuck man. That's incredible," said Ray.

David continued licking Ray's ass. Ray writhed in pleasure as David explored between Ray's legs, licking his taint and balls. He wanted to get him nice and relaxed and ready. David really wanted to fuck Ray good and hard.

"Fuck man. David, I want you to fuck me." Ray looked up at David who was smiling. He was more than willing to take him up on his invitation.

"You got any rubbers?"

"Yes, I do," said David. He hopped off the bed and pulled a condom and a small tube of lube out of his dresser drawer and handed it to Ray.

Ray ripped open the foil packet and pulled out the condom.

"Let me put it on you," said Ray. He rolled the condom over the head of David's aching cock, slowly inching it down the hard shaft. David thought he could come right then and there. Ray lay back down on the bed, raising and spreading his legs.

David squeezed the lube over his index finger and aimed for Ray's pucker, slowly fingering him and loosening him up. He inserted another finger inside Ray, and he Ray began thrashing.

"Come on, David. Give it to me. Fuck me."

David climbed back onto the bed and positioned himself between Ray's legs. David leaned forward and pressed the tip of his cock against Ray's sphincter. Pushing harder, Ray opened up, and David was inside.

"Fuck me, David. Fuck me."

David steadily inched his dick inside Ray as he moaned louder and louder.

"Oh fuck, David. Oh fuck."

Ray squirmed forward and David's cock slipped all the way inside him. David sucked in a deep breath. Lying motionless, David felt Ray's breath against his chest. David pulled back, snaking his cock back out of Ray, and plunged it right back in, grinding his pubes against Ray's ass.

"Fuck, man. Fuck, man," yelled Ray. His head rocked back and forth on the pillow. "Give it to me harder."

David pulled out of Ray and rammed back into him. His balls slapped against his ass cheeks as David built up a steady rhythm, pounding over and over, in and out of Ray's tight ass.

"Oh. Oh. Oh," moaned Ray.

David was getting close. His cum boiled up and churned inside him, as he pumped deeper and deeper into Ray's hot bowels.

"Damn, I'm getting close. I'm going to come." David clenched his teeth as he pounded into Ray's butt one more time. He cock erupted, filling the rubber with a huge load.

"Oh, fuck. Yeah. That was great," said Ray. They were both out of breath.

Ray pressed his lips against David's, kissing him softly. His eyelashes fluttered, and he closed his eyes. Ray opened his eyes as David pulled his softening cock out of his ass. David rolled off the condom and tossed it on the floor.

Ray grasped his cock and began to jerk off. David watched as Ray worked his foreskin up and down his shaft. He seemed lost in pleasure.

"I'm going to come," said Ray. He arched his back and a thick stream of cum shot out of him, splattering across his belly and chest.

Physically drained, Ray and David snuggled together without saying anything. Ray smiled and pressed his lips against David. David grasped Ray's hand and squeezed it tight.

David shut off the light, and Ray soon fell fast asleep, snoring lightly. David lay there next to him, trying to sort out the events of the evening. David listened to Ray snore, wondering what, if anything, could develop between them.

David wrapped his arm around Ray's shoulder, curled up close to his warm naked body, and fell asleep until morning.

AFTERNOON EXAM
By Jay Starre

When they first started seeing each other, their friends wondered what they had in common. When Jordi moved out of the frat house and in with his professor, they were appalled. One of them was using the other, one of them taking advantage, one or both of them were out of their minds to think a relationship between two men so different could ever work out. What could they possibly have in common?

All that negativity hardly phased the pair. As for what they had in common, they didn't bother explaining. The bond they shared had begun unexpectedly, from a simple college exam offered by a professor to his student.

Jordi, a freshman that year, was not exactly innocent. Young and naïve in a lot of ways, but no virgin, not at all. He'd fooled around with his share of other college boys on campus, wagging his cute butt across the quad on warm autumn days, flaunting his taut body and teasing freshmen to seniors alike with his direct smoky-amber eyes and smart-ass smile.

Jet-black hair, a cute dimple in his chin, a heart tattoo just above his left tit, and a row of glittering gold studs in his right ear accented his lush flesh and cocksure personality.

The Professor chose him.

Dressed neatly but casually in a short-sleeved open-necked dress shirt and grey slacks, Mack Dawson lectured the class on ancient Roman politics in his quiet baritone. His bulked-up build underscored his more obvious traits, quiet confidence and controlled power.

A blond with bright blue eyes and a slow, white smile, he watched and waited as Jordi lingered after class and slowly gravitated toward him across the emptying lecture hall.

"You wanted to speak with me, Prof?" Jordi offered the Professor one of his teasing grins and just managed not to follow it with a saucy wink.

Over the past few weeks of class, Mack had sized-up the college tease and made his decision. Leaning in as Jordi hovered just below the lectern, the Prof spoke softly but clearly.

"The Romans were experts in bondage. They controlled their vast and diverse population with it on all levels, both physically and mentally. Would you be interested in a private exam on the subject? If you perform well, it'll mean a passing grade or better for the entire semester."

Jordi's interest was definitely piqued. He already felt a huge attraction to the blond older teacher. Peering up into those direct blue eyes, a pulsing thrill teased both his cock and his asshole at the same time. Bondage? Would the Prof tie him up and fuck his ass? Or what? His imagination ran riot.

"Sounds cool. Now?"

The spur of the moment decision was typical of Jordi. But what he got himself into was far from typical. After this afternoon, he would be changed forever.

It was Charleston in early October. It had been an early class, and as the pair, prof and student, walked out of the Hall, it was just noon. A whiff of cool sea air swept across them. Mack's large hand on Jordi's shoulder steered him into a quiet residential area of the college where many of the professors and administrators were housed. Neither spoke, although Jordi was hard-pressed not to blurt out something entirely inappropriate or flippant.

Truthfully, he was nervous. Excited, of course, and curious as hell.

"We're here. Get your butt up the stairs."

The voice was calm, but the hand that cupped Jordi's ass-cheek was firm. Jordi shivered, even though the day was warm. What was he getting himself into?

That hand on his ass shoved him up three flights of backstairs until they reached Mack's apartment. The big body pressed against his, hot breath on his neck as Mack let them in.

Inside, Jordi was struck immediately by the riot of plants along the walls and the smell of fresh air wafting in from French doors that opened out to a balcony. Two shaded lamps offered soft lighting while a broad band of light from the slanting October sun bathed the hardwood floor from the balcony.

136

In the center of the room, a kind of sling-swing hung, all other furniture was back against the walls amidst the plant life.

"You were prepared, Prof. Is that for me?" Jordi blurted out as he gawked at that hanging leather contraption. It gleamed with black leather and silver chain. It definitely looked nasty. Jordi's dick grew stiff just looking at it.

He turned to see the Professor already stripping. Dress shirt on the floor and his arms high as he tossed off his undershirt, his burly chest was practically in Jordi's face. A light sprinkling of blond fur slithered down to a flat stomach and disappeared below the belt. A moment later as Mack stared him in the eye, that belt was undone and down came the slacks, loafers kicked off at the same time.

Mack was in his underwear, a bulge tenting them as he leaned down and grabbed one of his discarded loafers. With nimble fingers, he quickly stripped the shoe lace from it as Jordi watched perplexed.

The blond Professor stood up, running that lace between his fingers and staring directly into Jordi's eyes. "I want you naked for your bondage exam."

"No problem. I want to be naked, Prof."

The words came out in a nervous rush as Jordi gawked at those big hands playing with that shoe lace. What was that all about? His own hands trembled as he followed Mack's orders, tossing aside his book bag, stripping off his shirt, and kicking off his shoes. His cock leaped out to bob in front of him as he pulled down his pants and underwear.

He was so hot for the big prof! The shock of discovering this kinky side of the cool and calm teacher only increased his randy need to see where it led. A bondage scene? Who would have thought?

Mack dropped to his knees on the hardwood floor in front of Jordi. The professor's hands were sure as he took hold of Jordi's balls. "From slaves to gladiators to nobles in their fine mansions, everyone experienced some kind of psychic bondage in Rome's heyday. Tonight, you'll get a taste of how that felt, just a taste."

The voice was quiet, but there was no denying the power behind it.

"Nice sack, Jordi. Time to bind 'em. Spread wide with your hands behind your neck."

Jordi obeyed with a small gasp as those hands began to work on his nuts. With his arms up and his hands clasped behind his neck, he was virtually powerless to prevent whatever the blond Prof had in mind for his vulnerable nut-sack. His feet spread wide apart, he was defenseless as those hands worked down his crotch.

Mack knew what he was doing, which was no surprise. The teacher exuded confidence backed up by a wide-ranging knowledge that seemed boundless. The word among his students was, if he said something, it had to be true.

Jordi watched, shivering and gasping as fingers expertly twined shoestring around each of his nuts, separating them into swollen globes, then surrounded the pair with a final twist at the base of his stiff dick.

He was done. Jordi's nut sack dangled between his legs, swollen and warm, bound in shoelace. What a turn-on!

"Get over in the sling, Jordi."

The dark-haired college boy turned and walked the few feet toward that odd swing contraption with his bound nuts bobbing between his legs, aching pleasantly. The anticipation of what would happen next had his heart pounding. The wrapping of his nuts in that string was totally unexpected.

Anything might happen this afternoon! Of course, in his mind, he imagined kinky, twisted sex mixed in with a lecture about the Romans. Yeah, sounded awesome.

What Jordi didn't expect, not in his wildest dreams, was what happened after the sex.

He stood in front of the sling, which was strung up with the back higher than the front, just like some kind of swing. Jordi had actually seen pictures of slings in porn magazines but never anything quite like this.

He turned and sat back in it, feeling the slick leather against his naked butt-cheeks, his strapped balls sliding over the front edge, excitingly sensitive in their binding.

Mack was right there, still wearing his white underwear with a monster boner tenting the front, gooey wetness all along the fly where the crown pressed against the cotton material. The bulky blond took hold of one of Jordi's calves and lifted it. Jordi was pushed back into the sling against the leather as one leg was raised high.

"Ready for this?"

He spoke quietly, his blue eyes boring into Jordi's. The hand on his calf had slid up to his ankle and along the chain the sling was suspended from. A leather cuff awaited it.

Jordi realized it was decision time. In moments, he might be cuffed and bound. And helpless. At the mercy of his professor, the big blond who seemed to know everything. Was he ready for this?

"I want it. Yeah. Do it to me."

The words came out before Jordi even realized he'd made his decision. His ankle was trapped in a soft leather cuff before he took another breath. His heart pounded in his chest. His balls throbbed.

Mack took his time, gazing down into Jordi's amber orbs as he moved to cuff the other ankle. As that leg rose, Jordi felt himself wide open, his ass exposed, his balls and cock dangling between, more than ever at the mercy of Professor Mack, who now seemed to have him entirely under his mental control.

As the second ankle was restrained, Jordi realized his hands were still behind his neck as the prof had earlier ordered. A little moan escaped his lips as he recognized his willing participation in his own submission. It was unreal!

Large hands all of the sudden fondled his dangling nuts. He looked down to see Mack, who stood directly between his spread thighs, playing with his bound balls. He lifted his hips, pushing into those hands rather than away from them, but with his ankles raised up and constrained, he could only move so far.

That was the moment he realized he was no longer able to do what he wanted. His ankles were buckled into leather cuffs; he couldn't move his legs!

"A taste. Yes, a taste of what the Romans experienced in their daily lives. Controlled. In bondage."

Jordi gasped as the quiet words were followed by a fingertip stroking his asshole. With his feet in the air, his ass was wide open and his hole pouted helplessly. That fingertip ran across the distended ass-lips, teasing them without penetrating. A moment later, he felt something wet and slippery ooze out over his splayed butt-crack. The Prof was lubing him up!

His nuts bound tightly, his ankles in the air and cuffed, and now his wide-open ass coated in slippery lube, what was next?

"Fuck ... oh yeah ... put a finger in me ..." he heard himself beg.

Was he begging? His face flushed as he recognized the plea in his voice. He lifted his ass and pushed against that well-lubed finger. It moved with him. Tickling his hole, that finger did not go inside regardless of how much he wanted it to.

He looked into the prof's eyes. They stared back. A slow smile crept over the broad, handsome face. A curl of the lip, a flash of white teeth, and Jordi felt his will power melting away.

"Now your hands, Jordi. Then, perhaps, your holes will get some satisfaction."

Holes? What did the big prof plan? His mouth watered as he glanced down at the bulge in Mack's underwear. Was that hidden cock going to fuck his mouth before it fucked his ass? Whatever, he had no say in it.

Mack's fingertip tickled his asshole for another second as he writhed in the swing, the other hand massaging his swollen ball-sack. The blond prof moved around to his side and took hold of one of his hands, pulling it out from behind his head.

He continued to offer that crooked half-smile, not saying a word but his eyes boring into Jordi's as he raised a wrist and slid it into a cuff along the chain above. In a moment it was snuggled within smooth leather. Mack immediately reached for his other wrist, removing it from behind his neck and lifting it high.

He heard a whining moan and realized it came from his own mouth. The final surrender! His naked body shook as that last cuff snapped around his right wrist, and he was utterly powerless.

"Oh my god! You can do whatever you want to me!"

The dark-haired student wasn't sure what his own words meant. A statement of fact or surrender. Both, he realized.

But there was more. As he dangled in the swing, ankles and wrists far above his helpless body, the prof leaned in even closer and pulled something out from behind the sling. Another strap slipped between leather cross-straps and then fitted snugly across Jordi's forehead. The strap tightened, pulling his face and head back against the sling as Mack buckled it securely. He was unable to move his head away from the sling, his vision restricted. He couldn't see down to his crotch, or his splayed thighs and vulnerable cock, balls and ass. He couldn't pull away from Mack's hovering crotch, which pressed against him from the side, even if he'd wanted to.

He found himself greedily inhaling the heady odor of male crotch and leaking dick. Encased in cotton, that full package grazed his neck. He felt the swing dropping slightly as Mack released the crank at the ceiling. The contraption moved up and down, apparently.

The prof's underwear-encased package pressed against his cheek. He couldn't turn away; he couldn't turn toward it! A second later, he felt a fingertip back down in his ass-crack, once more stroking the pouting lips of his asshole.

He began to writhe and buck, all at once determined to test his bindings. He struggled, pushing against that maddening fingertip stroking his asshole, his ankles pulling helplessly against the cuffs that held them. He tried to move his face toward that wet bulge in Mack's underwear, but his head was secured. He tested his wrist-bindings and found he couldn't move his arms.

"Fuck ... oh fuck ... I can't move ... what are you gonna do to me?"

Underwear muffled his words, and his moans as the blond Prof pressed his crotch against the smart-ass college boy's lips and nostrils. He moaned and grunted, opening wide to lick and tongue at the bulge in those underwear, snorting in air around the cotton skivvies.

"You're all mine. Mine to fuck, mouth and ass. Until you come. I'm going to feed both your holes until you can't take it anymore and shoot a load for me. You won't be free until you give me your cream. A true Roman slave."

The nasty threat/promise sent the bound student into a convulsion of writhing, yanking and squirming. He pulled on his restraints wildly as he attempted to impale himself on that tantalizing finger teasing his asshole and gobble up the dick that remained hidden under cotton underwear.

He couldn't say anything with the prof's crotch muffling his mouth, but he was screaming inside. Screaming for more! Screaming for satisfaction! Fleetingly, he wondered if that was how the Romans felt in their lives, just as Prof Mack was telling him.

Actually, he didn't give a fuck about Romans. Right now, all that mattered was the big blond prof and his own aching holes.

Mack stared down into Jordi's wide eyes, as if reading his mind. He still smiled, a deceptively gentle grin. One burly arm stretched downward over the bound student's naked torso, a hand splayed wide in his lubed crack, and that tantalizing fingertip stroking his asshole. His other hand gripped the waistband of his underwear and slowly peeled it down so that his thick cock bobbed free.

Jordi's tongue was out as he felt the first hot caress of cock-head. He moaned and stretched his tongue, his forehead straining against the leather strap. The prof seemed to relent as he offered up the dripping crown, playing it over the college boy's tongue and lips.

He slurped it in, but then was deprived of the fat knob only a moment later as Mack withdrew to rub the slippery head over his lips and then his flaring nostrils. He snorted in the stench of raw cock, muttering little pleas that were barely intelligible.

"Gimme that cock ... please ... I want it ... uhhhnnng ... gimme ... cock ..."

The fingertip down in his ass-crack was busy tickling his pouting asshole, but he couldn't see it. Every time he pushed toward it with his ass, the fingertip moved away, stroking the distended center but never going inside. It was driving him crazy! And he could do nothing, absolutely nothing, about it.

Mack's smile grew broader as Jordi's squirms grew more animated. It was obvious to Jordi the blond hulk loved having his lush body trapped and helpless and at his mercy. And it was plain as day the big prof loved the fact Jordi wanted it so badly he couldn't stop moaning and squirming.

Seemingly happy with Jordi's enthusiastic response, he relented somewhat. He fed Jordi the head of his cock just as he slowly inserted a blunt fingertip between his straining ass-lips. The squirming student responded by lifting his body off the swing as much as he could, dangling from his ankles and wrists as he tried to swallow as much cock and finger with his holes as possible.

For a delicious few moments, Mack pumped cock and finger into his squirming body, probing hole with that big slippery finger, twisting and stabbing, pumping cock beyond sucking lips and toward throat.

The bound college boy fought against his restraints, loving that cock in his mouth and finger up his ass, but not finding it enough and wanting more. The prof's quiet smile broadened as he suddenly withdrew. Cock and finger pulled out at the same time.

He was left empty and abandoned. "Please! Give me that cock! I need you to fuck me," he gasped out.

"You'll get cock. A lot of cock."

The promise sent a wave of shivers up and down his bound body. The thick cock rearing in his face pulsed pink, wet with his own saliva. Mack had shoved down his underwear beneath his large ball-sack, and the thick shank bobbed in his face. Muscular arms reached up to crank on the swing, raising it higher before the blond teacher moved down to stand between his raised thighs.

He strained to see what was going on down there, but the band across his forehead restricted his view. He felt him down there, though. Big hands pawed at his swollen nuts. He groaned. He wanted those hands to stroke his cock, to finger his asshole again.

Something thick and slippery slid into his exposed ass-crack. It had to be the Prof's big boner. A column of heat rubbed in his spread crack. He immediately humped against it, causing the swing to rock and twist.

The prof's handsome face was visible, along with that tantalizing smile, as cock continued to rub up and down his wide-open crack and hands fondled his bound balls. He thrust up with his dick helplessly, aching to have it touched, stroked, pumped, anything.

He heard the sound of squirting. More lube, thank god. Then, something big and blunt pressed against his butt-lips. Cock!

"Oh yeah ... please fuck me," he begged.

That cock-head pressed against his gaping asshole as he again tested his restraints, pulling and squirming, humping powerlessly against that fat crown, wanting it inside him so badly he felt like either crying or screaming.

"Here it is."

The quiet words were followed by a deep thrust and a sudden aching stretch that gored him to the balls. The Prof had shoved his cock all the way home in one lunge.

"Gawd! I've got cock in me!"

His entire body ached. Cock filled him, stuffed him. His writhing ass was lifted off the sling and hovered in the air, impaled on his professor's impossibly fat prick. He reveled in it, the sensation of being fucked to the hilt, having that enormous tool inside him. His anal muscles quivered, clamping the length of the hefty meat he cradled inside his pulsing gut.

But it was yanked out, and he was abandoned again, his asshole gaping empty and hungry.

"Please ... please ... I need your cock in me ..."

He'd never begged for cock like that before. He loved the feel of a big one pumping in and out of his ass, no question about that, but he'd never found himself wanting it so much, and afraid of not getting it. It was entirely up to the confident professor how much cock he got. He could do nothing but beg for it, helpless and shackled.

Professor Mack leaned over the dark-haired college boy as he planted his cock back on target. As the fat meat began to slowly slither inside his wide-open slot, the hulking blond wrapped his powerful arms around him, encasing him sling and all. A smile hovered over his trapped face as he grunted and squirmed around dick driving into his guts.

The smile descended, pink lips parting and tongue snaking out to slide into his grunting mouth. Tongue drove deep as cock slammed completely home.

He was fucked!

The prof began to pound in and out as he tongued Jordi's mouth, slobbering noisily, his own mouth wide open as it encased the college boy's steamy maw with hot lips and stabbing tongue.

Both holes were being used! He swung helplessly in the sling, wrapped in burly arms, heavy naked body over his, cock up his ass and tongue down his throat. He gurgled and moaned, writhing in the sling, attempting to slam his body against the one burying him. His own cock dripped and slid between their mashed bellies. His bound balls ached where Mack pressed his steamy crotch against them as he pummeled his asshole.

No matter how he squirmed, he was trapped, trapped in heated flesh, helpless against the power of leather restraints. He opened wide at both ends, totally surrendering. Cock rammed his prostate, violently, savagely, relentlessly.

The approaching orgasm hit him like a punch to the stomach. His cock, slithering between their mashed bellies, swelled and pulsed. His nuts, tied with shoe lace, throbbed and ached.

It seemed as if orgasm poised and held off for a breath-taking, overpowering suspension of time, before the ramming cock in his guts drove him over the precipice.

He flopped in the sling, trapped, on fire from head to toe, his cock emptying in a spew of cream. The fat dick up his butt continued thrusting as he achieved release, driving more cum from his aching, bound balls. Lips sucked his tongue into hot mouth. He snorted for breath, arms wrapped around him.

It went on and on.

Eventually, he'd spent his load, and the prof withdrew with a slurp from juicy ass and wet mouth.

The blond teacher stepped back, abandoning the exhausted student in the swing, cum on his belly, asshole pink and distended lips wet.

"I think you liked that. We'll have to go another round later. But only if you've learned the lesson you're here for."

The soft-spoken promise instantly rekindled the burned-out flame of guttural excitement in the fucked college boy. His arms and legs trembled in their bindings. His ass was still wide open for his Professor's direct gaze. His thick cock jutted from his crotch out of his underwear. He grinned that crooked smile as he walked away, hefty butt encased in cotton swaying slowly.

The dark-haired student was left alone, suspended in the air, his head trapped, his vision restricted. What was Professor Mack doing? When would he be back? Down in his spread, hairless crack, his just-fucked and dripping asshole clamped and pouted in expectation. His balls ached, the string around them making them throb.

He was bound. He was trapped.

But now, for the first time he realized it wasn't leather cuffs and strings that were the real bonds. It was his own desire. He was in bondage.

Bondage to the stocky blond teacher. Praying for his return. Praying for more.

When would he get more of what he wanted? Soon, he hoped!

He called out to the vanished teacher, his voice pleading.

"I've learned my lesson, Prof! I have, really! Did I pass my exam?"

There was only a light laughter from the other room.

Jordi finally left later that night. He walked out the door physically, but mentally and emotionally he remained there with his new teacher and lover. From that afternoon on, the unlikely pair were partners. To friends and acquaintances, it was a mystery. Neither seemed to change even after they began living together. Jordi was just as flippant and flirtatious, Mack still the quietly smiling Professor so capable at his job.

And that was the real secret to their successful relationship. They shared that intense sexual bond, yet were still free to be themselves. Who cared how others judged them?

Not Jordi. Not Mack.

NICK AND HIS AMAZING RUGBY PLAYER ASS
By Armand

"Hey, the party can start now," someone yelled. "Nick's ass has finally arrived."

There was a sea of raised plastic cups and a rumble of drunken cheers. The Kappas were throwing another one of their infamous parties, and most of the coeds were already half-lit when Nick Harrison, a rugby player and one of the Kappas, arrived. He constantly endured a ribbing over his massive ass. It started one day when he bent over to plug in a game controller, and one of the guys made a flippant comment about his fleshy, round butt, and it just never stop. Because of his tree trunk thighs, his ample booty wasn't disproportionate, so the endless barrage of jokes just seemed juvenile.

Nick flipped double birds and held them high, and the crowd roared louder. To his credit, he took the jokes in stride, but I knew the relentless jibes had to get to him sometimes.

"So you must be smart if you're an engineering major." The woman in front of me was in one of the Christian sororities, but she was half-baked and looking for action. Next, she giggled, then she burped, and then she hiccupped and looked like she was about to upchuck.

"Listen, I've got to talk to my friend," I replied.

I deftly moved through the crowd – a high five here and a short conversation there. Because I'd given up drinking, I was able to look upon the melee like an anthropologist studying an indigenous civilization.

"Carter, my man, you scoping out the pussy?" Rashid said loudly.

I looked at him and decided it wasn't worth an answer. Rashid, like most of the Kappas, was a buffoon when he was drunk. Sober, they were alright, but drunk …

After an hour, I was ready to leave. Cutting through the sweaty, horny crowd I noticed Nick in the kitchen snacking on some chips when Eddie, one of his frat brothers, came up behind him and grabbed his ass with both hands. Nick whipped around with fire in his eyes. The semicircle of guys that goaded Eddie was laughing like they'd just witnessed a Jackass stunt.

I quickly maneuvered myself between the guys.

"Eddie, fuck off," I said.

At 6'2" and 215 lbs, I towered over Eddie. He looked up and started to laugh until he saw my stern expression. Realizing I was serious, he suddenly lost a bit of his buzz.

I turned back to the rugged rugby player and said, "Hey, Nick, can we talk?"

"Sure." He dropped the last of the chips in the bowl and led me upstairs to his bedroom.

"I gotta hit the head," he said. "Make yourself at home."

His room was small and tidy. I didn't know what I was going to talk to him about. I'd simply said that to get him away from the morons downstairs. My anthropological observations of drunken coeds had made me a little tired, so I plopped face down on Nick's bed. When I curled my hands under his pillow, I felt something cold and plastic-y. I grabbed it and pulled it out and found I was holding a dildo – flesh colored, about six inches, with balls at the base.

That's how Nick found me, lying on his bed holding a dildo, when he returned to the room.

I don't know what reaction I expected, but it wasn't the one he gave me. "You going to tell everyone?"

I looked at him, and a million thoughts jammed my brain. At first, I thought the dildo was left behind by a girlfriend, but he didn't have a girlfriend at college, though he talked about a high school sweetheart back home. I thought maybe it was a joke, maybe a prank gift from some douche bag. I expected him to say something funny or to get pissed. Then I realized what the dildo meant.

I finally uttered, "No."

"Just go," he responded.

"Nick, I ... uh ... I ... uh ..."

He looked humiliated, and I didn't want him to feel that way. I genuinely looked up to this guy. He wasn't a fucking tool like most of the guys downstairs.

"Nick, I don't want to leave."

He shut the door and locked it. "You want an explanation?"

"No." Actually I did, but I wouldn't admit to that.

"Go ahead and give me your best shot."

Perplexed, I just stared at him.

"Come on. I know you want to make fun of me – my big ass and that dildo. Give it to me."

I was looking at him in a new way, and I wasn't entirely sure what I was feeling or thinking. "How does it feel?"

Now he was perplexed.

"Does it hurt?"

He shook his head, and then walked toward me. By this point, I was sitting up on the bed, and he was right in front of me, his entire 225 lbs of bulldog frame overshadowing me. "Nah. It feels good if you let it."

"Can I borrow it sometime?" What was I saying? What kind of stupid fucking question was that?

"Maybe I could show you how to use it."

"Yeah?"

I didn't know if I meant the words coming out of my mouth. I just wanted to let him know that I wasn't judging him. Then he really fucking blew my mind when he reached and tenderly touched my cheek with his hand. I'd never been touched like that by a guy.

My head was buzzing. *I should feel uncomfortable. This should feel strange. I'm not even bi, I don't think. What the hell is he planning to do to me? Shouldn't I fucking run like a madman?*

"You okay?" he asked. "It's not freaking you out?"

It was a little, but I didn't really want him to stop.

Nick reached down and pulled my T-shirt over my head, and I laid the dildo on the pillow. Next, Nick ran his hand gently over my chest and lightly tweeked my nipples. I closed my eyes and tried to enjoy. When I opened them, I could see Nick's pants straining from his bulge.

Why didn't I scream, 'I'm not gay?' I mean, I had let two guys blow me in the past, but they were drunken one-offs. This was a sober me with another sober guy. This might mean something I didn't want it to mean.

Nick knelt, and I decided I should say, 'I like you, Nick, but I can't do this.' Before I could utter the words, though, he rubbed his hand down my stomach to my crotch and said, "Tell me if you want me to stop."

He was being so nice about it, how could I tell him? And I didn't really want it to stop. He hadn't crossed a line yet.

By the time he opened my fly, my cock was almost fully erect. That should tell me something. Then he tugged my jeans and briefs off and smiled like he'd discovered El Diablo. He looked at me for permission. Hearing no protests, he leaned forward and took my cock in his mouth.

Fuck it felt good, and I've had some top-notch blow jobs from guys and girls.

While he sucked, I tried to clear my mind and enjoy, but I kept thinking things like, 'Should I think of Brenda Snyder and her luscious lips? I'm not gay if I imagine a woman, am I?'

Nick moaned as he sucked, and I raised my head to look down. Maybe it was supposed to be weird to see his big biceps and short hair, but in reality it was fucking hot. That's the moment when I began to relax. I'd figure out what all this meant after it was over. For now, I was going to enjoy.

The next thing, I knew my legs were in the air, and Nick was licking my crack. Most straight guys act like they aren't turned on by a little ass play, but that's fucking bullshit. They're afraid it will mean they like penetration, which might make them seem gay, but every guy loves a little tongue action. Nick's tongue pressed up against my asshole, and I couldn't help but whimper like a porn star.

"I'll go slowly," Nick said as he dropped my legs and reached for the dildo.

Okay, I was a little afraid at that moment. This was going too far. And what if it hurt? What if Nick thought I was gay?

Nick put one of my legs over his shoulder, pushed the other away to expose my hole, and then he pushed the head of the lubed dildo into my crack. "I promise you'll like this." And he playfully pumped it against my hole without penetrating. It did feel good. He licked the underside of my cock from base to tip and then kissed the sensitive part of the shaft. The most bizarre thought crossed my mind: 'Big fucking Nick is one of the most tender lovers I've ever had.'

That's when he took my swollen cock back in his mouth and sucked down as he pushed the head of the dildo into my virgin asshole. He continued to suck, but he didn't move the dildo. I reached up and put my hands on his head and rubbed his hair, and then I felt him working the dildo slowly inside me.

When he stopped to lick my balls, I could tell he'd put the whole six inches of his toy inside my ass. Okay, I was totally turned on. I felt him work it out and back in as he whispered, "Oh fuck, that's hot."

"Yeah. It feels good."

"Yeah? You like it?"

"Yeah, I do."

"See, I told you." Then he pumped faster and harder. "You okay, Carter?"

I moaned instead of answering, and he began to suck me again while he fucked my ass with that flesh-colored dildo. I was getting close, and I didn't want it to be over so quickly.

Sensing my impending explosion, Nick stopped sucking. Then he took my hands and pulled me upright. I was sitting with the dildo as deep in my ass as it would go as he knelt and sucked my cock. I could see his massive back and the curve of his beefy ass. I didn't want to be turned on by his body, but I was.

I don't know that I've ever surprised myself more than at that moment when I asked breathily, "Can I fuck you?"

He looked up and replied, "I've never been fucked. I've only had a dildo inside me."

"It's okay. I ... I ... I just thought."

"No. I want to do it. I've fantasized about it."

Then he stood and started to strip. While he did, I fucked myself on that dildo just to turn him on more. He smiled as he freed his thick, rock-hard cock and beefy, rugby ass.

He walked over to me and pushed me back on the bed. Next, he slowly pulled the dildo out of my ass, and I was surprised by how much I missed it.

"You want to use the dildo on me first? Your cock is bigger, so it might help loosen me up."

"Sure."

We switched places. With considerable strength, I hefted his massive legs in the air and looked at this tight asshole. It just looked perfect – pink, tight, almost hairless. He grabbed his knees and I reached for the dildo. I added more lube and then positioned the head against his tight hole.

"Put it in me, Carter."

I obeyed. Once his asshole was stretched around the head, I worked the rest inside at a slow, even pace. I felt the need to ask, "You okay?"

"Better than that." He laid his head back as I started pumping, and I knew this must be better than fucking his own ass.

He dropped one leg on the bed and the other over my shoulder and raised his head to watch me. "Fuck me."

His thick cock was inches from my face. Once, on a dare, I'd touched a guy's penis to my lips, but I'd never sucked cock. So far, I could convince myself that I hadn't done anything too gay – another guy had sucked me, and I'd taken a toy in my ass. Lots of straight guys do those things, but if I sucked cock, then I'd have to admit that I was seriously crossing into gay territory. *Fuck it*, I decided.

He saw me eyeing his cock and said, "You don't have to, if you don't want to," which made me want to do it all the more.

I licked his cock first. Unable to multitask, I stopped pumping the dildo while I took his cock head between my lips and sucked like a lollipop. It wasn't bad. It was just as hot as licking a woman's clit, except there was a bit of a salty taste. Still, I knew I could give a good blow job if I tried.

When I went further down his cock, he moaned. It took me a minute to figure out how to work it straight over my tongue and not rub it against my teeth on the way in or out, but I got the hang of it soon enough and also got back into pumping that dildo in his tight ass.

"Fucking hell," he moaned.

I felt his hand on my head, but he didn't push me down on him. Instead, he rubbed my hair gently. 'Tenderest lover I've ever had.'

"I'm getting close," he said, so I stopped.

I stood up and was shocked to find my cock was still at full mast. Nick watched me slide a condom on and lube up.

"You want me in doggie or on my back?"

In doggie I wouldn't have to look into his eyes. Maybe I could convince myself this wasn't so gay. But I liked the way he looked lying on that bed. "Nah. You can stay just like that." Then I eased the dildo out of his ass, knelt between his legs, put one leg over my shoulder, and then rubbed my cock head against his asshole.

He looked nervous and excited at the same time.

"Tell me if it hurts, and I'll stop."

He nodded.

Then I pushed. At first nothing happened, but then I pushed a little harder, and I felt the most amazing sensation as the head breached his hole. As I slid inside, I watched his face the whole time, and if he grimaced, I paused for a while.

He breathed deeply. "Ooh, it's bigger than the dildo."

"You okay?"

"Yeah."

I started to pump slowly in and out, and it felt unbelievable. He stroked his cock while I fucked, and we got into a rhythm. Then I leaned over him and actually kissed him on the lips. Might as well go all the way. I kissed him more and sucked on his big lips while I fucked him. When I rose back up, he had a blissful look on his face, and I began pumping in earnest.

Soon I was pounding away, and I was worried that I was getting too rough. "You want me to ease up?"

"No. You're hitting the spot. Keep going, just like that." His breath was irregular, and he let go of his cock. "I can't hold back."

While I pumped into his muscle ass, jizz started shooting out of his cock without him even stroking. That sent me over the edge, and I shot into the condom.

Un-fucking-believable!

After I pulled out and stripped off the condom, I plopped down on the bed beside him. Panting like we'd just finished a rugby match, we basked in our post-fuck bliss, my head on his arm, his fingers stroking my chest.

"Can I stay here tonight?" I asked.

"Sure."

"So there is no girlfriend back home?"

"No."

Thinking of what had just transpired, I was quiet for some time. I'd gone full gay sex and loved it. Guess I was more bi than I thought. Finally, I asked, "Let's go take a shower."

Nick raised up on his elbow. "Someone might see."

"So. I don't give a fuck. Let 'em think what they want."

He kissed me – whether to test me or because he wanted to, I'm not sure. It was nice and started my cock stirring again.

"You really don't care?"

"Nope. I say we go out there and kiss right in front of everyone. Fuck with their drunken minds."

He chuckled. "Maybe next time."

I shrugged.

"And maybe later, I can fuck your ass." I looked at him with a blank expression. I didn't know how I felt about his proposal."I ... uh ... It's just that ... I thought maybe ... Forget I said that."

"Sure, we can try it." I started to add, "As long as you take it easy on me," but then I knew I didn't really need to say it. And if I had the same reaction as Nick, then the harder he pumped, the harder I might come.

As we lay quietly, the rumble of the party could be heard through the door, and I smiled as I realized how good it felt to be doing gay things.

PADDLE BOY
By Landon Dixon

It was a tight game, 20-19, for me. One more point and I'd finally beat Andy at his own game – ping-pong.

We were in the rec room of the frat house, just me and the tall, thin redheaded fraternity brother. His handsome face was flushed, beads of sweat dotting his tall forehead. He prided himself on his ping-pong, like some guys pride themselves on their beer pong, when they remember.

"Match point, A-man," I taunted, raising the ball in my left hand, the paddle in my right. "Your streak is coming to an end."

"Shut up and serve," he growled, crouching, bouncing side to side on the balls of his feet. He was wearing a white T-shirt and jeans, an expression of intense concentration.

I grinned. Then I darted down my left hand, as if I was dropping the ball, swung with my right. Faking the guy out. "Ready?" I taunted, as he spasmed.

"Bring it," he gritted.

I smacked the ball, cutting my paddle down across the white plastic sphere for maximum back spin. The ball bounced off my side of the table and onto Andy's side, within the lines. Then leapt backwards almost right into the net.

Andy rocked back, jumped forward. He'd been expecting me to try to blow a smashing serve right by him, like I'd done on the two previous points. By the time he recovered, it was too late. The ball pocked his side of the table a second time and was swallowed up by the net.

"I am the champion!" I sang out. "Pong live the new king of table tennis!"

I danced around like I'd won miniature Wimbledon, pumping my paddle and fist into the air.

Andy stared glumly at me. Then his expression hardened. He raised his paddle. "Hey, Roger Frauderer, you know what week this is?"

157

I halted my moonwalk mid-heel and toe.

"Pledge week," Andy went on. "Paddling week." An evil grin spread across his freckled countenance.

"Hey, just because you're sore, doesn't mean you have the right to make me sore."

He wasn't listening. He was advancing, smacking the rubber-dimpled ping pong paddle against the palm of his hand. "Grab the table and take your punishment like a man."

I dropped my paddle, filled my hands with the inch-thick green edge of the ping pong table. Andy got in behind me, reached around me, unfastened my jeans with his free hand, yanked them down. He skinned my Jockeys down, to join my pants at my knees.

I looked back at the guy, my pale, smooth, mounded bottom exposed. He raised the ping pong paddle up high over his head, slashed his arm downwards. I shut my eyes, tensing for vicious impact.

The red dimples just kissed my electrified skin.

"Ready?" he taunted, as I spasmed.

"Bring it," I gulped.

He drew the paddle back, whistled it down onto my bare ass. The crack of rubber against skin went off like a gunshot, exploding inside my ears and body. I rocked forward, stung, heat and hurt flashing through my reddened cheek.

Andy whacked my other cheek, harder. I jumped at the fearful smack, sparks shooting all through me. He crashed the paddle down across both my trembling buttocks at once, raising me up onto my toes, making me moan.

"Hey, Andy!" Brent called from upstairs. "We're going on a beer run. Get your ass in gear – you're the only guy whose driver's license isn't suspended."

"Lucky boy," Andy hissed in my ear. "Or unlucky?"

He gripped my rock-hard dick, and tugged. As he blasted my right cheek, my left, both together.

I jerked with the blows blistering my bum, with the ecstasy blistering my body. Semen jetted out of my prick, Andy jacking me, whacking me.

"See you later," he said, tossing his instrument of recreational pleasure and pain onto the table.

He ran up the stairs. As my fingernails scraped the surface of the ping pong table, the last few spasms of sperm rocking my body. My butt smoldered, hardly ablaze, needing beating much worse.

# # # # #

Trevor and I were studying in the library, at a table way in the back behind the stacks. "Hey, what'd you get on the chemistry quiz?" I asked, looking across at the big, green-eyed blond.

He grinned, glancing up from his computer screen. "Ninety percent, ace; not bad, huh?"

I nodded. "Not bad. If you want a job cleaning test tubes at some high school chem lab. I snagged a ninety-eight percent, myself."

His grin faded. "Think you're pretty smart, huh?"

"Don't think it – know it," I replied. "Ninety-eight percent positive."

He glared at me, his big fists clenching on the table.

"He sassing you, too?"

Andy, come up from behind.

"Yeah," Trevor replied. "He thinks he's pretty good." His eyes glinted. "Maybe we should knock him down a peg or two?"

"I'm game," Andy said over my shoulder. He held a wooden ruler up in his right hand.

Trevor shook his head. "I've got a better idea. You watch Poindexter."

He got up from the table and jogged down the hall.

I looked back at Andy. He grinned back down at me, smacking his palm with the ruler.

Trevor was back in short order, clutching a pair of wooden measuring sticks; only bigger, longer than the mere twelve-incher Andy was gripping – yardsticks. He handed one to his frat brother. "We'll see how you measure up now, pal."

I opened my mouth to protest, was cut off by Trevor adding, "It's paddling week."

Andy pulled my chair back. I stumbled to my feet, gripped the edge of the table. Trevor unfastened my jeans, and both guys took a pants leg apiece, and pulled. My briefs quickly joined my jeans puddled at my feet.

My butt was exposed again, still a little sore from the spanking Andy had dished out the night before. It got a whole hell of a lot more sore, but fast, exhilarating.

The men took up position on either side of me in behind, Trevor being a southpaw. "See anyone else around on this floor?" Andy asked the bigger man.

"Nope. Just us three." He raised his yardstick. "We'll have all the privacy we need – to beat the smart right out of this ass."

I twisted my head around and gaped at him. He flicked the flexible stick against my butt, stinging my cheeks. I jerked. Then jumped, when Andy laid his lumber across my bum. The guy was obviously still warmed up from the night before because he hit hard.

The table rasped against the cement floor, my breath coming in gasps, as Trevor swatted my behind again then Andy. I bit my lip and quivered from tip to toe, inch-wide, quarter-inch-thick wood lashing across my buttocks, making my booty and body and brain boil.

The blows came faster, harder, the air singing with the slashing song of the three-foot rulers, exploding with the cracking reports of impact. They were well-coordinated, one blow leaving off, leaving a stinging stripe across my tail; the other landing before the white-hot flash of pain and pleasure had a chance to subside, punishing me anew. My ass lit up a fiery red, criss-crossed with the markings of the brutal blows.

"Look who's enjoying this almost as much as we are," Trevor said, tapping the tip of his yardstick against the underside of my wood.

I moaned. I was poled out as hard as those butt-beating devices, almost as long. Trevor ran the flat surface of his yardstick all along the swollen undersurface of my cock.

Then he cracked my ass. And Andy stroked the bottom of my shaft with his yardstick.

That's how they did it. One guy whacked my butt, the other ran his heated wood along my cock; vise-versa. It was breathtaking, butt and ball and mind-blowing. They smacked and jacked.

I quivered up on my toes, taking the beating front and back. My butt cheeks blazed raw with painful pleasure, my cock seizing up cum-hard.

"Fuck!" I cried, one man's wood whipping my ass, the other man's wood whittling orgasm out of my wood. Semen shot out of my cock and striped across the table, spurting in rhythm to the banging on my butt. I rode the waves of punishing ecstasy, blasting and getting blasted.

It was enough hard knocks education for any one man. If that man wasn't pain-greedy me.

# # # # #

It was Friday, end of the week. The successful pledges would be picked for brotherhood that night. I was leaning up against a tree in back of the frat house, holding court with some wannabes.

"Piece of cake," I opined. "The fraternity's short of guys. Too many flunked out of school last year, couldn't meet the academic standards. You guys have nothing to worry about."

"Think so?"

That wasn't a pledge asking. That was Roger, head of the house; a small but powerfully-built black-haired man with plush red lips and a dimpled granite chin, hard grey eyes. He was a leader, with a leader's strength and will.

He was flanked by five other brothers, Andy and Trevor included.

"Before we announce any successful candidates," he went on, "I think we better show these pledges just what kind of discipline and obedience this fraternity demands – on our big-mouthed friend here."

He had his hands behind his back. All the brothers did. Now, on his word, they brought their hands out into the open. They were all carrying cricket bats.

I gulped. The pledges moved away from me.

Roger lifted his bat and rested it on his shoulder. The big, ball-hitting club had a foot-long handle, a three-foot long, nine-inch wide flat wooden blade. It looked as if it could really do some serious damage – on and off the pitch.

"Paddling week isn't over yet," Roger reminded me. Then, in a harder tone, he said, "Turn around and grab some bark, while we see about tearing a strip or two off you."

I stared at the grinning brothers, the varnished clubs they were wielding. I turned around, dug my fingers into the tree trunk, and shook like a leaf on that big old oak.

Somebody popped my jeans open, pulled them down. I was quickly bare-assed, sans briefs tonight. The cotton only cushioned the dull pain still throbbing through my butt cheeks from the previous two paddlings.

The pledges oohed and awed, staring at the wicked red stripes on my buttocks. These were the dark sides of the moons, my sexual deviance revealed for all to see. My cheeks glowed in the starlight, flushing with the heat that was suffusing the rest of my body, in anticipation of the beating to come.

"Normally, we don't go to this extreme," Roger explained to the pledges, prolonging my agony. "But this guy is an extreme case."

He smacked my bottom with the cricket bat. My blistered ass burst with raw sensation. I gripped the tree trunk and waggled my war-ribboned bum at the brothers.

They formed a line, my exposed rear end at the front. Andy cracked me; Trevor, Ethan, Tony, Marcus, Roger again. They slammed me one after another, not so hard at first, really just tapping my derriere; then, as they got into the swing of things, harder, and harder.

I was jolted repeatedly, polished wood jarring my buttocks. My cock jumped along with my body, hard as any one of those bats. It was a warm, humid night, and sweat poured down my face and armpits, my ass getting burned, bashed.

The blows kept coming, rocking me over and over, each smack uncorking electric agony and ecstasy in my ass cheeks, sending searing currents of delight shooting through me. It went on and on, the men moving faster, striking quick and ruthless. The heavy air clouded with the wet splatting of wood against skin, the rasping of men's breath.

I clung to the oak, battered and breathless, white ridges rising up all over my butt cheeks – the telltale signs of a truly brutal, beautiful beating.

My head swum, and my body seemed to sail, propelled upwards into the night sky on the end of those paddling cricket bats. Only my cock kept me secured to the ground, and reality, hard as that tree trunk.

"Trevor, Andy," I vaguely heard Roger call out, "get alongside, lay some wood over the poor guy's wood and give it a log-roll. While we finish knocking some sense into his brains."

Trevor appeared on my right side, Andy on my left. I looked at them through glazed, tear-filled eyes, barely conscious; and grinned. As my butt was thumped again, and again, and again.

Andy slid his cricket bat over top of my jutting prick, while Trevor slid his in underneath. The guys sandwiched my dong, squeezing me where it counts. I felt the sweet pleasure even over the merciless beating my bottom was taking.

Trevor pumped his bat back and forth one way, Andy the other, the men rolling my cock between their two flattened slabs of wood. My fingernails sank deeper into the bark, my balls surging from simmer to boil.

I shook with a thunk to the ass, shuddered with the pressing roll on my cock. I could hardly feel anything, could feel everything. The savage ass-assault had catapulted me to a higher plane, where lay pure, molten joy never experienced by the faint of punishment.

I lunged, and yelled. Andy and Trevor tried to stem the tide of my ecstasy, by slamming my cock almost flat between their bats. But it was no use. I was coming, hard and heavy and heated, from far, far away. One more thud up the backside, and I was shooting.

Semen spouted out of my prick, blowing my balls apart, rocking my body and soul more violently than any blow to the ass ever could. But the blows kept on coming, Roger wielding the thunder all alone now, destroying my derriere. As I poured out my blessed, bone-rattling orgasm, sticky starburst after starburst.

It took three guys to help me back to my feet afterwards, Andy and Trevor under my arms to keep me upright.

"Okay," Roger said to the stunned pledges. "Now you see how we enforce discipline at our frat house."

Pledges gulped, gaped.

"And-and the thing of it is," I croaked, numb now from head to haunches, "I'm not even a pledge, or a brother. I just hang out at the house, help the guys out during paddling week."

I glanced from Andy to Trevor, at Roger, tremors of phantom butt blows still rippling through the empty spaces of my wasted body and mind. "Th-thanks for helping me out, guys."

AN ORAL TRADITION
by Mark Apoapsis

Hear me, you youthful recruits
who have begged to be our brothers,
now hanging here helplessly,
surrounded by your shredded T-shirts and torn shorts:
You pathetic pledges are far from the first
this fraternity has stripped and strung up
like so many sides of beef being prepared for butchery.

Year after year have our youngest brothers,
having pledged to endure the ordained ordeals,
met with much more than they'd imagined.
Yet every experience you've endured this night,
every unexpectedly intimate indignity,
every petty pain or unsought pleasure,
all the degrading discipline, has a dual purpose.

Those who seek the bond of brotherhood
must submit to the same strenuous torments
inflicted on their brothers before them
by their brothers before them. Better yet,
you young men who once yearned to equal
the fortitude of the fellow beside you
have witnessed him whimpering, humbled and humiliated.
As for any among you who believed you were better
than those who will be your brothers:
Your bravado has been broken and beaten out of you.

Now! Every man must memorize the sacred saga
of his fraternal forebears.
Until we tease from every tongue
the flawless repetition of our sacred story,
your torment will not be terminated.
Every pause will be punished with the paddle.
Every omission will endanger your private parts.

Every mistake will mean fresh manly misery.
And until every one of you
can call our hallowed history from his memory,
your pledge brothers must hang, every major muscle aching.
My brothers beside me now could tell you how many times
I tried repeatedly to recite it right
as they hung heavily by raw wrists!

# # # # #

Although the bond of brotherhood lasts a lifetime,
brothers leave campus to seek their fortune each year.
Yet, yearly, young men yearn to fill their abandoned beds.
So it came to be that a band of brothers began
the annual initiation rites for the few recruits
winnowed from the many men willing to pledge themselves
to their famous fraternity.
Liking loyal, brawny brothers,
they had chosen the cream of the crop
that is sown every autumn and selected in spring:
well-muscled men who'd meant their oaths
when they vowed very seriously to submit
to the will of those they wanted as brothers.

In the dead of night they descended on the darkened dorms,
where defenseless students, stacked in standard bunks,
lay sleeping an unsuspecting slumber;
dragging, half dressed from their beds,
a dozen drowsy freshman pledges,
a batch of boys, barely men.
Bound and blindfolded, the kidnapped candidates
were bundled onto strong shoulders
and carried into the cold night.
Their captors were comfortably clothed:
the wakeful jocks were wearing warm jackets.
But the night could numb the naked flesh
of a student stripped down for sleeping.

The frightened freshmen finally found themselves
in a familiar house, walls decked in dark wood,
where once they'd visited voluntarily

and vowed to return as residents.
But none had been in the basement before.
Their wrists were roped together,
and hefty housemates helped hoist them.
Strong hands soon suspended them
from the cement cellar's ceiling,
set in a semi-circle so each could see his fellows.

Bound there in their briefs or boxers, bare-chested,
or bellies uncovered under untucked undershirts
uplifted by unwillingly upraised arms,
the fettered freshmen hung in helpless humiliation,
dangling defenseless – displayed
to the fully-clothed fraternity of beer-swilling brothers
– toes not touching, but grazing, the grimy ground.
Those still clad in T-shirts when stolen from sleep
now found the sleeves seized and ripped away at the seams,
leaving wispy hairs curling over ragged white cotton.
Now all had armpits equally exposed
to the invading fingers of their fiendish captors,
and very vulnerable to the viciously cold cans
with which their tormentors tortured them.
The men moaned in shared misery.

Hairy-chested Steve, star quarterback of the college,
usually quite confident and cocky,
had looked bewildered from the beginning.
Now he began to look beaten,
bearing his brief torment badly.
His chin on his chest touched a triangle of tangled hairs
that turned into a tenuous trail down his trembling torso,
bisected by his belly button just above his boxers.

Brawny Barry, his muscles made meaty
by long hours lifting large leaden weights,
was a bit of a bully, unused to being at other men's mercy.
His bared biceps bulged as he resisted,
squandering his strength against unrelenting ropes,
until he dangled, dejected and defeated,
dripping with sweat in the chill cellar,
his tight T-shirt turning transparent.

167

Carlos, whose coffee-colored belly
was no longer quite covered by his undershirt,
kicked bravely with his brown legs.
The strong student's stomach muscles strained;
his heel hit a captor's chest and grazed another's groin.
Calmly, his captors kept his flailing feet
from doing damage, simply by seizing his sensitive soles.

Tony's carefully trimmed and tended hair
had been tousled by sleep and struggles,
and then by tens teasing hands.
He looked particularly pathetic
in plaid pajama pants and torn T-shirt.

Lean and lanky Lorenzo limply dangled,
handsome head hanging in defeat,
all defiance disappearing from his dark eyes.
He too wore pajama bottoms, but was bare-chested.

Peter had looked imposing at parties
in a pressed suit and silk tie.
Now he was clad in patterned powder blue boxers.
His disheveled shirt was ruined,
ripped to reveal the prisoner's pale pecs.
The modest muscles the man's accustomed attire had hidden
were merely run-of-the-mill,
compared to the collection of captured brawny bodies
that hung half-bare all about him.

Charles was a study in contrast, with his chocolate chest
set off well by his brilliant white briefs.
The brothers had hung him next to blond Billy,
pale but buff in his black boxer briefs.

Sharp-witted Matthew had mocked the men
who had kidnapped and bound him,
but his laughter had not lasted long.
Shoulders shaking, shivering shirtless in his undershorts,
he gradually grew as quiet as his fellow cowering captives.

Kevin, considered the coolest man on campus,
seemed scrawny in his skimpy shorts,
compared to the classmates captured with him.
He looked a little lost, hanging by his skinny arms,
every rib revealed for his rivals' review,
glumly gazing at the beefy bodies beside him
as they silently sized up his slight form.

Barry, in his boxers, was blushing.
He was well-built, but bashful at his near nudity.
He had hair next to his nipples and near his navel,
nowhere else on his chiseled chest.

Red-haired Rich had recovered his composure,
looking overconfident in his underwear,
but the freckled freshman had been first to beg
when his helpless hairy armpits had been attacked.

Some were strangers,
But several had buddies bound beside them.
These friends were forced to watch
their classmates' clothing ripped away,
their trembling teammates tormented with tickling,
respected roommates reduced to writhing, red-faced wretches
as ribs were ruthlessly rubbed by rough hands.
Rarely does a man feel so profoundly powerless
as when he watches a faithful friend fondled familiarly
while he himself is held back by hard hands, helpless.

Men impervious to tickling managed to stay silent
only until their broad backs were beaten with belts,
the leather lashes soon shredding their shirts.
A senior student stood ready to stop this striping
the instant a helpless pledge pleaded miserably for mercy.
No humiliation is harder for a man
than being made to beg before a buddy's eyes
as respect is replaced by pure pity.

Any who dared to demonstrate defiance
quieted quickly when warned their bodies would be bathed
by a gallon of golden liquid –

for every hour, fraternal fingers
fumbled with freshman flies
and fished out their flaccid cocks,
coaxing all to empty their bladders into a common canister
to which the beer-swilling brothers contributed copiously.

Hours of taunting torment later,
the few remaining ragged shreds of shirts
were ripped from their bare backs.
Now the nineteen-year-olds all were naked to the waist,
twelve trembling, well-toned teenage torsos
to be teasingly tortured by sadistic sophomores
wielding whips of twisted towels.
The whipped men whimpered, then howled
as icy beer sprayed their shirtless spines
and cold cans cruelly caressed naked nipples.

Presently, pure oaken paddles were produced –
solid wood sliced into slabs –
and brought to bear on buttocks
covered in cotton briefs or boxers:
Poor protection against solid oak!
A few were wearing flannel pajama bottoms,
briefly buffering the blows to their buttocks.
But pajama pants were promptly pulled partially down,
exposing pubes and penes to their peers,
and leaving the buttocks bare.
Now a stinging, unstinting paddling
readily rendered those rumps red and raw.

Tradition demanded that the hairiest he-man of the bunch,
in front of his captured comrades,
be shaved smooth, from shoulder to shaft,
not sparing any hair that trailed from navel to pubes.

That year the young quarterback, Steve,
was chosen for chest shaving.
As the lingering lather was washed from his hairless torso,
the cocky quarterback, quivering, started to sob.
The brothers jeered at the dejected jock,
running rough hands over his chiseled chest,

170

now smooth as a baby's bottom,
their nails not neglecting to nick his naked nipples.

Once again, a senior sought each freshman's manhood,
fishing it out through his fly with his fingers.
This time, each fondled the flaccid member until it firmed,
hardening helplessly in his hand.
Each captive's captured manhood,
once massaged, was meticulously measured
and its length listed in a leather-bound ledger
whose dog-eared pages documented decades
of incoming initiates before them.
Marty, the man measuring Barry the body builder,
laughed at the large lug's meager man meat
lying limp in his hand, leaking a little
as the enforced erection slowly subsided.

In cases where clinging cloth came between
the base and the ruler,
the fellow's fly was ruthlessly ripped wide open
and his manhood measured again.
The nut sacks of many men now lay exposed.
Powerless to put this to right,
they passively endured the jeering
of the junior, sophomore and senior jocks.

Marty belittled the beefy Barry, who he'd thus bared.
The big freshman was far fitter than him,
so he knew he would never again
have this giant jock in his power.
Pulling aside the badly tattered boxers,
he lightly scratched his captive's silken scrotum
in a teasing, tickling torment.
Casually, he cupped two tender testicles
in his calloused hand,
cold from quaffing cans of frothy beer.

The tough man knew his testes were trapped
in his tormentor's power.
However the big body builder begged, Marty's only response
was to jiggle the jock's junk gently.

171

The feeling of his family jewels
being jostled in such a familiar manner
brought tears of helpless rage
to the strapping student's eyes.

He hooked his free hand into the band of Barry's boxers
and pulled. It promptly parted with a painful snap,
and the ragged remains of cloth clinging to it
came free in his hand, leaving the big body bare.

At this signal, every student was stripped
by a hundred hands as he hung helpless.
The partially-pulled-down pajama pants were pulled
entirely free of flailing freshman legs.
The remaining tatters of torn shorts
were ripped away from limbs and loins.
Utterly naked now, the students stopped struggling
and dangled defeatedly, chests heaving heavily,
powerless to prevent the fraternity's final inspection.

Any hopes for a hands-off inspection was, naturally, naive.
Nut sacks, now denuded of shorts,
were kneaded menacingly in men's hands.
The fettered freshmen feared for their family jewels,
yet their captors did not crush them,
but carefully caressed them,
until the pledges pleaded for an end to the pleasure.

Stroking the students relentlessly,
organisms were wrested from resisting bodies.
Penes were pumped, or teased by tongues.
Testes were tasted.
Try as they might to distract their minds,
their bodies betrayed them.
Semen is trivial to tease from teenage testicles
in the final year of their second decade.
They each ejaculated into a giant jug,
one made to hold a gallon of milk,
not to gather the mingled milk of multiple men.

They then hung limply, wretched and unresisting,
as their genitals were gently grasped
and the last precious drops milked from their manhood.

Seven seniors coated their forefingers for finger-painting
with the milky mixture made moments before.
They smugly smeared each freshman's chest
with long lazy lines of liquid
drawn down the nude students' stretched stomaches.
The first contrasting canvas chosen for the chalky fluid
was Charles's chocolate chest, but paler pecs than his
were soon painstakingly painted, from nipples to navel,
with pearly patterns of their peers' penis proteins.

It was midmorning before the recruits were released,
having recited the required stanzas
recording the historical humiliation of youths of yore.
The brothers, shedding their own shirts,
at last lowered the limp bodies
and lifted them unresisting onto their strong shoulders,
leaving the bare basement floor splattered in man juice,
the jellied jism of jocks coating the concrete
and soaking the scattered scraps of shredded sleepwear.
The pledges, plastered with each other's spent seed,
were next carried naked to the third floor restroom,
where the musky men were muscled into massive tubs.

Some of the sticky students struggled in vain
as they were brutally bathed in warm water,
scrubbed clean by the hard hands of countless captors,
careless of the cherry-red welts
crisscrossing their chests, backs, and buttocks,
oblivious to the tenderness of their testicles.

Afterward they lay exhausted, resting together
in the great hall of the fraternity house,
piled on a pair of mattresses pushed together,
pink bodies covered by collective blankets,
each unshaven cheek
nestled on a naked neighbor's shoulder or chest.
The freed freshmen felt that their shared shame

had forged a friendship among former strangers,
an unbreakable bond of brotherhood
that would last a lifetime.

Even before evening fell, when finally
they were clad in clothing borrowed from big brothers,
and permitted to proudly pull fresh shirts
printed with large green Greek letters
over their bare, abused backs,
they knew they had become brothers,
both of their erstwhile captors
and, better yet, of the comrades sleeping beside them.

# # # # #

Listen up, losers! You youths yesterday night
saw seized and stripped, subjected to a similar saga;
you current crop of captives, now naked,
dangling in defeat, your bare bodies decorated
with congealed cum collected from your comrades:
Know that I and this band of brawny brothers before you –
all your cruel and confident captors,
even your tallest, toughest torturer
– once hung helpless here,
as bound and broken as we have now made you.
Once, we all knelt, nearly naked, at our captors' feet.
Once, we were raised by roped wrists to be whipped raw,
vulnerable to the very men who now know us as brothers.

I too once wore dried drops of jellied jism,
the joined juices of the juniors here tonight,
drawn upon my ticklish belly and bare chest.
I carried this sophomore, shivering in his shorts,
on my shoulders, and strung up his struggling body.
Before his eyes, I tenderized his buddy's bare broad back
brutally with a twisted towel.
This strapping senior stole me struggling from my bed,
this one stripped me of my shredded shirt,
and that one gently grasped my unprotected testicles
while his brother pumped my penis dry.
I would lay down my life for any of these men,
and I truly trust any of my brothers to guard my back.

174

Our humiliation is burned into each brother's memory,
permanently, for one purpose: so you younger brothers,
and your younger brothers in the years to come,
will all know us utterly as your equals.
That is why we will make every man here,
on pain of male misery at our hands,
memorize each humiliating moment of our humbling ordeal
before we are willing to welcome you
into our warm fraternal embrace forever.

Bonus Novella
FRAT BRATS
By R. W. Clinger

PART ONE – DANE

1.

"Impressive. Butch. Hulking. I rather like it," I rattled off, and consumed the monster of a frat house. The Theta Chi edifice was everything I imagined it to be: wraparound porch, three stories high, expansive windows, frat brat cars parked to the right, couch in the front yard next to a Weber grill.

"Let me take you inside, and you can meet some of the guys," my older brother, Nash, told me.

"I'll follow you, Scooby Doo."

Inside Theta Chi was like being in a young gay man's dream: battered furniture, massive flat screen television set, beer bottles strewn everywhere with pizza boxes, locker room smell, and half-naked male bodies relaxed on Goodwill sofas.

"That's Blaine," my brother introduced.

Blaine was flopped in a ragged Danish Modern chair and supplied a wave. He looked like Taylor Lautner, which included the actor's ripped torso, dashing smile, and superstar eyes.

I waved back and said, "Hey."

Nash pointed out a guy named Goalie who looked like Zac Efron. We said "hey" to each other and nodded our heads in a brotherly manner. Nash introduced me to Pecker, Lance, and Tom, all of which were dark-haired cuties with nicely built chests and thick thighs. Nash said, "Sixteen guys live in the house. There are six bedrooms, three baths, and a pool table in the basement."

"Comfy," I chanted, pleased to see my brother's habitat, and added, "Show me where a bathroom is; I really have to take a piss."

Templeton College was the home of two thousand young men, an all-male college with enough testosterone and semen to start a XXX media company. The campus consisted of three hundred and ninety-three acres, two dorms (Chase Hall and Tanley Hall), a dining facility called West Hall, a library (Minster Hall), a gymnasium, planetarium, and a small chapel where Christian men prayed on Sunday mornings … after they were naughty and sinned on Saturday nights. The college sat near Lake Erie in Pennsylvania, surrounded by thick oaks, pines, and maples. The

179

small town of Templeton was populated by fourteen thousand residents, most of whom were blue collar and worked at the local paper mill. The town was collectively quiet, subdued, and only a nuisance when the college boys threw obnoxious parties in the surrounding woods.

My brother, Nash Biggs, was a junior at Templeton. He majored in political science and Italian girls. He was twenty-one years old, two years older than I. The sexy smartass was a spitting image of me: strawberry-blond hair, five-eleven frame, intense green eyes, a dimple on his right cheek, and showcased a lean build with a two percent fat ratio. The only difference between the two of us was our mass: Nash weighed one-eighty and had a lined torso. I, on the other hand, was muscular in size with a thick neck, palm-sized pecs, and biceps of steel. I weighed in at two-twenty and could lift three-hundred-fifty pounds. Football had abducted me at a very young age, and I had played a tight end in junior high through high school, and carried the nickname Tackle, even though my real name was Tyler Roderick Biggs.

There was one other valid difference between my brother and me. While he trampled the tri-state area for dark-haired bellas, I preferred the company of sexy, well-built gentlemen. My difference was self-acknowledged at age eleven when I helplessly fell in love with Joey on *Friends* and endlessly masturbated to a glossy picture of the star for the next five years.

Julia, our widowed mother, as well as Nash, accepted my diversity with very few questions. We were a close family with keen survival skills. Mother was a psychologist at The Woodrun Facility, a special needs school in downtown Pittsburgh. I worked at Lord's Gym as a physical trainer's assistant. Nash obtained a scholarship to attend Templeton, which he gratefully accepted and used. In truth, we were as happy as we could be, still united as one, and loved each other.

Templeton College was a three-hour drive north of Pittsburgh. I had saved up enough money to purchase a ticket and take a Greyhound north. On the bus ride, I read a John Patrick collection of naughty gay stories, which caused a boner to sprout between my legs. By the time I reached the college, a long and tedious ride, I was ready to fuck a dozen or more college dudes and release my load.

Minutes before: late September offered a beautiful Indian summer. The air was fresh and warm next to the lake, and the temperature was mild, in the high seventies. Nash picked me up at the Templeton bus stop in a frat brother's banana-yellow Mustang. I hadn't seen him for five weeks, and he gave me an exceptional man-hug. After our hug, he drove us to Templeton College and parked in front of a massive Victorian-style frat house among oaks and maples. He turned to me in the passenger seat and rattled off, "Welcome to Theta Chi, bro."

2.

One of the three bathrooms sat on the second floor in the frat house, which looked like a nest for rats, among other dirty creatures of the wild. The porcelain sinks were chipped. Pubic hairs were sprinkled everywhere. The two toilets looked as if they hadn't been cleaned in what looked like seven years; both were trimmed in brown and smelled like urine. I stood over the toilet, released my junk from Diesel jeans, drained my hose, shook the goods off, and began to button up.

The bathroom door opened behind me, and one of the frats entered. The guy moved up to my side, spun me around by my hips, and peered down at my denim-covered package. He reached out, cupped my goods, and whispered, "Tackle. Nash's queer little brother ... We finally meet."

Wood started to grow in my cotton briefs. A smile formed on my face with pure delight. As the guy massaged my goods, I gave him an awestruck look and consumed his handsomeness: twenty years old, onyx-black eyes, medium build, five-eleven frame, one-hundred-ninety pounds, thick black hair with sideburns, ruby red-colored lips. I knew the guy as Dane Larkson from my brother's Facebook page. Dane was from Cleveland, Ohio, a third generation Templetonite. He was one of my brother's friends for the last three years.

"What are you doing down there?" I inquired, enjoying his fingers at work on my boys.

"I'm just checking to see how gay you are. By the feel of it ... you're pretty headstrong about fucking dudes."

"Don't you mean dick-strong?"

Dane laughed at me and jostled my beef.

"I didn't know you were gay," I said; it sounded more like a question, but whatever. "My brother didn't tell me that."

He man-handled my pouch with a firm palm and started to stroke the fabric up and down in a feisty manner. In doing so, he said, "There's a lot Nash doesn't know about me."

"Aren't you close friends, though?"

The Robert Pattinson look-alike continued to stroke my jeans-covered beef in a north and south fashion. He chanted, "Not that close. Obviously you're mistaken. Nash chases the girls, and I chase ... whatever jock I can get my hands onto, and my cock into."

"Are you a slut?" I asked, overjoyed with his handjob. Elation flooded through my system, and I pumped his palm two times in a row.

He shook his head and shared, "Only if you want me to be."

Before I could answer, he leaned over, took a sniff of my product, dragged his tongue against my cotton briefs, along a sliver of my Diesels, and eventually pulled away. After his show, he asked, "What are my chances of getting you naked?"

I sort of laughed at that: heartily, wide-eyed, broad-smiled. "You're a total flirt," I admitted and covered my package with denim.

"You don't have to button them. I actually have other plans for your cock."

"What kind of plans?" I had the four buttons secured and turned around. A twin looked back at me in the mirror: mussed hair, glittery-green eyes, cutest cheek-dimple on the planet.

Dane reached around my right shoulder and tried to handle my chin with three fingertips, but I pulled away from him. Surprised by my reaction, he asked, "Do you have a boyfriend in Pittsburgh?"

I shook my head. The last boyfriend I kissed, hugged, and fucked was last February, then he dumped me. Ricardo Gonzalez broke my heart; he cheated on me with a high school swimmer. As far as I knew, Ricardo (Dick, as I referred to him) still dated the guy and never thought about me.

"I want to lick you from head to toe," Dane confessed. "Something tells me you want to be fucked, and I'm the guy to get the job done."

"What makes you say that?"

He circled me as if I were his prey. Once he faced me again our lips almost touched. Dane attempted to cup my goods a second time, but I pulled away.

He said, "Face it, you're hard for me."

"I could be. I'm just not sure about your forwardness as of yet."

He laughed at my comment. Fingers on his right hand discovered my bottom lip, and he gently caressed its red plumpness. "I'll have you by the end of the weekend."

"I'm leaving tomorrow. If you're going to fuck me, you'd best quickly figure out how. That gives you about twenty-four hours."

"I won't disappointment you," he confessed, smiling like a superstar.

I moved up to the sink, gave my hands a quick wash, and wiped them on my jeans. In doing so, I said, "Try your hardest, Dane. I like when a man works for me."

"Trust me ... I'll do my best."

"I would hope so," I responded over my right shoulder and exited the bathroom to find my brother.

3.

I played pool in the basement with a few of the frat brats: Nash, Tom, and Goalie. Bo Nassy also joined us. He was a big sophomore guy with muscles like me, completely bald, sported his Native American skin, and stood at six-three. Nash and Bo were experts at pool and kicked our asses. We drank some Jack Daniel's shots and smoked weed during three games. I wasn't a big fan of smoking pot, but once in a while I did partake at parties. Between games, my brother pulled me aside and whispered in my ear, "What happens at Theta Chi stays at Theta Chi, so don't tell Mom."

"I got your back, bro," I said and promised not to tell our mother about the antics at Templeton College.

Dinner was around five in the evening; Goalie was a master on the grill, and he barbecued hot dogs and hamburgers. Two coolers filled with beer welcomed three dozen or more unexpected guests. A late afternoon party ensued around the house. Music blasted. Drugs were taken. Clothes came off, and young men sported their late-summer tans.

I drooled over hairy navels, bulging biceps, and sweaty pecs. There were a dozen or more different types of young men: thick and thin, muscular and twigs, blonds and brunettes, bald guys with Greek noses and kissable dimples, Polish and Russian dudes, Irish lads and Jamaican soccer players. My eyes took in those frats as if they were all in a candy store and I was nothing less than a hungry boy who craved sugar.

Discreetly, I pushed my boner away and felt pre-spew leak into my cotton briefs. The last thing I wanted to do was embarrass my sibling among his peers/brothers. Truth was there was so much sticky substance at my privates that I believed I had accidentally shot an entire load inside my shorts. Moisture collected around my cock, balls, and the tangles of blond pubic hair. I felt ridiculous and wet, yet I was turned on to the fullest.

Dane was present among those dashing and young-spirited frat brats. As I continued to feel uncomfortably sticky-moist between my legs, he glided up to my side, took a swig of his beer, swallowed it down, winked at me in a rather sexy manner, and demanded, "Follow me."

Why not? What did I have to lose? Honestly, I just wanted to find my backpack with a fresh pair of Unico briefs, a shower, jerk off under a hot spray, and clean myself up.

Dane walked away from me. And like a little puppy dog, I followed behind. In a matter of seconds, we were inside Theta Chi, and traveled up the wide flight of stairs with its rickety steps and found ourselves inside his room. There, I took in four beds, books everywhere, a rank smell of jock-sweat and spew-dribbled sheets. I consumed the clutter with such ease and zeal, and enjoyed the ghastly sight for some odd reason. One window was broken, cracked from north to south. An empty pizza box decorated the top of a walnut dresser. Clothes were strewn in all directions; my brother's among them. I saw a bong, glass ash trays, more of my brother's things, and a guitar.

Dane locked the door behind him and removed his shirt. He informed, "It's only fair that you see what you're going to get yourself into."

The man was gorgeous in my opinion. Biceps gleamed with natural sweat. Solid pecs looked edible. Strawberry-colored nipples hid among close-cut black fur. Lined abs decorated the student's stomach and caused a pool of saliva to nestle itself in the back of my mouth. A trail of treasure hair fell from the base of his puckered navel into his jeans/underwear. Intoxicated by his appearance, I helplessly licked my lips and whispered, "Nice."

"There's more," he chanted, unzipped his jeans, and pushed them down to his knees where they stopped. What was hidden underneath was a pair of white 2[X]ist boxer-briefs with a mounded package of semi-hard beef.

I licked my lips. How couldn't I? Dane Larkson was beautiful from head to toe; a model just waiting to be found and strewn over fashion magazine covers. The guy was perfect in every definition of the word.

"Do you like it?"

I nodded my head and studied his semi-limp cock under its material: six inches of presumably uncut tube grew by the seconds. Balls the size of Christmas bulbs on a festive tree looked absolutely delicious. Then, I confessed, "I really want to fuck you."

Dane laughed while he pulled up his jeans and zipped them closed. He shook his head and chanted, "Not here. My roomies always come and go."

"Where then?" I inquired, ready for whatever could happen between two young men in small college town.

"Follow me," Dane said again. This time, he grabbed his T-shirt, slipped it over his head, and we exited his bedroom together.

4.

The screen door at the back of Theta Chi banged against its frame as we scurried outside, through the lot of partiers, and found a narrow trail at the edge of the woods. There, I followed Dane on a rocky pathway for quite some time. Nature welcomed us with hungry mosquitoes, shade under the green canopy, and the occasional oak, birch, or maple limb brushed against our arms. We walked for a considerable length and eventually steered right, off the trail, and deep into the woods.

Some nine hundred yards or more off the beaten trail, we came to a small clearing. There, sat a fire pit built out of God's stones. Hefty-sized logs surrounded the pit; I assumed they were seats. Against a hulking oak leaned a half dozen roasting sticks. The ground was decorated with pine needles, exposed tree roots, and dirt.

"This is our getaway place," Dane confessed.

I smiled, and teased, "Do you bring all of your masculine finds here to fuck around with?"

My new friend blushed. Then, he pulled off his shirt and dropped it to one of the log seats. Again, I took in the deliciousness of his model-perfect chest and licked my lips. Helplessly, my temperature rose as well as the cock in my pants.

Dane teased me. He licked two fingertips and pinched one of his nipples. The fingertips then spread, and he fanned his right palm down and over his chest, and discovered his navel. Eventually, he stopped its travels at the top of his jeans and said to me, "You up for giving me a blowjob, Tackle?"

I liked a man who knew what he wanted, which I always thought flattering. Drawn to him, I closed the space between us, found myself on my knees in front of him, and nuzzled my face against the fraternity brother's denim-covered package.

Dane was not at all shy and removed my T-shirt. He leaned over, pulled up on its cotton sides, and released it from my torso; it was dropped to the woodsy earth somewhere. While that act carried out, he ground his goods into my face, and chanted overtop me, "Bite it."

I listened, opened my mouth, took in as much denim that could fit inside, and bit down on his material-covered goods.

He let out a grumble of satisfaction, and demanded, "Do it again, Tackle."

I was keen for instruction and bit into his covered cock again. In that process of naughty behavior, firm meat-bolts came to life between both of our legs.

Dane moaned above me and swirled in deep satisfaction. In a matter of seconds, he gently pushed me away, unzipped his fabric, slid denim jeans and boxer-briefs down to his ankles, and exposed his rigid timber for both of our pleasures.

What flopped out of his V-covered man-area was nothing unpleasant. Eight steeping inches of uncut cock thwapped against my face, decked me in my right eye, across my nose, and fell to my semi-parted lips. Since that opportunity arose for easy access to his shaft, I simply opened my mouth, consumed the tip of it, and passionately sucked.

My brother's roommate/friend gripped my shoulders. In one heated moment of fiery delight, he pushed all eight inches of tube into my mouth, down the back of my throat, and whimpered, "Suck me off."

As a friendly weekend guest at his college campus, I cordially obliged. One suck turned into many as I clamped my palms on his hips and prompted my mouth to ride back and forth on his swollen rod.

Of course, Dane was not shy about his face-blasts. He rode my mouth with such zeal and built up a fine orgasm. Grunts and groans echoed in the dense woods. Slurps and moans resembled ghoulish and monstrous sounds among the foliage. Both of us were having the time of our lives. And, helplessly, we worked each other over and shared a vibrant motion of to and fro, continuously and wildly, until he explained in a rather hungry manner, "I want you to shove your jock-cock into my ass, Tackle."

5.

Dane had his jeans and underwear pushed against the ground as he faced a hulking oak trunk for his pleasure. Again, he begged over his right shoulder, "Fuck me, Tackle. I like it hard and fast."

I stared at the most desirable ass I had ever seen: bulbous, tight, and hairless. The thing gawked at me with its own needs, perhaps hungry for my nine inches of engorged beef. But, before I decided to shove my pole into its taut center, I had other selfish intentions in mind, which I knew would spin my naked cohort deeper into his realm of queer bliss.

Cautiously, I looked to our left, right, and over my shoulders to see if we were alone. Once I determined our privacy, I knelt down behind the frat guy's winking core and spread his ass apart with my fingertips. Momentarily, I outstretched my tongue, leaned my head forward, and rolled the tip of my tongue along his pink core.

Dane went spastic in front of me. He constricted and released his asshole, moaned with satisfaction, and eventually whispered, "Lick me, Tackle ... Do it ... Don't be shy."

Of course I was not shy. The Biggs boys were far from timid and introverted, and we were awesome at fucking. Slowly and steadily, I swirled my tongue around his opening, pulled away, and swirled around it again. As Dane's moans became louder, I then dabbed the tip of my tongue into his hole, pushed it inside as far as it would go, and kept it there for the longest of moments as he whimpered like a little boy.

After that surge of joy for the both of us, I released my tongue from his hub, slid it back inside, released it again, and continued that act of ass-pleasure for the next five … seven … nine minutes, until Dane confessed, "I want to ride your cock."

Upon that decisive invitation, I immediately pulled my mouth away from his pink-tensed midpoint, stood, and discovered a square of plastic in my rear pocket. Rushed, horny as hell, I unbuttoned my Diesels and pushed them down to my ankles and Nike runners. In that process, my nine-inch tube of beef decked his ass, which caused me to grunt with excitement.

Seconds later, I had my tool covered in plastic and the head of it at his hungry entrance. There, I slapped the tip of its beefy cap against his crack a number of times, and chanted along the fraternity brother's back, "You ready for it, pal?"

"Bring it on," he whimpered and attempted to back into my stiff pole and lodge it into his man-fissure all by himself.

After applying the lube tube to my dong, I leashed my left palm onto his hip for balance and shoved four of my nine inches into his gap. Quickly, I yanked the inflated tube out and pushed seven of the nine inches inside.

In front of me, my new friend gasped with wanted pain and clenched the oak tree trunk with both palms. Eagerly, he begged, "All of it, Tackle … push all of it into me."

Again, I listened. On his demand, I pumped his body with my nine inches, pulled out, pummeled it inside again … again … again, and built up a refined orgasm of my own.

We worked together in synchronized bliss. Man connected with man so easily. When Dane backed into me, I pushed forward. When I backed out of him, he willingly pulled away. Together we blended with such zeal, besieged with the masculine power of our bodies in motion.

Truth was I didn't even have to wrap my right palm around his middle and stroke his lumber off. Dane was so mad and swept away by our man-link that he came on his own. I knew three lines of cock-juice flew out of his stick and drizzled his jeans and underwear at his ankles. Positioned in front of me, he gasped and groaned in orgasm, and emptied his system in utter elation.

My own orgasm was discovered in a matter of heated seconds. I found his euphoria as an aphrodisiac, and a quiver of excitement raced through my body. I shivered behind him with one … two … three last pumps, and felt my own orgasm sweep throughout my system. On fire, I backed out of his tight ass, ripped the used condom off my rod, dropped it to the woodsy clearing, and began to jack myself off onto his back.

"Spray it, Tackle," he coached me.

Frenzied pumps to my shaft ensued. I bucked my hips forwards, raced my right palm up and down on my meat, and …

I gasped a final time as white cream shot out of my post and splashed against his ripped back. The ooze glazed his skin, spine, and bare shoulders. All of my goop was released and caused me to moan with deep fulfillment as I became spent, exhausted.

6.

In the distance, after our post-sexed connection, a branch cracked at our far right. Both Dane and I steered our attention in that direction and …

Bo Nassy stood approximately twenty feet away from our twosome. He was half-hidden behind an oak tree. In his hands was a cell phone/camera. Obviously, he shot video of our entire scene in the woods.

Dane rose from his position and yelled, "Bo, what the fuck are you doing over there?"

Bo heartily laughed, waved his recording device in midair, and yelled back, "Making some money, faggots! Thanks for the fuck scene!" He then spun around, sped off, and headed toward the narrow trail and Theta Chi.

"You sonofabitch!" Dane screamed at the top of his lungs. With my wet spew drizzled on his back, and his fresh semen on his briefs and denim, he pulled up the fabric, zipped up, and took off after Bo through the woods.

Honestly, I didn't know what the fuck was happening. Confusion found me and toyed with my emotions. I looked down at our T-shirts on the ground, spun my view to Dane and Bo among the thickets and branches, and stood helpless in the clearing. My junk was limp between my legs. A bubble of sap hung on the tip of my rod and dropped into my briefs.

Dane called out to Bo, "I'm on your ass, fucker!"

The two were a blur among the tree trunks, gnomes who scurried in the woods. I yanked up my briefs and jeans, buttoned my denim, grabbed our T-shirts from the ground, and chased after Dane.

The three of us zigzagged through the late afternoon woods. Bo was the leader of the pack, some one hundred meters away. Dane was approximately fifty feet in front of me and shifted from left to right around trees. Both were faster than I in the woods. My muscular mass seemed complicated to steer around green thickets, over fallen trunks, and moss-covered stones. I charged through thick ferns, broken branches, and blackberry tangles in hopes of not losing the two frats. The last thing I wanted to do was spend the night in search of Theta Chi as twilight discovered nightfall and then morning.

Honestly, my woodsy lopes were totally different compared to those physically fit brothers. I did not run on Astroturf to the end zone and score a touchdown. Instead, I covered rocky and mossy earth with sloppy leaps and bounds. I zoomed left and right, accidentally dropped our T-shirts to the ground, and attempted to miss fallen pine limbs and rotted stumps.

Again, I studied the frats in front of me as they darted like wild buck or flying fairies through the thick brush. To my surprise, I heard Dane call out at the top of his lungs, "I'm coming to get you, Bo! You'd better run faster!"

The two were maniacs in the woods. Each acted as if they were superheroes as we all headed toward the nearby trail and ...

Accidentally, I tripped over a stump's fresh root and fell to the earth. My face landed in a plume of ferns, saving me from a broken jaw. My weight hit earth with a sudden thud as my legs stopped their movement under me. Pain arched through my right ankle, swelled, and then began to subside. I lay dizzy on the ground, pressed against ferns, another fresh root, and Mother Nature's timbered tummy. There, I tried to sit up, but couldn't. Dizziness had found me, and I was at a loss of motion. Instead, I merely lay still on the warm ground and waited for most of the pain to subside from my right ankle.

"Way to go, Tackle," I said to myself. "That was a nice fall." I looked into the distance and watched Dane's waving and fogged back vanish into the woods. Part of me wanted to scream for help, but I didn't. Why cry wolf when I didn't have a broken rib, arm, or ankle? I simply took a spill among the ferns and roots; no harm was done. Instead, I kept still and quiet on the earth, and simply attempted to pull myself out of that clumsy tumble. Once I could stand, I brushed myself off, took a deep breath, and attempted to find my way back to Theta Chi.

7.

How I became lost in those woods, I will never know. A purple-blue twilight had discovered me and somehow turned me around. I walked in the wrong direction: north, east, south, west – somewhere. I believed I walked a mile or more in those darkening woods, unsure of my whereabouts. Things moved around me: an owl on a walnut tree's branch, squirrels at play before bedtime, and a badger that looked for a boyfriend. The silver-white moon rose as the sun set, and I no longer felt safe. Half of me believed a handsome vampire would find me inside the woods and fall in love with me, or mutilate me to shreds. The other half of me was paranoid of the new dark, unsure of its movements, life, and secret whatnots. I feared headless men, serial killers, and trolls. I walked in circles, unable to find Theta Chi, Templeton, or even Lake Erie.

Again, I tripped and fell to the ground. My chin banged against something hard and abrupt pain skied throughout my face. My jaw stung with new arcs of soreness, and my lips became swollen. There, I lay for the longest time in a state of uncertainty. How was I going to find my way back to my brother's fraternity? And, how would I survive throughout that night in the wild with not a single Boy Scout badge on my chest? I cringed at the thought of sleeping on the ground under a pine tree, hungry and cold. My world consisted of a comfortable mattress, pillows, and happy dreams, certainly not what I had arbitrarily gotten myself into that evening. I liked the cozy amenities of life: the warm bed and tasty food; clean clothes and a hot coffee for breakfast; my cell phone and …

I remembered my cell phone in my front pocket. I sat up, dug out the phone, and flipped it open. What I discovered prompted my heart to fall to my middle and turn into heated ash. OUT OF SERVICE flashed on the cell phone's screen. At that point, I realized two things: I was doomed and … shit out of luck. Night held me inside its firm grip, and I became its prisoner. Dawn was many hours away, I knew. Food was probably not sparse, but my days of Girl Scouthood were long over. I was a princess of the woods by the nickname of Tackle, lost and hungry, exhausted and panicked – Dear God, what would happen to me by morning?

There I sat and listened for familiar sounds: partiers, music, a Mustang's engine rumbling, a door slamming – anything real. To no avail, that didn't happen. Night circulated around me, silence. And, it was then that I realized how alone I had become, surely lost and on my own.

Not ten minutes later, I saw a beam of yellow light to my right, which split through the tree trunks. Alarmed and in a state of glee, I stood and called out, "Over here!" My voice echoed throughout the night, and a gold-bright feeling cascaded throughout my core that clarified I was going to be just fine.

The flashlight's beam discovered my upright body and kept me inside its sun-like ray. In the distance, not even twenty feet away, I heard my brother call out, "Tackle?"

"I'm okay. I just got lost." Elation flooded throughout my core; it was better than sex with an entire football team, honestly.

Nash moved through the woods and up to my side. Once he found me in that darkness, he grappled me to his chest, kissed me on my cheek, gently shook me, and scolded, "Don't ever do that again."

Honestly, I didn't want to let him out of my reach. He pulled away, though, and inquired, "What happened? Walk me through it."

I told him everything: my escape from Theta Chi into the woods with Dane; our long walk; the way we messed around; and Bo Nassy's naughty videotaping. I said to Nash, "Bo ran away. Dane chased after him. I tripped and fell, which left me behind. Before I knew it, I couldn't find the trail and was lost."

"How long have you been out here?"

"Before twilight."

"Were you scared?"

I never lied to Nash and confessed, "I was. It's not like living in the city."

He gently pulled away from me and said, "It's far from the city. I'm just glad I found you."

"Me, too."

"What do you say we get you back to the house, and you can shower, take a nap, and join us later for a party?"

"Sounds like a super idea," I said and walked with him through the thick woods and darkness, back to the narrow trail, and then to the frat house, where I again felt safe.

8.

Once back at Theta Chi, I chugged down two beers, ate half a bag of potato chips, and found myself upstairs and in the bathroom for a relaxing shower. Inside that dirty room, I stripped out of my Nikes, Diesels, and Rufskins underwear. A pile of my clothes lay on the middle of the floor. Next, I checked myself out in the mirror: bloody lips, stump moss collected on my forehead, and a small cut next to my left eye came into view. I ignored my Fight Club appearance, turned on the hot water in the shower, and allowed the room to fill with steam.

Approximately two minutes later, I stepped into the shower and felt life again. Hot spray covered my torso and pricked at my skin. There, I placed my head under its fall, closed my eyes, and felt the hot liquid warm my shoulders and the top of my head. I stood like that for the longest time and sucked in the hot spray. A small smile formed on my face and offered a sense of contentment.

Suave shampoo sat on a shelf to my right, and I scrubbed my hair. In the process of a speedy rinse, I listened to the bathroom door squeak open and close a few seconds later. Had I opened my eyes, shampoo would have leaked into them, and they would have burned. I was careful for that not to happen. Instead, I took the time and finished my needed rinse.

To my surprise, the shower curtain was pulled back and a naked Dane said, "Your brother said you were in here." He stepped into the shower and cuddled up behind me. His chin found my right shoulder and his limp cock snuggled against my bottom. He asked, "Can I soap you down?"

"Hell yeah. Go for it." I was not shy about a shower buddy. In fact, I enjoyed the company, the soap, and whatever else could happen between two naked men under a steamy spray.

Dane also seemed to enjoy his time with a shower buddy. The Irish Spring was easily found, suds were lathered on his hands, and he applied them to my chest in a matter of seconds. Nipples were soaped and pinched. Abs were decorated with suds. The treasure trail beneath my puckered navel was soaped up and petted. And, within minutes of our shower fun, he found the knob between my legs and began to harden it up with soapy strokes.

I confessed, "You'll make me come again."

He laughed behind me and said, "Maybe that's what I want."

"Now, you're teasing me."

"Enjoy your ride, pal. Just so you know I'm not getting out of this shower until you blow."

True to his words, Dane labored over my pole in a vigorous conduct. Soapy stroke after soapy stroke ensued, which caused my head to spin and my temperature to rise. He was not about to seize his action, though, and wanted nothing less than to see and feel me blow my load into the shower. Steady hand movements jacked me with an exceptional accomplishment and sent me into a nonstop frenzy. Suds flew off his right hand and my dick. Dane Larkson, I realized, had me exactly where he wanted me, and wasn't about to free his hand from my staff until I erupted.

I huffed and puffed in front of him, and felt a siege of wonderment shift throughout my body. The frat manipulated my pole with exuberant skill. He applied licks to the side of my neck and right earlobe. I also felt his hard shaft slip between my legs, but not into my core. Dry humps were heatedly applied to my bottom in an animalistic manner; an action I craved to the nth degree.

Quietly, without any trepidation whatsoever, my brother's roommate whispered niceties to me, and called me steamy hot, sexy as hell, and XXX material. My chest rose and fell as I attempted to find oxygen. Helplessly, I bucked my hips into his right hand and felt my release.

"Come on, boy. You can do it. Shoot your load," Dane coached me as he nibbled on my earlobe.

No longer could I hold my white cargo in. With one last huff and puff, and a final thrust with hips into his right palm, seed rushed out of my wanker and flew against the shower's turquoise tile.

After my blow, my new sex-friend chanted, "You're shivering."

I spun around and said, "That was amazing, Dane. Nice work with your hand."

"Just imagine what I can do with my mouth."

With that said, I reached around his naked body, collected him into my massive arms, squeezed him against me, and collided my lips with his under the shower's warm spray.

9.

We dried off together with cotton towels inside the locked bathroom. Dane had his left foot plopped up on the toilet's closed lid and showcased his droopy balls. He confessed, "I'm sorry I left you in the woods. Bo really had me pissed off. The guy is always doing shit like that. Sometimes he doesn't know when to mind his own business."

"My brother found me."

"Were you petrified out there?"

"I was. A city boy doesn't really know what to do in the dark unless he's in the back room of a gay bar."

Dane laughed at my joke. He switched feet on the toilet and continued his task with the cotton towel.

"Honestly, I was glad to see Nash."

"That was my bad," Dane confessed. "I should have gone back to look for you. Once I decided to, Nash had already found you. Will you forgive me?"

"Only if you tell me what happened between you and Bo when you went chasing after him."

He now brushed the towel over his firm chest. "That's an interesting story. I chased Bo clear to his room, ripped the cell phone out of his hands, deleted the video, and passed the goods back to him. Fortunately, we have the same kind of cell phone, so I knew exactly what to do."

"So, there's no video of us fucking in the woods?"

"Not a chance. I was quick to respond."

"Why did Bo do it?" I inquired while running the towel back and forth along my skull.

"Bo is just a wiseass. He's a prankster. Someone who likes to have fun. The guy everyone laughs at, and with. The only problem with his created video is simple: only your brother knows I'm gay. The other guys in this house think I like girls, but I'm a little too geeky to nail one."

"Trust me," I confessed, "you're hardly geeky. Everything about you reeks of sexiness. I could pop another boner again, here and now, just by looking at your goods."

"That was nicely said. Flattery will get you everywhere, Tackle. Keep that up, and I may just have to take you home for Thanksgiving break and show you off to my family."

"I'll keep that in mind," I replied, and finished with my post-shower duty. I wrapped the towel around my middle, found my clothes on the floor, picked them up, and told Dane, "I'll meet you in our bedroom."

He informed, "I'm right behind you, man."

I sort of laughed at that and replied, "Just like you were in the shower, right?"

Dane chuckled, became a shadow behind me as we left the bathroom together, and discovered our shared bedroom again.

During the next half hour we dressed together, fixed our hair, brushed our teeth, and were ready for that evening's radical party off-campus. Although I needed a nap, there wasn't enough time to take one. Instead, Dane handed me a pink pill called Zoom and told me to take it.

"Is it an upper?" I asked.

"The best out there. Trust me. You'll fly on this thing."

"Will I know what I'm doing?"

"You don't have to worry about that. I'll be right at your side to take care of you."

I believed him. Why not? The weekend was short, and I wanted to play hard. There was no reason to be a pansy and no fun.

We both took a pill. Each of us did a shot of Jack and swallowed the pills down. Once that was accomplished, I asked Dane, "How long does it take to feel the side effects?"

"Twenty minutes. Maybe less."

I looked down at my watch and saw that it was just after nine o'clock in the evening. At nine-forty I would probably start to feel the pill's little adventure. Good for me. And, good for those around me to know I wasn't about to be the blandest person among them.

10.

Zoom kicked in exactly when Dane said it would. My eyesight outlined everything in a rich pink hue, a twang was heard between my ears, and I became very figidity. I did know exactly what I was doing, conscious and alert, perhaps almost too alert.

Dane checked up on me, which I felt fortunate for. He wanted to be held accountable for my behavior, since he fed me the pill in the first place. Downstairs, among a majority of the brothers, he asked me over a shot of Absolut, "How are you feeling?"

"Wired. Alert. Massively important."

He laughed at me and rubbed a palm through my hair as if I were his special pet. "Do you bite?" he asked while he patted my head.

I leaned into him and whispered, "I only bite hot guys."

A broad smile formed on his face, and he went in search of two beers for us from the kitchen.

The living room was scattered with jockish Theta Chi fraternity brothers. A *Girls Gone Wild* DVD played on the forty-two-inch Sony. Female boobs and asses flashed on the screen as easy girls screamed. Like me, a guy on the opposite side of the room had no interest in the soft porn, eyed me up and down, and took me in like an iced cake. The hottie was model-perfect with ginger-colored hair, sea-deep green-colored eyes, stood at six-two, weighed approximately one-seventy-five, sported dimples, freckles, and a reddish goatee.

I winked at him. He winked at me. I smiled. He smiled. We were just ready to click when Dane walked back into the room with two beers. He passed me one and kept the other one for himself. We both took swigs from our bottles and I asked, "Who's the gingerhead across the room?"

Dane knew without looking. "Niner."

I sort of laughed. "Is that his real name?"

"Nicholas Baker-Roddington is his real name. He has a nine-inch cock when it's soft. That's why he's called Niner."

"Love it," I responded, and took another swig of my beer.

"He'll break you if he fucks you."

I leaned into Dane and asked, "How big is his cock at full mast?"

"Ten inches."

"I'm willing to take it on." I received a playful punch in the shoulder by that statement.

Across the room, Niner still watched me. What did he want with me? What exactly was he in search of? Honestly, I wanted to blow him a kiss but thought it inappropriate in front of the straight frat guys. Instead, I took another swig of my beer, faked my interest in the female anatomy on the Sony, and eventually decided it was time for a piss.

Upstairs with my beer, I did what I had to do in the bathroom, washed my hands, exited the teal-colored room with my beer and …

"You're a fag; aren't you?" Niner stood in the hallway with his fingers in the loops of his jeans.

"What if I am?"

"I'd probably take you to my bedroom and fuck you over my bed, but … there's very little privacy in this house."

I found some extroverted mentality and moved up to his cuteness, snuggled my chest against his firm chest, breathed in his Axe scent, cupped his junk in my right palm, and inquired, "Are you really nine inches soft?"

He laughed at my question. "I could be. You want to find out?"

Truth was I already had. His junk filled my palm. In fact, his goods overflowed in my hand. And, they started to grow hard under my touch. I gave them a quick massage with my fingers, looked into Niner's deep green eye-pools, and confessed, "I found a pot of gold down here, friend."

He leaned into me and kissed me: unexpectedly, roughly, and opened his world up to me.

I was dizzy in the upstairs hallway, lost in his wet kiss. His hands strayed to my sides and touched my cotton shirt and hidden torso. Sexual slobber was added to my lips, teeth, and tongue. I didn't know if Zoom was finally at work on my system or Niner. All I really knew was that I had somewhat lost my balance and fell against his solid mass.

Niner quickly pulled away from me and asked, "Whoa there, guy."

Mickey Erlach

"It's Zoom," I confessed. Honestly, it wasn't. It was Niner, every inch, slobber, and breath of him. He excited me to no end.

"Is Dane passing out his magic pills again?"

I nodded my head.

"Shame on him. Watch what he gives you. The guy likes his pills."

I was just about to tell him that I would do that, but my brother interrupted our twosome in the hallway. Nash called up the stairs, "Hey, we're all leaving now."

"Where to?" I asked Niner, attracted to his good looks, his temporary kiss, and whatever else I could find myself falling into.

"Phi Kappa Theta is throwing a party tonight. It's supposed to kill."

I joked around and asked, "What should I wear?"

"Nothing, I hope," he responded, and pulled me down the hallway at his side to experience a night I would never forget for the rest of my life.

PART TWO – BO

1.

Dane said all the guys at Phi Kappa Theta were the hottest at Templeton College. He added, "They're uppity sweethearts with too much money. They reek of charm and dignity. But … when they throw one of these frat parties, they are totally different. The guys become out of hand, wild, and fun. It's a crazy kind of party. I'm talking passed out bodies on the lawn and unexpected threesomes. Extreme stuff. You can find any drug you want, and all the alcohol you can possibly drink will be there. P-K-T rocks all the way."

I was tucked between both Dane and my new friend Niner, who carried the Duracell flashlight. We walked through the woods to the Phi Kappa Theta house. Some of the Theta Chi fraternity brothers drove, like my brother. Others decided to take to the woods and travel with flashlights through the dark. The hike was over a mile long and off the narrow and beaten path. We headed north, then east, and north again in the autumn time darkness.

The night was very warm for late September with low humidity, a light wind, and a smiley moon overhead that offered splinters of silver-white light through the branches and leaves. Primal young men chattered, laughed, and yelled in the obscure dimness. Owls hid in overhead trees, unsure of our existence. Crickets were silent but still underfoot, hidden behind ferns.

Our group of ten walkers broke up into three smaller groups. Dane, Niner, and I were the last group on the trek. Dane was on my left side. Niner was on my right side and had his left hand in my back pocket. I felt his fingers rub against my rump. Each footstep allowed friction between the two and offered a sense of pleasure for me, and possibly for Niner, but I wasn't sure.

Dane had his right arm wrapped around my waist as we walked in our trio. He informed Niner, "We can share Tackle if you want."

"What if I don't want to share him? What if I want him all for myself?" Niner responded in a rather rough tone.

"We either share him or neither of us are allowed to have him."

I was flesh between them, easy muscle for their wild fantasies, and meat for their heated urges. I asked, "What are you two talking about?" and chose not to pull away from them. Instead, I continued to walk between them, and rather enjoyed being the center of their frisky attention.

"We're boyfriends," Dane confessed. "I thought you realized that."

"Boyfriends? For how long?"

"Almost a year," Niner responded. "We want to take turns fucking around with you or maybe at the same time."

I was speechless. Never had I been in a threesome before, certainly not with two hot jocks from a northern college. "What if I don't want to be your pet?"

"Trust us, Tackle ... You like us both and want us."

I did. Was it written on my face, even in the darkness? Did I wear my conceded attraction on the sleeve of my cotton T-shirt? Was I that transparent, horny, or easy? I admitted, "I never fucked around with two guys at the same time."

Niner was quick to respond in a tone of delight, "There's always a first time for everything."

I didn't reply. Instead, I stopped in the middle of our trek and listened to distant sounds in the woods: house rock, masculine voices, bottles clinked together, a girlish scream. I saw lights through the woody tree trunks in bright yellow-gold and soft orange. Excitement rose in the back of my throat as well as in my jeans, and a smile seemed to surface at the edges of my mouth. I was delighted to attend the party and believed that I would be up all night with my frat brat friends.

"We're here," Niner whispered beside me, always calm, cool, and collected.

Dane responded with cheer, "Let's get the party started."

The three of us tromped forward, elated and inspired by the sting of fun that hung in the late September air.

2.

The party at Phi Kappa Theta was top-notch stuff. Cars and numerous partiers littered the front lawn. The four-floor Victorian was wall-to-wall jocks, drunks, cheerleaders, princesses, and students of every race and color imaginable. Bare-chested hunks were on every floor. Some pressed pretty blonde girls against walls. Beds on the second and third floors were occupied by naked football players and risqué girls. Corners were taken over by young lovers with unstoppable libidos and extended tongues.

Nash, Pecker, Lance, and Tom were already at play in the living room area. A Cornhole tournament took place between Theta Chi and Phi Kappa Theta. Most of the young men had their shirts off and beers in hands. All boyishly laughed and wagered bets.

The battered walnut table and chairs were removed from the dining room area and exchanged for a ping pong table and paddles. Four Phi Kappa Thetas were at serious play, drunk off their cute asses.

Dane, Niner, and I walked through the house, room by room. Cigarette and pot smoke lingered from one room to the next. Pills in different colors, shapes, and dosages were easily accessible.

Chips, pizza, wings, and three kegs of beer stocked the kitchen. All three of us helped ourselves to a keg and filled plastic cups with cheap beer. Two minutes later, Dane bumped into a pusher and was given six purple pills called Blitz; he immediately took two with his foamy beer.

Music vibrated in the night and rocked the house: Eminem, Rhianna, and Lil Wayne. My ears stung with the loud music, but I loved it at the same time.

Inside the kitchen was a pantry stocked with canned goods, boxes of cereals, and bottled water. Dane pushed me into the small room and pulled a string that hung down from the high ceiling. White light brightened the room. Niner followed us into the room. Once he was inside, the pantry's door was locked behind him, from the inside.

"What's going on?" I apprehensively asked.

Niner pushed down on my right shoulder and instructed, "We want you to blow us."

"At the same time?" I inquired, daunted by their plan.

"Fuck yeah," Dane chanted, and beamed a boyish and mischievous smile from ear to ear.

Two minutes later, the boyfriends stood shoulder-to-shoulder in front of me. Jeans were pushed down to their ankles with ease. I was on my knees with an opened mouth and stared up at their muscular chests comprised of tight abs, firm nipples, and delicious treasure trails. Dane's eight-inch cock showcased a thick and black thatch of triangular hair and two tight balls. I lapped at the tip of his rod, pushed it into my throat, sucked on it a few times, and came off for air.

Of course, I was cement-hard between my legs. In fact, bubbles of pre-sap leaked into my Unico cotton and glazed my skin.

Dane said, "You got that shit down pat."

"Suck me," Niner was greedy and pushed his ten swollen and uncut inches into my face. His meat slid down into my system and gagged me. He positioned his hands on the back of my head and rode my mouth. The guy was like a jackhammer on my face.

"I'm next," Dane insisted, and pushed his lover out of the way in the pantry. Within seconds, he had his dick in my warm mouth and started to fuck me.

More dribbles of my shaft-juice leaked into the cotton and soiled my skin and fabric. I let out a snivel of my own in pure delight, perceptibly besieged by the moment.

Sweat built on their plated chests as they took turns in my mouth. Niner liked to gag me while his lover behaved in a smooth and rather slow manner. The two worked side by side on my face, in and out, and panted loudly above me. I held the base of one steam and then other. At one point inside the pantry, I wretched on both of their poles as they simultaneously began to throttle my throat with their pumped and veined tools. Spit erupted from my mouth as I grumbled and gagged in pleasure; the wet stuff covered both of my cheeks. The masculine duo laughed above me in their discovered bliss and informed me that they were going to blow.

Dane pulled out of my mouth first, then Niner. I took a deep breath, sucked in a considerable amount of oxygen, and knew our three-person party was just getting started.

I was politely instructed to jack them off with both hands. Still positioned on my knees, I grasped their shafts with both fists. My right hand wrapped around Niner's ten inches, and my left hand discovered Dane's eight inches. Together, with skill and enjoyment, I applied friction to their spears. Heatedly and quickly, I cranked the boyfriends off and sent them into states of erotic lust.

Hips were untamable and shifted to and fro. Gasps and groans echoed inside the pantry. I swear, Niner whimpered like a little boy with deep satisfaction. Perspiration on their lined torsos flung against my forehead and neck.

Dane chanted, "Finally."

And Niner roared, "Blasting."

Within seconds, they both provided me with a facial and exploded their sticky loads on my cheeks. Thick, white drizzle decorated my face; none splashed into my mouth or eyes, though.

Post-sexed, after our spicy threesome in the pantry, I used Niner's shirt to clean off my face. Cotton rubbed ooze away from my pores. Following my self-clean up, I dropped the T-shirt to the floor and informed Niner, "You look better out of the T-shirt, anyway."

Niner decided to kiss me: with tongue, intoxicated warmth, so very close.

And, Dane joined in. He pressed his body into our twosome and all three of us flicked our tongues together and connected lips.

3.

Bo Nassy was at the Phi Kappa Theta party. I saw the six-three man of muscle with a Sony Bloggie video camera in his right hand and a big-breasted brunette in his left hand. The two heavily smooched in a nearby corner of the living room while the Cornhole game continued with my brother and his frats. Bo's two-hundred-twenty pounds looked as if they were going to crush that poor girl; but maybe she knew what she was getting into and wanted to be sexually crushed.

Dane fetched another happy pill, freshly grown pot, or something naughty for his body. I was left alone with Niner and his ten-inch cock among the other fraternity brothers. Both of us stood inside the living room and watched my brother and his pals play Cornhole while Bo molested the female brunette in the corner.

I asked Niner, "Tell me what you know about Bo Nassy."

"He's a spoiled rich kid. The only child. His father owns a greeting card company."

"How old is he?"

"Twenty-one?"

"Why does he always carry a camera around?"

"He makes movies. Shorts that are about seven minutes long."

"It's bothersome," I said.

"A lot of frat brats think that."

Dane returned to our twosome and smelled like pot. He studied Nash, Pecker, Lance, and Tom at their Cornhole game and asked, "What did I miss?"

"We're watching Bo," Niner responded.

"What's our plan?" Dane inquired.

"I want to fuck him," Niner responded. "Straight guys always turn me on."

"I knew that," Dane replied, and snickered. He added, "We follow him, pin him down, and provide him with a fuck-show because of his little camera antics from this afternoon in the woods."

"Sounds like a plan," Niner added. "Tackle, what do you say?"

I turned my attention to Bo in his corner with the brunette and watched him at work on his female prey. For some reason, I liked the brother and thought him over the top bold and rather cute. There was something richly arrogant about the guy and essentially tasty with regards to his dark skin. I really couldn't place why I liked him. I found him easy on the eyes, though, a morsel of meat I wanted to kiss, lick, hump, and spray my load over. I thought him delicious for all the right reasons. What slipped out of me was pure magnetism for the beefy man, and my cock's demands: "I'm game."

Dane lightly punched me in my shoulder and said, "That's my boy."

Niner laughed, enchanted with his boyfriend's comment, and with me.

We heard Bo tell his lady friend, "I need some fresh air," and watched him escape the living room.

The prissy brunette nodded her head and replied, "I have to go to the bathroom anyway."

"We'll hook up later," Bo said.

The girl agreed.

We followed Bo outside, through the night, and to the house's back garage and drive where more cars were parked. There, he crept into the garage, found a light and turned it on. Yellow-white illumination filled the garage.

Dane, Niner, and I hid outside the garage area in a set of oak trunks and studied its interior shadows: paint cans, stacked lumber, a wall filled with tools, a vintage snow blower, wheelbarrow, stack of newspapers, and a parked 1972 Nova. Bo leaned against the Nova's hood, lit a joint, and enjoyed a puff. After observing three drags, Dane said, "Fuck this. We're going in."

Dane entered the garage first. Niner followed. And, I brought up the rear.

Once inside the garage, Bo put out his stick of weed and shoved the toke in the front pocket of his jeans. Frankly, he didn't look surprised at all by our unexpected intrusion. Bo was playing a game with us, and we had become his tokens with such ease.

Out of the blue Dane said, "Dude, we came to fuck you up." Instantly, he rushed forward and pinned the Native American musclehead to the Nova's hood by his throat. He pressed the jock's skull against the car's metal.

Bo lay still on the Nova's hood with an unspeakable greedy smile on his face. Truth was he had a controlled look about him that said: I led you three out here like little sex puppets. Take advantage of me. Do what you want to me; it's what I crave. He was cool and sneered with a sense of politeness at our trio. His grey eyes shimmered with zeal as he responded, "I want all three of your cocks inside me at the same time. Let's get the show started."

4.

"It's payback for your little scene in the woods this afternoon with your camera," Dane rattled off; the evident leader of our trio. He released his grip from Bo's throat and slipped his hand into the front right pocket of Bo's jeans. He drew out the frat brat's Sony Bloggie and toke. Dane handed both to Niner, who set them down on a nearby table saw.

Bo said, "It's three against one. What are you guys planning to do to me?"

Although Niner was not the head of our group, he interjected, "Unzip your jeans, pull out your cock, and make it hard. I want to watch you jack off."

Dane said, "Listen to him, pal," and lifted Bo's T-shirt. He exposed a clean-shaven navel and washboard stomach.

I watched Niner help Bo with his Nike shoes, white cotton socks, Levis, and teal-colored Hanro briefs; all were pulled free from Bo's skin and dropped to the garage's cement floor. What flopped out of the Hanro fabric was something similar to one of the Eight Wonders of the World: eleven hard and thick inches of pick was revealed, and leaked a few droplets of man-goo. The shaft was veined with purple lines and sported a perfectly cut cap.

"Fuck," Dane whispered in astonishment, "that thing is huge."

"Jesus," Niner chanted, mesmerized by the joint's size.

And, I vocalized rather smoothly, also taken aback by the sight at hand, "That's the biggest cock I have ever seen."

No matter the size of Bo's massive rod, we wasted no time and found pleasure with the man. Niner fell overtop the filmmaker's middle and started blowing Bo's eleven inches; the poor bastard could only get seven inches down the back of his throat, but who could blame him, right?

Dane and I fell to the Nova's front bumper, shoulder-to-shoulder. Our twosome escapade discovered a hairless, pink hole and smooth balls. Bo Nassy truly was clean-shaven from head to toe; Amen to him.

In unison, we licked and lapped at Bo's tight ass. Dane and I met tongues and lips as we sucked the jock's baby-soft rump with pure elation. Our fingertips pulled at the frat's hole and spread his chute open, so it showed off his pink niceness. There, passionately hungry for the Native American, we took turns on his man-cave with our tongues. Dane was first, and I followed suit with sloppy seconds. We giggled at our diligent work, just like mischievous boys.

"Eat me," Bo moaned, lost in his own splendor of man-connected-to-man-connected-to-man jubilation.

Dane spanked Bo with an opened palm.

Bo let out a yelp, and then added, "More ... Do it again ... Please."

Above our action, Niner gobbled up the eleven inches, or as much as he could fit into his mouth, of course. Together, we worked over Bo with heated slurps, smacks, kisses, and sucks.

Bo, lost under our care, inebriated by our relentless connection, garbled congenial sounds beneath us.

Again and again, Dane and I licked and lapped the man's rigid hole. And, critical of his labor, Niner continued to blow the filmmaker on the Nova. Our trio worked with ardor and unspoken commotion.

Eventually, I pulled my tongue and lips away from Bo's core and turned my attention to Dane, and asked, "Do you have your cell phone on you?"

Dane also pulled his face away from Bo's hairless opening and said, "Yeah. Why?"

I sneered from ear to ear, and shared, "We fuck him and take a video of it ... just like he took his video of us."

Dane was pleased with my suggestion and gave me a high five. In a matter of seconds, he reached into the front pocket of his jeans and pulled out his Verizon, pressed the video record button, passed it off to his boyfriend above us, and told Niner, "Film us while Tackle and I fuck Bo. It's time to make our first porno together."

5.

It wasn't rape, violence, or a flurry of uncivilized events in the garage. I have to point out that Bo Nassy begged for us to fuck him while Niner filmed our show. No, we didn't have to pin the two-hundred-twenty pound man to the Nova's hood and pull his legs apart for our duo of plastic-covered cocks to carry out a train on his rump. I knew that Bo purposely led all three of us to that garage to take advantage of him, to restrain him to that vehicle's metal hood and use his dark-colored skin ... the way he wanted us to use it. Bottom line: Bo desired us as much as we desired him.

Frankly, Bo's size was unfathomable, massive and muscular, and he could have wrecked havoc on our sexual group. If he wanted to, the jock could have swung his fists and belted us into unconsciousness. In self defense, he could have butt-headed our skulls or kicked us in our nads, if he wanted to. He could have ...

That wasn't the case, though. Bo craved dick and wanted our lengths and girths inside him. His appetite desired nothing less than a fresh pounding and relentless sex between young men.

Niner stood to the left of us and filmed our action with Dane's phone. Between his legs, hidden under his denim, was an engorged piece of ten inches that was surely ready to be played with by either him or one of us.

Dane bolted his condom-covered dick inside Bo, pulled Bo's legs apart, tugged out of the man, and bashed inside him again. He instructed, "You're up, Tackle. Give him your best work."

It was my turn to be a skin star. I plunged my nine inches of solid mass into Bo, backed away, and pushed forward. Sweat clung to my chest, hips, and shoulders. My breath intensified and I gasped with pure stimulation. Euphoria was discovered. Ripples of deep contentment rushed throughout my middle. I became numb between the beefcake's legs and heavily panted.

"My turn," Dane challenged behind me. He tapped me on my right shoulder as if we were tag team fuck champions, and told me to exit Bo's center.

Cordially, I moved out of Dane's way and allowed him to nail Bo. Dane was swift and sturdy. His movement was vibrant and almost carefree at the same time.

"This is what you want," Dane urged, caught up in our moment of ecstasy.

"Fuck me," Bo murmured between his clenched teeth. His eyes were closed, and his arms were spread out at his sides.

It was a smooth ride, and endless. Dane blasted into Bo, released his weight from the man in speedy motion. His balls thwapped against the filmmaker's ass in a skilled manner. Dane zoomed towards Bo's bottom, quickly pulled away, and careened forward again.

"Ride him," Niner coached his boyfriend behind his small video tool. "Cram everything you have inside his ass."

Dane did as he was told by Niner. In fact, he performed so well that Bo came a little. Two drops of white splash ejaculated from the jock's spike and dripped next to his navel. In that process, Bo whimpered with agreement.

Dane then asked, "Are you hungry, faggot?"

Bo replied, "Feed it to me ... whatever you scoop up."

Dane found Bo's pre-shoot with two fingertips and fed it to him. He applied the appendages to the man's lips and whispered down to him, "Lick your spew up, dude."

Bo listened. One lick turned into three licks, and the sap had instantly vanished. A soft mumble escaped the jock, which proved his pleasure with the evening snack.

I was up at bat. Dane quickly jacked himself out of Bo, and I took over. With one quick thrust, I jammed my nine inches of meat into Bo's tight crevice and started to shift east and west. My ride was extensive, velvety, and just right. He and I moaned together, into our shared gig.

"I have to shoot," Bo challenged; his face turned a dark reddish hue, and his cheeks puffed.

"That's my cue," Dane cheerily said, and moved up to Bo's waist, reached his right hand out, firmly grappled the eleven inches of Bo's beefy center, and started to jack it north and south, willing the stick to explode.

6.

Dane jacked Bo off and sucked the tip of his dick at the same time. Growls escaped my new friend's mouth as his hands and face worked at the same tempo.

Bo quivered under Dane's touch. He vibrated in joy beneath Dane. Masculine moans lifted from Bo's clenched teeth.

Caught in that act of our three-man pile, I lodged my pick inside Bo's ass, uncorked it from his hole, and continued that motion for the next minute ... two minutes ... three minutes, until Bo exclaimed, "Coming."

Dane quickly rose from the jock's spike, but kept up his handy pace. He said over Bo's succulent body, "Spray it, buddy."

My blasts to the Native American's ass increased. I hung fiercely onto his ankles and banged him without candor. One blast. A second blast. A third blast.

Bo finally exploded. Three arcs of sticky seed spun out of his hose and splashed against his torso. He grunted with glee and emptied his interior of spunk with zest.

After Bo's release, Dane asked him, "Do you want to eat it?"

"Feed me," Bo replied. "I want all of it while Tackle fucks me."

I was not at all alarmed by Bo's request and continued to thump his bottom. My bangs and humps became more wicked, and my grapple on his ankles only tightened.

Dane was naughty and scooped up Bo's gluey seed with three outstretched fingers. Next, he pushed the three tips into the man's mouth. Again and again he fed Bo until our victim's torso was completely free of shoot.

Dane was next to come. He moved up to my side and began to crank his beef up and down. The guy swished his hips to and fro, and manhandled his eight inches. In that process of pleasure he gurgled, "I'm going to squirt my load all over you, Bo."

"Do it," Bo approved while he munched down his own goop from his lips.

Graciously, Dane doused Bo's cock and torso with his cargo. After numerous fist-bolts on his flag, added humps, and a continued growl, white spurt shot out of his dog, twirled through the air, and decorated our Native American pal.

Sweat, huffs, and tears mixed chaotically within the room. As I continued to ride Bo's tight cave, Dane used his right palm and smeared his spunk into Bo's tight and hairless torso.

Niner still filmed our work. I believed he had a giant pounder inside his denim, which was most likely ready to burst all on its own but didn't.

I, too, was ready to burst. No longer could I contain my creamy freight. In a matter of seconds following Dane's blow, I released my joint from Bo's rump, removed its plastic, and used both fists to spank myself off.

There, I became woozy by my own work. My legs wobbled and my chest shuddered. Perspiration spun off my flesh and practically sizzled against Bo's drooping balls and eleven-inch shaft. My chest rose and fell with intensified action.

"Come, Tackle," Bo coached as he sat up. "I want to wear your jiz."

I huffed and thrashed my hips forward, backward, and forward again. Both palms worked crazily on my tool. Seconds later, guy-ooze shot out of my hose and decked Bo's balls. Sticky lines formed droplets and dripped to the Nova's front bumper. Most of the gunk hung on Bo's orbs, though.

"Lick it off," Bo demanded of me.

I listened, famished for my own shoot. Quickly, I leaned over, held his cock with my right hand, and extended the tip of my tongue against his droopy balls. As expected, I lapped my own spurt away and cleaned his scrotum off. The bittersweet juice stuck to the roof my mouth, gums, and the back of my throat.

Beside me, Dane told his boyfriend, "Wrap it up, Niner." He patted Bo's tight stomach and said, "Blackmail always works in my favor."

I was finished with my treat, stood, and pulled up my briefs and jeans.

Bo looked over at Dane and asked, "Blackmail?"

Dane pointed at Niner and his cell phone. "It's all recorded, Bo. One more fuck up with your Bloggie, and I will let everyone at Templeton know how you fuck around with faggots and eat shoot."

"You wouldn't?" Bo confessed, rather surprised. His grey eyes widened and his mouth formed a perfect O.

It was an act; I knew that. Bo was putting on a little pony show for us. He wanted to be filmed, and he didn't give a fuck if it spread all over the college or Internet like some godforsaken disease. The dude was a star in his own way and he knew it.

"Trust me, I would." Dane smiled and nodded his head in an exigent manner.

Bo didn't even have to think about the consequences. Whatever seemed to skit across his face. The guy's eyes clarified that he didn't give a flying fuck if his integrity was questioned. Nor did he care if his sex life was exposed and broadcasted to all of the student body, which included his fraternity brothers. Bo was straight, or gay ... or something ... and his actions were extroverted and on the fly. Smiling without guilt, he replied, "I get it. No more fuck films of you."

"Or any of the frats," Dane added.

"Deal," Bo replied, hopped off the Nova, found his pile of clothes on the garage floor.

Minutes later, we were all dressed and found ourselves back inside Phi Kappa Theta's frat house, and acted like our foursome in the garage never happened.

7.

Nash sat on the front porch of the house without his shirt on. Under a yellow-gold light, two blondes were all over him: one had her lips against a pointed nipple; the other one rubbed a palm between his legs and shared a tongue-kiss with him. When I walked up on the porch, he connected eyes with me that said: What can I say, chicks dig me.

Behind me, Dane said to my brother, "Way to go, buddy?"

Bo ignored us and didn't say anything. He passed us and headed into the frat house in a hurry.

Niner brought up the rear and coaxed Nash on, "You're getting laid tonight, dude! Nice!"

Nash gave a thumbs-up while in action. As I stepped into the frat house, I watched one of the blondes unzip his jeans and go where many women had gone before. Nash released a moderate groan of pleasure, and continued to play with the two dames.

Bo zoomed upstairs for some unknown reason. Maybe he had planned to borrow a laptop in the house and write in his blog about his sexual adventures in the garage with three guys. Or, maybe he was going to take a shower and clean off the post-sex ick from his body. Honestly, I didn't know what the guy was up to and didn't bother to find out.

Dane went in search of a pill to pop. He hunted down a guy by the name of Wizz, collected an orange pill with lime-green stripes, and took it down dry.

Niner followed me into the kitchen to tap a beer. I pumped the keg, let the beer flow, and filled two plastic cups. I gave Niner one of the plastic cups, and …

He was in my face: tips of noses brushed together, lips gently grazed, tongues could meet with such ease. The guy was so close to me our chins almost touched. Eyes met with eyes and cheeks almost caressed. Our denim-covered cocks brushed together. A devious glow of happiness spread over his face and he said, "You thirsty for me?"

If memory served me right, which it clearly did, I had just popped my creamy load on Bo's droopy balls and licked it off. Niner was present for that scene, of course. Maybe he was just looking for something to talk about: my affection for him; my hearty interest in his body, mind, and soul; my attraction to his good looks.

I responded in a positive manner, "I do want you … But not just yet."

"You'll let me know when I can fuck you, right?"

I promised I would. Honestly, I really wanted to ride his ten healthy inches. My ass begged for his tool to plummet inside and force whiplash upon me.

Just to seal our kitchen deal, Niner reached for my free hand and cupped its palm and fingers against the swollen mass between his legs. He confessed, "Everybody blew their loads except for me."

Poor baby. I hadn't thought of that issue, even if it was the truth. Bo jacked his load out of his system. Dane shot his rocks off. And, I creamed Bo's package. Unlucky Niner was the cameraman in the garage and was completely untouched while our naked threesome unfolded. Nor did he jack himself off, which I knew.

"Later, I'll get you off," I confessed, molded my fingers around his pumped log, and gave it a jostle.

While that moment of hand-fun was shared, Dane walked into the kitchen and carried two orange pills with lime-green stripes. He broke our twosome apart and said, "What's up, gentlemen?"

Niner turned his attention to his boyfriend and confessed, "I'm trying to talk our city boy here into riding my cock."

Dane laughed and lightly punched me in my right shoulder. "We should ride it together. Wouldn't that be a fucking hoot, Tackle?"

Niner took the two pills from Dane and popped one in his mouth; he chewed it up with skill and swallowed it down in a matter of seconds. He then fed me the second pill and said, "Down the hatch, buddy."

I listened. Why not? The orange and lime-green pill vanished into my mouth without water, slid down the back of my throat, and into my stomach.

8.

"The pill is called Moosh," Niner confessed as he attempted to kiss me at the kitchen counter.

I pushed him away because I didn't want the two of us to be the center of attention next to the kegs of beer, among other places of interest.

"It will make you super high and then you'll feel like you're falling off a building. You'll need some sleep in an hour or two."

The room spun in circles. In the next half hour I felt giddy and wild. I told Niner I wanted to go for a run, which he suggested I didn't. Instead, I drank an entire plastic cup of beer, then a second one. Three Niners floated around me, danced, did somersaults, bounced off the walls, jumped and smacked their heads off the ceiling, and simply vanished from the kitchen.

There, Niner didn't move at all, and asked, "Are you alright, Tackle?"

Of course I was alright. I was fucking Superman and Batman and Aquaman mixed together. I could leap buildings, fly like a bird, and tame killer whales. Hell, I could take on a train of twenty-five men, one after the next, as they consistently banged my ass.

"Do you need to lie down?" Niner questioned.

"I'm good. There's no reason to be concerned."

"You're swaying. You do know that, right?"

Of course I knew that. It was just a sliver of my new superhuman powers. I could see through steel, swing from bridges, and hold my breath for almost two hours under water.

I had just realized that Dane was in the room. He said, "Follow me, Tackle."

"Where are we going?"

"To the attic. A sofa is up there, and you can lie down if you need to."

Niner was pulled away from our threesome by Tom; a Cornhole team needed an extra player, and Tom headhunted down Niner to fill the position.

Dane tugged on my right hand, and we climbed three flights of narrow stairs and ended up in the dismal attic. There sat a scruffy sofa for my use, a dusty Oriental rug, a shabby recliner, and a hatch to the roof, accessible by a piece of hanging rope. A diminutive window hung at the north side of the attic that overlooked the thick woods and nearby lake.

"What's up there?" I asked, pointing to the rope.

"A widow's walk. I'm going up. Are you coming?" Dane had a starry look of excitement tucked in the corners of his eyes. I didn't know if it was Moosh or something else, but it did seem to make him rambunctious.

I shook my head and admitted, "Thanks, but I'll sit here. Besides, I'm terrified of heights." The room spun around and around. Lights of many different shades popped on and off. A shrill buzzing sound flooded my temples, and my throat grew dry.

"Whatever," Dane announced, brushed me off, pulled on the string that hung down from the attic's ceiling, and prompted a set of stairs to appear. In a matter of seconds, he began to climb the stairs, pushed a hatch open on the ceiling, and vanished outside, into the night.

Safe in the attic, I visualized the widow's walk: a small enclosed cupola that encompassed a red brick chimney; a miniature porch of sorts perched on top of the frat house with waist-high white railings; a rectangle structure that was ten-by-fourteen feet in size.

"Dane!" I called out my new friend's name.

"You coming up?" he hollered down at me from above. I listened to his footsteps cross over the boards above my head; obviously he was already posted near the railing at the front of the house.

"No way, pal! You couldn't pay me to go out there."

High as a kite, he started singing a song about a shitty romance by Lady Gaga at the top of his voice. His tune carried out and through the Indian summer night, but was soon lost by the next few seconds with alarm and instant panic.

Above me, I heard a board crack and Dane yelped. His feet banged against the top of the window to my right and almost broke one of its four panes of glass. I then heard him yell out, "Help me, Tackle! The railing snapped free! I'm going to fall and die if you don't help me!" and knew he was in a state of petrified danger.

9.

The following events were a blur to me because of the pill I had consumed: frat boys of many different sizes and backgrounds careened into the attic to rescue Dane from his unexpected tumble. To my surprise, Nash was the leader of their shocked group. He rushed past me and zoomed to the single window in the attic.

All of us saw Dane's feet and shins as they hung in mid-air outside the window. I had guessed that Dane must have leaned a little too close to the widow's walk's railing, and it snapped under his weight. He obviously hung to the roof by a gutter, piece of heavy-duty shingle, or one of the widow's walk's upright wooden supports.

When Nash slid the window up and opened it, Dane screamed for his life. The attic's light was dim, but we all watched Dane as he swung left to right like a pendulum. One of his tennis shoes fell off and plummeted down four stories.

I handed it to Nash; he was a hero in the making. As Dane continued to scream for his life, my brother grabbed onto the frat brat's legs and rattled off, "Trust me, Dane. You're not going to fall." Nash didn't let Dane reply. Instead, he quickly pulled Dane down with abrupt force and tugged his entire body into the small attic as if the man were a mere domestic cat stuck in a tree.

Both Theta Chi and Phi Kappa Theta brothers roared with cheers during Dane's recue. Nash's name echoed off the walls by his elated supporters.

Dane was placed next to me on the sofa. Nash leaned over him and asked, "What the fuck happened out there?"

"I was on the widow's walk, and its railing snapped under my weight and gave out. I was holding onto the edge of the house. I think it was a gutter." Dane's voice quivered. He looked as white as a ghost, and his eyes were set deeply in the back of his skull. The guy's lips were dry and his brow was covered in a thick sweat. He mumbled, "Thanks for saving me, man."

Nash rubbed Dane's head as if the young man were twelve and responded, "What are brother's for?"

The rest was still more of a waving blur to me. Dane wanted to go back to Theta Chi. Nash said he wasn't drunk and could drive him. The two left minutes later, and I stayed behind with Niner, who decided we should have a beer together in the attic, and get cozy on the sofa.

"Are you going to seduce me?" I inquired. Both of us were seated on the sofa, shoulder to shoulder and thigh to thigh.

"Only if you want me to." Niner looked like a complete gentleman with wide eyes and serene warmth about his face.

"Shouldn't you be with Dane right now?"

"Trust me; he's had way too many pills tonight and needs to sleep it off. Pills have always been his weakness. Nash will put him to bed, and Dane will be fine."

I understood that and nodded my head. "So, I want to know why you're here with me right now." Our faces were inches apart, and I could feel his breath on my lips. Both of us smelled like beer and post-summer sweat. The attic was warm and cozy, private and semi-dark.

"I like you. What more do you want me to say?"

"Tell me a little bit about yourself. I should get to know you better if you intend to like me."

He told me he came out of the closet two years ago, he was the only child, and he was adopted at the age of four. He had no intentions of ever finding his real mother or father, since they were hippies who abandoned him. His favorite color was teal. He liked Oprah Winfrey. He enjoyed spending his evenings reading Pierce Anthony fantasy novels. He liked to collect stamps, and he really wasn't big on kissing. He considered himself a "bottom" in his relationship with Dane, and he gave phenomenal blowjobs.

We talked for the longest of hours until we started to yawn. I learned more about Niner in that short period of time than I ever thought possible. I found him reasonable, sexy as hell, and just a nice guy.

"You like me," he said, and rubbed two fingertips against my chin.

"I do," I confirmed. "Just don't tell anyone."

"Except for Dane. I tell him everything, since we're boyfriends."

"Except for Dane," I agreed, nodded my head, and yawned again.

Sometime later, long into the night, perhaps closer to dawn than we both imagined, our bodies tangled together on the sofa, and we fell asleep.

Light snores ensued in the attic, pleasant dreams were discovered, and a sense of serenity between two young men traipsed into the hours of restfulness.

10.

We woke shortly after dawn. Niner had his head on my chest. One of his hands was tucked between my legs. Both of us sported morning wood. I touched one of his shoulders with a palm and gently shook him. "You up?"

"For a few minutes. I sort of like being together with you."

"You're hard," I said, and discovered the piss-boner between his legs with my left palm. "It's harder than steel."

"Just the way you like it," he replied, reached between my legs and grabbed my inflated beef. "You have a nice chub going on. I could suck it if you want."

"A piss is in motion," I confessed, and supplied his body with a light push to get up. "We stink."

"I sort of like that, too."

Both of us stood, stretched, and yawned. I rolled a palm down and over his chest, caressed his bare navel, and said, "I think I'm still drunk."

"And terribly sexy," he replied, and moved up to me, connected our chests together, and shared a kiss with me.

I melted. Something wild and fluffy skittered within my stomach. I couldn't remember the last time anyone had made me feel that way. When I finally pulled away from him, I asked, "Can you remember anything about last night?"

He did. His shirt was in the downstairs closet; Dane had taken too many pills and almost fell off the roof; Nash drove Dane back to Theta Chi; we spent half the night talking and eventually fell asleep on the attic's sofa.

"My shirt, where is it?" I inquired.

"I can't remember that. I guess you're lucky to have your jeans on."

We both laughed at that, yawned, stretched again, and decided to head downstairs and return to Theta Chi through the woods.

Not two minutes later, Bo was seen on the living room floor in the far right corner between two half-naked jocks. All three young men were cuddled together and totally passed out. One jock had his mouth placed against Bo's dark nipple. The other one rested a flat palm against the Native American's puckered navel.

I decided to take a picture of them with my cell phone, dug the phone out of my jeans, flipped it open, and snapped a few frames. Next, Niner and I reviewed the pics, laughed, and then took in the rest of living room, which was completely trashed. On the left side of the room a floor-to-ceiling window was smashed into a million shards. The beer pong table was covered with vomit, cigarette butts, and an empty vodka bottle. Unfilled pizza boxes were scattered throughout the first floor like debris after a tornado. Plastic cups and puddles of spilled beer decorated tables and the floor. College bodies lined the walls and upholstered furniture. Some were naked while others were completely clothed. A pile of dog shit was found on the kitchen floor, which caused both Niner and me to look at each other in confusion. Once that was discovered, we agreed to leave Phi Kappa Theta and head towards the woods, back to Theta Chi.

Outside, thunder wrecked havoc in the heavens. Streaks of yellow-gold lightening zigzagged across the bruised skies. Rushed, we bolted to the woods for cover. To no avail, our bare chests became glistened with morning raindrops. Once under the pine, oak, and maple canopy, Niner said, "Let's take a piss."

I flopped out my cock first and Niner followed my action. Side-by-side, we stood in the woods and drained our tools. Yellow lines of piss emptied from our systems and decorated the fern-covered earth. Rain found its way through the late September treetops and splashed against our nicely built chests. I happened to watch droplets fall and lick at Niner's firm nipples and taut navel.

"Dude, what are you looking at?" he asked, overjoyed that he was the center of my current attention.

"A really hot guy whom I would like to fuck."

More thunder and lightning spruced up the day. Between kabooms and yellow-gold flashes of light, Niner replied, "I say we eat first, fuck our brains out, and then get into something else together. What do you think?"

"I'm also hungry," was my response and nodded my head.

Content with our decision, we secured our tools again, zipped up, and walked hand-in-hand back to Theta Chi through the pouring rain and the tempest's melodramatic upset.

PART THREE – NINER

1.

"Water. I need lots of water," Niner said, complaining about his hangover. We had returned to Theta Chi unharmed. The tempest outside was outraged and grew into a combative devil. Theta Chi's lights flickered off, on, and back off. Niner stood beside me in the kitchen and said, "Count to three."

I did. "One. Two. Three."

The lights flickered back on, and stayed that way.

"I'm fucking Harry Potter," he chanted. Half of his body was tucked into the refrigerator in search of provisions for breakfast, and bottled water for his minor dehydration.

"I would like to fuck that wizard," I confessed.

Both of us laughed.

He found eggs, bacon, sausages, and bread in the Kenmore. He pulled all the food out with both arms and carried the items to the counter. "You watch. I'll start to make breakfast, and every fraternity brother will be down here like a dog, sniffing my ass."

I stood behind him at the counter and brushed two fingers against his bottom. "Come on, you like to have your ass sniffed by hot jocks."

He laughed. "I will never admit to that."

"That is such a pity. I was thinking about sniffing your nice ass right now. Oh well, your loss."

He found a skillet, warmed up some butter, and began to fry a few eggs after cracking their shells open. "You're nothing more than a tease."

Truth was I was horny and desired him. Every ounce of my queer body wanted to rub against his body. "Not always. You finish up here and I'll prove to you that I'm not."

"Promises. Promises," he replied, and found another skillet to fry some bacon and sausage.

I was instructed to find the toaster and make toast. He told me to lather the slices in butter, which was the way the brothers liked it. I had the toaster on the kitchen counter in less than a minute and began to churn out slices.

Once the breakfast smells circulated about the frat house, as if on cue, Theta Chi brothers started to fill the kitchen. One by one they grabbed plates, glasses of orange juice, flatware, and whatever provisions they could devour. After an hour of hard labor at the stove, Nash decided to take over and give Niner a break, which prompted the two of us a moment to eat together on the front porch.

Side by side on the top step as rain poured down from the heavens, we gobbled down our breakfasts. Between bites we talked about the previous night and Dane's almost-fatal accident.

After our rainy breakfast, we dumped our dishes in the kitchen and found ourselves upstairs. Once there, we checked on Dane, who was in his bed and curled up in a ball. His closed eyelids twitched, which told us he was tucked away in his dreams, somewhere in a faraway place where men carried him on their bulky shoulders and called him a god.

"The baby at sleep," Niner said as he studied his boyfriend.

"The beautiful puppy at rest," I added.

Niner slipped his hand within my own as we stood over Dane's fetal position. He gave the hand a brief squeeze, turned to me, collected me in his free arm, and provided my lips with a kiss.

I was swept away to somewhere distant and loving and caring and peaceful. My soul seemed to lift out of my body and float above the room. The kiss was exotic and blissfully blue with smears of tainted yellow. I melted and became windswept, lost within that bedroom.

When he finally pulled away from me, semi-spent and out of breath, he said, "You want to get a shower together? The guys won't even know it."

I kept his hand within my own, nodded my head, and replied, "Lead the way. I'm all yours."

2.

"You're body fucking rocks," Niner critiqued as he gave me a once-over. His cheeks turned red, and his chest puffed out.

I was naked in the bathroom, and my pile of clothes sat at my feet on the dirty tile. I felt nervous for some reason, unsure of what I could conjure with his skin. My right palm found the space between my pecs and rolled down the center of my chest. I stopped the palm at my navel, twisted its flat surface to the left, then to the right, and moved it down to the V-area of blond pubic curls between my legs. My palm then traveled further south and discovered the nine-inch rod at my middle. There, I provided the pole with a stroke … two strokes … three strokes, and coached, "Strip out of your clothes, turn the water on in the shower, and then you can finally have me."

Niner listened. He unbuttoned his jeans, kicked off his Reeboks, removed his socks, and sported a pair of boxer-briefs, which outlined his pumped dog. Then, he pulled down his underwear to his ankles, slid them over his feet, and stood completely naked for me to take in.

The man was beautiful in every sense of the word: ten inches hard and upright, bushy strawberry-red thatch of man-hair above his knob, swinging balls, which were the size of golf balls, and a drizzle of hair above his cock that led up to his dented navel.

I swallowed saliva in the back of my throat and felt my shaft bounce up and down between my legs with fresh excitement. Inside me, bubbles of warmth meandered around: between my pecs and legs, under my arms and at the base of my neck, against the bridge of my nose. That tender and alive moment pushed me into irreversible lust and caused me to believe: I am in real love for the very first time … honestly.

He moved around me, started the shower, and prompted the spray of water to heat. Once that was accomplished, he turned to me and said, "Come on in, the water's fine."

"You going to play lifeguard and save me?"

One of my nipples was flicked, and he provided my cock with a tug. He rattled off, "It's suds time, buddy. Let's hop in."

Not even a minute later, we stood under the warm spray and kissed. Shower water poured down and over our heads, caressed our noses, lips, and chins. His spike pressed against mine as his tongue slipped into the back of my throat. Our nipples kissed, and our stomachs brushed together. Groans and moans were light, but present.

When he pulled away from me, he said, "I want to soap you up."

"Go for it. I'm ready." I grabbed the bar of Irish Spring and passed it to him as if it were a football.

Face to face, he took the soap and lathered it under the heated spray. Once that was achieved, he soaped up my nipples until they were knife-sharp, and then one ab after the next. My shoulders and neck and hips were all lathered in green-white soap. The bar moved steadily over my flesh and covered every inch.

I moaned, satisfied with his soap-tour. Helplessly, I gave into that shower moment with him and whispered, "Do my nuts. I love them soaped up."

He was a good listener; no, the best. Niner rocked. He caressed one ball and then the other. Soap was mixed with strawberry-red hair and water. The three combined with such ease and offered me more pleasure than I ever anticipated. My balls shifted to and fro in his palms as he lathered their rounded circumferences.

"How's that feel, buddy?" he inquired behind me.

"You shouldn't be doing this."

"What can I say? I'm a man with needs, and you have everything I need."

He left my pole alone, which told me he was a meager tease and wasn't about to shoot me off. A sinister smile spread across his adorable face that offered a suggestion of his sexual game.

"You're tormenting me, aren't you?"

"I wouldn't do that."

"You are. I know you are. Touch my cock. Stroke it off. I'm burning inside to come."

He laughed at my sexual fervor and shook his head. One of his soapy fingers found the tip of my nose, and he tapped it twice. "Not yet ... but soon. Hang in there."

Before I grew too disappointed by his sexual teasing, Niner pulled his hands away from my body, rinsed under the shower's warm spray, and exited my side in search of a cotton towel to dry off.

There, I was left with a club the size of a skyscraper between my legs, turned the hot water to a steady cold, stood under the chilly spray with my eyes closed, and waited for my guy-flag to deflate before I followed Niner out of the bathroom, in search of fresh clothes.

3.

Niner did not room with my brother or Dane, so we dressed in separate bedrooms. Most of the frats were still in the kitchen eating breakfast and reminiscing about last night's party at Phi Kappa Theta. Dane was still passed out; I studied his body at sleep while I slipped into a fresh pair of Diesel boxer-briefs, white bootie socks, jeans, and a sky-blue T-shirt that fit snug against my chest. Seconds later, Niner and I met in the hallway, and he checked me out from head to toe. He whispered, "Nice," and pinched one of my nipples through the tight tee.

"What are we doing?" I inquired. The guy was XXX stuff: broad shoulders, nice face, ripped chest, thick thighs, and flat stomach. I desired him in ways that I had never desired a young man before. My lust for him was immeasurable, and my ass actually twitched with hungry zeal for his congenial thrusts. Truth was I couldn't wait to feel him inside my body, all ten inches of his shaft buried into my bottom. I desired nothing less than his sweaty and firm palms to push into my hips and his perspiration to sting the plane of my back. There, in that hallway of discovered lust, I wanted him to uncontrollably rip my fresh clothes away from my body with his beautiful teeth and incessantly have his way with my skin.

He leaned into me and whispered, "You're hard."

The tube of meat between my legs had plumped into its nine inches because of my nasty thoughts of our bodies in frenzied motion. "Fuck me," escaped my lips without a single thought.

He looked to his left and right to see if we were alone, which we were, and he replied, "I like a man who knows what he wants."

The excitement of that impassioned moment was soon over. The thought of his seduction was lost. Briskly, he discovered my right palm, twisted me against his torso for just a mere second of time, and chanted, "Off to town we go."

"What's in town?" I asked.

"The coolest bookstore ever."

Before I could respond, I was tugged through the second floor hallway, downstairs, and outside.

The rainstorm had seized, and the day offered blue-yellow sunshine and warmth. A light wind kicked into motion as we walked towards Templeton and Nemo's Books.

Templeton was a charming and quaint town with oaks that lined sidewalks, awning-protected storefronts, and street-lined Tudors. I noted it as a walking community where people used sidewalks instead of local ways and avenues with vehicles. Niner led me down Cumber Way, and we entered Nemo's Books, which was decorated with a wrought-iron fence and gate, two gardens, and numerous ceramic gnomes that looked creepy.

Nemo's Books was independently owned by Alfred Nemo: bald head, horn-rimmed glasses, bushy eyebrows, and on the chubby side. Nemo greeted us with a firm hello, impetuous smile, and a stare of interest. "Young men, how can I help you?"

"We're just browsing," Niner said, and we escaped deeply into those many shelved books and topics, desirous of a certain tome for each of us.

Beekeeping, the life of Cleopatra, biochemical warfare, paleontology, and candle making were just a sliver of topics scattered about the store. Niner and I found the GAY/LESBIAN ISSUES at the back of the store. There, among that three-walled cove of Felice Picone, Michael Cunningham, Armistead Maupin, Edmund White, David Sedaris, Michael Craft, Milton Stern, Alan Hollinghurst, Logan Zachary, Wayne Mansfield, and other gay authors, I was pressed against the shelf, and Niner slipped his hand down into my jeans and discovered my plump joint. And there, among the naughtiest titles (*Eat My Cum*, *Bang My Hole*, *The XXX Adventures of Jacob Bigdick*, *Slams Against the Wall*, *Better off Laid*, *Spew Swallowing*, *Gay Train*, and *Eating Paulo*) I was kissed and fondled and cared for by him.

Three minutes had not even gone by when Alfred Nemo searched us out in the store and came upon our connected twosome. There, he witnessed a rather crude sight: my mouth opened with Niner's tongue inside; my friend's palm taking residence in my jeans; chests compressed together with such ease; sweat brushed over foreheads and cheeks. Alfred simply said, "Not here, gentleman … Please."

Niner backed away from me and cleared his throat. I was left against the bookshelf and felt embarrassed, numb, and rather dizzy. It was Niner who suggested we leave, which we did, and both of us smiled from ear to ear like tiny schoolboys.

4.

Our town adventure was rather short and brisk because both of us were horny and wanted to strip each other out of clothes. We became greedy for sweaty and muscled flesh. Firm rods were between our legs as we hiked back to Theta Chi, ready to burst and spray our loads all over each other.

The morning rain had dissipated and left the sky beaming with warm sunshine, a soft wind, and just a few clouds. Robins chirped with delight as local dogs barked in gated yards.

Most of the brothers had escaped the house. Niner told me they were out with girlfriends, relatives, or at a practice football game at Templeton Stadium, which was on the western side of the campus. Nash, Pecker, Lance, Blaine, and Tom were among those jocks at the field. Dane was finally up from his doozey of a night. He sat in the kitchen, enjoyed a cup of coffee, and milked his pill-popping hangover. The guy looked like hell: pallid skin, deeply set eyes, dried lips, and pitted cheeks.

Niner kissed his boyfriend on the top of his head and said, "I want to show Tackle the cold cellar, do you want to join us?"

Dane shook his head and muttered, "Thanks for the offer, but I'm going to pass."

I asked Niner, "What's in the cold cellar?"

"Wait and find out."

We escaped the kitchen and traveled down a narrow flight of stairs into the cluttered basement. Among spiderwebs, pipes, a boiler, and numerous junk, he led me to a navy blue painted door at the rear of the basement. He found a key in one of the overhead rafters and slipped it into the Yale lock, which secured the door. Then, he opened the door and ...

Heat lamps, white walls, and marijuana plants decorated the eight-by-seven square foot room. The plants were almost six feet high and showcased giant buds. Niner helped himself to a few leaves, smelled them, and informed, "You smoke?"

I shook my head and replied, "It does nothing for me."

"No problem," he said and pushed the leaves into one of his front pockets, willed to smoke a stick later. Then, he moved up to me, locked his lips to mine, pulled away, and admitted, "I'd rather smoke your dick instead, if you want to know the truth."

He directed us out of his pot room, and we returned to the basement area. Among moving boxes, two bicycles, empty suitcases, an arrangement of tools, and a cluster of other things, my back was gently pressed against one of the brick walls.

There, we became molded together again by lips, and he tugged on the joint between my legs. When our tongues touched, I felt wet and wild and whimsical and windblown. Our boners danced together in a heated crescendo. I honestly couldn't wait for him to plug my bottom. My crack was on fire for him, in need of his spirited man-motion. I simply desired nothing less than to have inch after inch of his naked erection inside my ravenous core.

Unable to contain my hunger for his shaft any longer, my fingers found the courage to unzip his jeans and pull them down to his knees with his cotton underwear. In that semi-darkness where investigative spiders and pesky mice watched our homoerotic needs unfold, his upright tool of ten engorged inches greeted my warm palms.

Infatuated with his skin, zealous for that iniquitous connection between hidden young men, I dropped to my knees and felt the underside of his cock glide against the handsome ridges of my face: unwrinkled forehead, gradually sloped nose, and plump upper lip. In need of his hard flag, I opened my mouth and allowed four of his ten inches to slip inside. With infatuation discovered, I thrust my head forward and backward in chaotic pleasure. Five … six … seven … eight … nine … ten inches entered my throat, became motionless there and gagged me, and eventually caused me to pull out and away.

Above me, Niner's breathing intensified. Sweat clung to the spot beneath his navel and rubbed off on my nose as I continued to blow him. His gyrations quickened, and he gripped his palms to the back of my head. The frat brat's balls – floppy and covered in thin strands of ginger-colored hair – smacked against my chin. His sounds of satisfaction spread throughout the basement's confines: melodramatic groans, a decorous hum, and an unexpected animalistic growl.

I continued to gratify him for the next ten minutes … thirteen minutes … sixteen minutes until my lips and tongue grew anesthetized. Once I surfaced for air, unattached to his knob, he instructed, "Turn around, drop your jeans, plant your palms on the brick wall, and spread your legs, so I can taste your ass."

5.

Was that upright and sexual adventure in the basement with Niner considered offensive to his lover/boyfriend upstairs who just happened to be soothing his previous night's drug and alcohol binge? I believed not. Niner seemed to have an open relationship with Dane and often scooped up attractive fuck buddies such as myself. Their bond had very minimal rules, which determined Niner's act with me rather harmless and innocent play.

Half of me wanted Dane to join our twosome in that square and empty space next to the basement's brick wall. Greedily, I wanted to eat Dane's junk and have his boyfriend's tongue in my wet man-crevice.

No, Dane did not find his way into the basement and strip out of his beer-scented clothes. Nor did he stand in front of my face while I attempted to rock his world with a glorious blowjob. Instead, I was alone with his lover/boyfriend who assiduously rolled the tip of his tongue around my furrowed opening and sent me into a spin of pure ecstasy.

What exited my mouth were murmurs of bliss by his tongue-escapade. Swirls continued on the circumference of my man-hole. After those teeth-together twirls, Niner affectionately flicked out his tongue, dabbed it to my bottom, and sent me into sporadic gasps. The wet and warm tool sprung into my hole, pulled out, and pivoted inside again. His fingertips spread my rear apart for deeper access. Flicks, swabs, and dabs developed, which caused me to shutter in front of him, and almost fall in a molten man-puddle to the basement floor.

I whimpered and grunted like an animal. Because I was so taken by his tongue-game, I shifted my ass into his face and ground its hole against his lips, chin, and nose. I rode his mouth with such ardor, charmed by his mouthy current.

Niner, blessed with prosaic motion in the company of another young man, finally pulled away from my rump and stood. After that abrupt act, he provided my buttocks with an open-palmed slap two times and chanted against my splayed back, "Hang onto the wall. I intend to buck the city boy out of you."

"Fuck me," escaped my pursed lips; words I had rarely uttered with a man, or men.

Seconds ticked by as a condom and packet of lube in his jeans was found and applied to his shank. Then, he warned like a gentleman, "Hang on, Tackle, I'm moving in."

As God is my witness, I confess here and now, years after that event at Templeton College, he bolted all of his ten inches of dick into my tight hole, whipped it out, and punched it back inside.

I gasped against the wall in desired pain. Helplessly, I clung to the painted bricks as he lodged his beef into my pit again. "Niner," echoed from my mouth as thunderous bats continued to affect me.

No, he wasn't about to end his erratic friction with my man-end. I knew he was skilled in boffing hot jocks such as myself, and had no intention whatsoever of concluding his rump-romp. Instead, his pace quickened, and he became on fire behind me. His fingernails dug into my hips for the longest time. Eventually, one of his hands found its way around my sweaty torso and located the cement-hard boner between my legs that begged to be played with.

To no avail, Niner did not disappoint me. In truth, he began to stroke my protein in a speedy and concurrent to and fro motion. The young man coached me, "I want to make you fire your load. Spray it all over the wall."

Together, we heaved back and forth. Our bodies were melodic in nature, connected by thick and long cocks, tender palms, and my eager rump. My flag rolled inside his hand, and I gasped for air. Repeatedly, he continued to bang my backside in a hyper manner. Bonded by our intense covetousness, we were inexorable together, steadfast and caught up in the moment.

I trembled against the basement's brick wall. A shallow howl abandoned my mouth as I felt an orgasm rush throughout my interior. No longer could I contain my sticky cargo inside. Quiver after solid quiver meandered from south to north within my veined prick and ...

"Explode, Tackle ... Do it for me," he chanted over my right shoulder.

An exasperated sound of homoerotic joy escaped my mouth as four arcs of white goop twirled out of my hose and decorated the basement's floor. Some of the oozy liquid garnished my feet and ankles because of my endless spray.

Niner slid his junk out of my ass. He knew I had released my churn and twisted me around with a swift tug. There, in the afternoon beams of sunlight that flooded in through the basement window, he rode both of his palms up and down on his meat in a hasty manner. The ginger-haired jock bucked his hips into his fists, let out a roar that I found alarming, and popped cream out of his man-gadget.

Within seconds I sported a chest covered in his sap. Coils of his gooey spent clung to my perky nipples, rigid abs, and creased navel. His white splatter even glazed my shoulders and the base of my chin.

After his blow, he said with a blistering smile, "Let me clean you up, pal."

I agreed wholeheartedly, into his mouth gig. Niner moved up to me and held me by my hips again. His extracted tongue lapped every drop of his glop from my flesh. Between his pleasurable licks, he chanted, "I like you too much ... and my spew."

6.

Niner continued to remove every drop of his creamy, pearl-colored sap from my skin. Light whines of likeness drifted from his mouth. I knew he was still granite hard between his sturdy legs, possibly ready to thump my bottom a second time. Aches still meandered in my ass region, though, because it was ever so tender. As his tongue-adventure continued, previous boyfriends flashed through my mind:

Ricardo Gonzalez: I dated him for the shortest period of time. He was a player built like an XXX Colt model, almost too bulky with his biceps and lats and delts, Peruvian-colored skin, molted chocolate-colored eyes that often dropped me to my knees with an opened mouth, older than I, and more experienced. He was a man who enjoyed soccer, working out at the gym, and showering with other naked men, particularly high school swimmers; the reason for our relationship's sudden demise.

Jake Harlow: a summertime fling last year, the Texas lifeguard who visited his Aunt Helite and worked at the Shottenmyer Pool. He was everything I desired in a young man. Someone I found compassionate, thoughtful, and exceptionally brilliant. I craved his dark thick hair, bronze chest, thin arms, and crooked smile. On summer nights, under the moonlit city that glittered and gleamed a silver-white brilliance, when the wind was nothing more than a sticky heat that fondled our bare flesh, I toyed with his dark treasure trail with three fingertips, and eventually replaced them with my extended tongue. A part of my soul had opened for that Texas lifeguard, among other intricate body parts of random pleasure. I fell weakly in lust for his animated blue eyes and narrow chest. Perhaps that was the first time I had fallen in love, even if I didn't exactly know what love was. How quickly he left my side after that heated summer of young man connected to young man in the secret confines of a busy city. My cowboy/lifeguard fled my side rather speedily and returned to his Texas, his different life, forever lost from my soul; I haven't seen him since, of course.

Bernard Stephen Ludowski. Because I despised his name, I simply called him B. He was thirty-five years old with auburn-colored eyes, a block-shaped chest of thick hair, dick the size of a skyscraper. The man was married to Sophia, a beautiful Polish woman, for seven years. He had a five-year-old daughter named Madeline, two Labradors, and drove a Volvo wagon. He discovered me in Ashton Park on the North Side of the city, bought me lunch, invited me to spend an afternoon with him at a local hotel, and desired my skin. I was a senior in high school, mind you, a virgin with supple skin that had never been touched, licked, or fucked. I was a fling for B, that fatherless boy who lived on Merchant Street with his mother and older brother. He purchased numerous gifts for me: food, CDs, movie tickets, books to read, trinkets to wear around my neck. He admitted that he hadn't fallen in love with me, although I did with him, faultlessly and with much ardor. He confessed that he had accumulated other "boys" such as myself: Paul, Carlos, Billy, and Philip. A list of high school boys he frequented with his skin at various hotels/motels in the city. B claimed he wasn't gay, which I didn't believe. And, he had simply vanished from my life as quickly as he arrived, which left me with a broken heart, loneliness, but as a much stronger young man.

"You're shuddering," Niner whispered as he finished his tongue-game on my chest.

I only shuddered because: I had inadvertently and weakly fallen into him, and for him, in an imprudently and questionable manner throughout that northern two-day trek. Shame on me for allowing emotions to transpire for him in that dirty and dusty basement after our bodies so easily twisted together as one.

I could effortlessly see Niner as another boyfriend on my list of men I had fondly fallen for. And, if his current lover/boyfriend, the pill-popping Dane, wanted to join our twosome, I would have undoubtedly agreed to such an alternative possibility. Indeed, I could see the three of our skins molded together in a sexual tangle, combined by friendship, lust … or something most heart-tugging.

"You drive me mad," was my response to his question.

"Mad is sometimes good, Tackle."

As a matter of fact it was, I surmised, and allowed him to hold me in his arms and dab warm and moist kisses to the length of my neck.

7.

We kicked off shoes, socks, jeans, and left piles of clothes on the basement floor. Niner snatched up my right hand and led me through the debris inside that cement tomb. We weaved left and right among battered furniture, moving boxes, and an assortment of bicycles. On the west side of the basement we came upon a wooden door with a cracked window. The window was smudged with dirt and dust and looked flimsy. Positioned there, he convinced me in a rather easy manner to join him for a swim in the lake, and added, "There's a pathway down to the water through this door. None of the brothers will see us."

I agreed. Why not? My chest was still sticky from his shoot, and my dick and left hand were lathered in my own spew-dribbles. A good swim in the lake, with an added clean-up, seemed like a great idea.

Secretly, he opened the rickety door, and we passed outside and emerged on a dirt path with blackberry tangles. The pathway veered to the left, sloped downwards, and led us to the lake, just as Niner said it would. Hand in hand, we stood at the lake's edge and studied its magnificent serenity: at peace, yellow-red bliss, beaming with extraordinary life. Naked, among brush, berry bushes, and tree limbs, I followed him into the lake. We moved cautiously, one step at time, hidden from the frat house and its straight brothers.

"Careful now," he said, and finally released my hand from his own.

"I'm good," I replied, and waded into the fresh water, which was cool and refreshing, clean and rather comforting. The water rose around our bodies as we walked deeper and deeper into the lake: up to our knobby knees, inner thighs, navels, abs, pecs, and nipples.

The current took us under and lifted us above its surface. We swam for the next hour or so like freshwater dolphins. Side by side we glided in the deep. Occasionally a muscled thigh bumped into another muscled thigh, and our fingers swam together. Under the water, hidden from those above, we became immortal and kissed in bliss. Our mouths connected as well as our bare chests. The limp cocks between us also kissed.

I wanted that moment in the lake with Niner to last forever. Heaven never felt so close, if the truth be told. My heart fluttered within my chest and all of my limbs became numb. The soothing water that surrounded our bodies felt like a blanket of sorts, shelter from those hypocrites in the breathing world, above the lake's surface. There, as mermen under that gentle current, I held him close to me, almost too close, and wished I were his husband, legally married to him, just the two of us locked together in harmony, lust, and faithfulness for the rest of our queer lives.

We surfaced. Our heads bobbed in the lake like inflated balls. We smiled and laughed like young boys, and we treaded the deep water. And, Niner admitted, "I'm hooked on you, Tackle. Just so you know."

I did know. I could see it in the oval brilliance of his green-perfect eyes and the uplifted smile on his face. Closer to shore, still hidden from the frat house, in the shadows of shoreline oaks and maples, we kissed again: with tongues and teeth and saliva and lips in motion, fused in glee, but only for a short period of time.

How long did we swim in the lake together? An hour? Two hours? I wasn't sure. The yellow-gold sun slipped a notch overhead and passed throughout the day. We laughed and played and acted immature. Our fingertips became wrinkled, and our dicks shriveled up to tiny muscles. We choked on water when our sexual wrestling ended up risky. Carelessly, we tugged each other under the lake's surface and kissed. For someone not big into kissing, he sure liked kissing me. Balls and cocks were gently pulled. Nipples in the deep were pinched. Asses were patted and licked. Then, exhausted by our horseplay, still naked, dripping wet with water, we found the narrow pathway up to the basement again, gathered our clothes, and escaped upstairs, as if nothing sexually erotic had occurred between the two of us.

8.

Niner escaped to the bathroom for a shower. I found myself inside Dane's bedroom, where I checked on him. Although I thought my brother's roommate was asleep, he wasn't. He lay on his bed with his eyes closed, obviously in a state of naked excitement. His eight inches of stick lay flat against his stomach. Its cut cap covered his hollow navel. Two pearl-white bubbles of pre-sap decorated his pisshole.

"Dane?" I whispered his name and closed the bedroom door behind me.

"Come here," he chanted, and patted the sliver of bare space next to him on the bed.

My footsteps carefully led me to the full-size bed and his side. He opened his eyes, reached out, and caressed the limp mound of denim and underwear between my legs. His other hand gripped his own cock, and he asked, "Can you help me out here?" as he gave both of our beefs healthy strokes.

I looked over my right shoulder in search of an invisible Niner and replied, "What about your boyfriend?"

"It's alright. You're not the first guy we have shared. Lock the door and strip out of your clothes."

Truth was I don't think I could have blown another creamy load because of my previous hot action with Niner in the basement. But, that didn't mean I couldn't help Dane get his rocks off. Apparently, he was a man in need of another man, and I just happened to be there to fulfill his desire, which was a total turn-on for me. Without another thought, I walked over to the closed door, twisted the knob to a locked position, and removed all of my clothes.

Not a minute later, I stood on the bed over Dane's face, bare of clothes. My balls rocked to and fro between my thighs. Beneath me, I studied his good looks: upturned smile, freshly shaven sideburns, interested onyx-colored eyes, pink-red cheeks blossomed with pure excitement. He mumbled, "Sit on my face, Tackle. I want to fuck you with my tongue."

Intoxicated by that moment, I lowered my balls to his chin and felt my man-chute open for both of our pleasures. Within seconds, I felt the tip of his tongue rush inside me, pull out, and dive back into my sweet and tight ring. Hunched above him with my hands planted on my muscled hips, I ground my center to his face and felt the tip of his nose, with his tongue, slip inside my warm system. Quickly, I pulled off, allowed him to find oxygen, and pressed my bottom to his face again.

Both of us panted with deep satisfaction. Up and down I rode his face and felt my fully erect knob bounce between my legs. The mattress squeaked under my constant motion. Dribbles of fresh dick-sap sputtered out of my shaft and glazed the space between his medium-built pecs. A moan of pure elation surfaced from my own lips as our rapid motion sustained.

On cue, behavior very much like a porn star's, Dane jacked himself off with one fist. In a feisty manner, he bolted his hips upwards into his palm and fingers, which continued for the next few minutes.

To my surprise, his other hand latched onto my extension of protein, and he began to stroke it off with the same vibrant motion as his own tool. Together, his hands worked in succinct action, and devised mutual orgasms for the both of us. Consistently, audaciously, and keenly, Dane manipulated our poles. Minute after minute of our bond grew into fine orgasms. Both of us moaned and grunted. The bed rocked up and down. Sweat flew off of my torso and splashed against his nipples and abs. Continuously, I rose and fell onto his face.

No, I could not hold my load in much longer because of his tongue lodged into my bottom. Joy surfaced, and a bolt of pure energy swept throughout my torso. Honestly, I didn't believe I was capable of coming a second time after my naked affair with his boyfriend/lover against the basement wall. To no avail, a shiver of exultation ripped through my organs while he persistently whacked me off, and ooze fired out of my staff and glazed his perspiration-covered pecs, nicely built shoulders, and toned abs.

At that same time, he left out a final howl of conviction and released his own gooey shipment. Strings of the white shit looped out of his pipe and adorned my hard cock, swinging balls, and his chin.

After our fuck-session, I unlocked the bedroom. Nash stepped into the room and saw my naked body, then Dane's on the full-size bed. He shook his head with glee, smiled, and said to me, "Glad you found a way to fit in around here."

"Trust me, Tackle is the shit," Dane said from the bed, and wiped himself clean with a cotton towel.

Nash told me, "We have to get you to the bus stop, bro. If you miss your Greyhound, you're here for another two days."

I thanked my brother for the information.

Dane said, "Niner and I can drive him, if you don't mind, Nash."

My brother was fine with that idea and replied, "Find me before you leave, Tackle. I have something for Mom that I want you to give her." He tapped me on my bare, right shoulder with three fingertips.

I nodded my head, and said, "Will do, Shamoo."

Nash dropped his fingers from my shoulder and walked out of the room; I shut the door behind him.

Dane finished his clean-up.

I found a cotton towel and began my own clean-up, then decided to take a quick shower, and pack my bag for home.

9.

Before leaving for the Greyhound bus stop with Dane and Niner, I had two things to accomplish: one, I wanted to tell Bo Nassy goodbye, and leave him with a remembered kiss; two, I had to tell my brother so long, and retrieve a package from him for our mother, which I would haul all the way to the city and eventually present to her.

After a long search in the obnoxious-sized frat house, I finally found Bo in the backyard, down by the lake. There, he was bare-chested with a pair of canary-yellow Rufskin shorts nestled against his cock. Bo lounged on a cotton beach towel in the toasty sun, baking his pecs and abs. Upon my arrival, he lifted his faux Oakley sunglasses, squinted, and offered, "You again."

"That be me," I challenged, and took in his six-three frame yet again: perfectly round nipples, solid chest, Native American hue, pumped muscles lathered in a generous late-summer sweat, gleaming bald head, thick thighs, and the delicious package between his legs.

"My cock's been missing you, pal."

"Maybe I'll visit it sometime soon again."

"Why, you leaving?"

I nodded my head and replied, "I'm heading back to the city in a few minutes. Dane and Niner are taking me to the bus stop."

"You come to say goodbye to my cock?" Bo looked behind us to see if any of the brothers were around; it was just he and I along that picture perfect lakeside scene. He pulled down the Rufskin and sported a semi-boner.

I honestly don't know what came over me and walked up to his side, bent over, took a sniff, lick, and suck of his cock's head. Quickly, I pulled away. Then, I decided to kiss him. My mouth blended with his while I grabbed his rod with my left palm and sporadically jerked it up and down. Pre-spew gathered on my fingertips, but I didn't care.

That kiss was the most amazing one I think I have had in all my life. Fireworks exploded between my temples. My pulse raced, and my heart barely kept up with it. I almost lost my balance and fell overtop his succulent and motionless body in the sun's rays, but voluntarily found my composure at that very last second before an accident between us occurred. Tectonic plates shifted from his kiss. Our planet shimmied off its axis for just a second or two and …

I pulled my partially numb mouth away from his and removed my laborious hand from his granite-hard shaft. Then, I wiped the back of my hand across my mouth and confirmed, "When I come back here again, I want you to fuck me."

He grabbed his junk between his thick legs and gave it a jostle. "It's going to hurt, Tackle."

"I'll be ready for it."

"If I don't find you in Pittsburgh first."

"My ass is ready for you anytime you want it," I replied, told him goodbye, and vanished from his side, where Bo stayed in his cozy sun and baked, and possibly thought about me all that afternoon, perhaps even longer.

After my short visit with Bo Nassy, I went to find my brother. He and three other frat brats were in the kitchen, cleaning, which was something that rarely happened at the house, I surmised. Tom washed dishes and Pecker dried them with a tattered hand towel. Lance wiped down the table and countertops. My brother used a broom and swept the floor. When Nash saw me walk into the kitchen, he stopped his chore, turned to me, and said, "You leaving?"

"Unfortunately."

"Too bad you have to go ... Niner and Dane really liked your ass," Lance said.

"And your cock," Pecker added.

"They'll miss you, buddy," Tom said.

The secret was out at Theta Chi that I had fucked around with Dane and Niner in the past twenty-four hours – and that they were a couple; so much for trying to keep my affairs – and theirs – discreet. Comfortable with the trio, I responded, "I'll be back soon. Then, I can finish my fuck games with the two."

Lance, Pecker, and Tom all cheered me on, hugged me all together, and told me goodbye. Each of them said I was welcomed back to their frat house anytime I wanted to return. After our farewell, Nash passed an envelope to me from his back pocket and told me, "Give that to Mom."

I looked at the envelope and asked, "What is it?"

"Just a letter to tell her that I love her. Nothing else," Nash confessed.

The trio behind my brother oohed and ahhed in play like little boys in grade school.

"That's nice," I said, folded the envelope in half, and slipped it into my back pocket.

Nash asked, "You need help with your pack?"

"I'm good," I said.

Satisfied with my response, he gave me a bear hug, kissed me on the top of my head, and said, "Text me, little brother."

"Will do, Shamoo," I rattled off, exited the kitchen, and went in search of my ride to the bus stop from my intimate friends, Dane and Niner.

10.

"Ready?" Niner asked in a rather unpleasant manner. He was somber-eyed with a crinkled brow.

"I am," I said.

"I'll take your pack," Dane said, picked up my single backpack from my bed, and tossed it over his right shoulder.

The three of us left Theta Chi and climbed into Niner's ancient Buick with its rusted trunk and missing rearview mirror. We sat together up front. I was in the middle. Niner drove, and Dane was positioned on my right side. The Buick bounced up and down towards town.

The day now offered a sort of bleakness about it: a still-life picture of blues and grays with limited sunshine and movement. I don't know why we were quiet, but silence seemed to rule. To break it, I reached my right palm out and grasped Dane's left inner thigh. My left palm discovered Niner's right inner thigh. I gave both thighs a squeeze and supplied, "I really had a good time at the frat house. Thanks for everything."

"All good things come to an end," Niner said that old cliché that caused me to roll my eyes.

"Such a pity," Dane added. "We were just beginning to get to know you and your cock."

"Don't be blue, you two. I'll be back."

Neither of them believed me, though. Again, I squeezed their inner thighs. More silence was found and caused me to feel a bit uncomfortable.

Eventually, out of the blue, Dane said, "You have an amazing dick. I think that is your best quality, Tackle."

Niner laughed, but disagreed. "I'm fond of his ass, if you want to know the truth."

"Do I have a say in this?" I inquired and smiled from ear to ear.

"Hit us," Dane said.

"I'm sort of fond of my abs," I responded.

The three of us laughed for no reason until we were downtown and at the bus stop.

Niner carried my pack to a narrow bench painted a forest green, which sat on the corner of Wilmington and Haring at the bus stop in Templeton. He plopped the pack on the bench and sat down beside it. I sat next to him and admired the streets: Tudor-style houses with well-

242

maintained yards garnished the sidewalks; the post office was one block up Haring; beyond that was the local grocery store and community park.

"Don't worry, I'll be back," I confirmed.

"Make sure you SKYPE us," Niner suggested. "I want to watch you play with yourself."

I laughed at that and agreed.

Dane passed me a piece of paper with e-mail addresses and cell phone numbers. "If you get bored, contact us."

"I promise to," I said.

Niner took out his cell phone and said, "Let's get a picture of us together."

The three of us all agreed. Dane joined Niner and me on the bench. Clumped together, shoulder-to-shoulder-to-shoulder, Niner snapped a shot of us. Dane took out his Verizon, flipped it open, and snapped a pic off, too. I was last to take a picture of our threesome. I dug my Sprint out and clicked a quick one of our unique bond.

By that time, the bus was on its way down Wilmington: its engine creaked and groaned; air brakes hissed at every stop sign.

"Kiss us," Dane suggested. "Something quick and sweet, so we can remember you by."

"Stop saying that shit," I warned, "I'll be back soon."

"Kiss me, anyway, Tackle," Niner demanded.

I gave in. Our mouths collected as one. Wet tongues and smooth lips combined in a threesome. The kiss was hurried and sloppy, but still real and needed. When we pulled apart, the Greyhound bus had fully stopped in front of us and its mouth opened.

I stood and reached for my pack.

Dane blocked my reach and passed the pack to me. Before he released it, he shared, "We sort of fell for you … just so you know that."

"And I, you," I said. It was the truth. I enjoyed the couple to the fullest. Not only had I gained their friendship, but I had also gained their lust; something I never anticipated twenty-four hours before. Truth was I had a crush on both of them, their college, and the small town of

Templeton. There was no way I could stay away for very long. My brother attended the school, and I had gained two very close friends (with benefits, of course). Plus, Bo Nassy was at Templeton College, whom I wanted behind me in the worst kind of way, and craved his eleven-inch cock inside my bottom. That small northern town in western Pennsylvania had obviously found a spot in my heart, crotch … somewhere.

Niner saluted me like a solider; sadness was locked at the corners of his deep-green eyes, and he wore a frown.

Dane smiled and finally realized that he would soon see me again.

"Off I go, guys. Wait for my return," I chanted, stepped onto the bus, showed the driver my ticket, and listened to the door close behind me as I welcomed my three-hour bus ride, a good paperback to read, and my life back in the city.

THE END

The Authors

Armand has had nearly a dozen stories – ranging from sports erotica to superhero stories to westerns – published in a variety of anthologies. His ultimate fantasy is to move to Europe, marry a nice Czech man, and write full-time

Derrick Della Giorgia was born in Italy and currently lives between Manhattan and Rome. His work has been published in several anthologies and literary magazines. Visit him at www.derrickdellagiorgia.com.

HL Champa is an extensively published writer of erotic fiction. Find out more at heidichampa.blogspot.com.

Jake Harding lives in Florida. He currently is at work on his first gay erotic novel. His short story in this anthology is based on true events.

Residing on English Bay in Vancouver, Canada, **Jay Starre** has pumped out steamy gay fiction for dozens of anthologies and has written two gay erotic novels. Contact: Jay Starre on Facebook.

Over 65 of **Jim McDonough's** erotic stories have been published on the web, in more than a dozen dirty magazines and in anthologies. Jim lives and writes in Albuquerque.

Landon Dixon's stories have been published in numerous magazines and anthologies.

Logan Zachary (loganzachary2002@yahoo.com) is an author of mysteries, short stories, and over forty erotica stories, living in Minneapolis with his partner, Paul, and his dog, Ripley, who runs the house. www.loganzacharydicklit.com.

The sexual fantasies of **Michael Roberts** have now been featured in almost a dozen anthologies, on www.cruisingforsex.com, in several leading adult gay magazines, and in the author's moistly fevered dreams.

R. W. Clinger writes for STARBooks Press and has written four novels and is working on a fifth. He resides between Pittsburgh and Florida.

Rob Rosen, author and Lambda Literary Award nominee, has been published in more than 125 anthologies. Please visit him at www.therobrosen.com.

T.A. Meeker studied created writing at the University of Iowa. His articles and stories span several genres and have appeared in numerous newspapers and magazines. He is the author of many short stories and a novel. He lives in Texas and can be reached through the editors at STARbooks Press.

The Editor

Mickey Erlach's is a full-time editor for STARbooks Press. He went to community college where there were no fraternities, but his partner, Eric Summers, offers to haze him weekly.

aring any underwear. "Excuse me," I said, having a hard time look

inded by that bulge in his crotch, "but don't I know you?" "Maybe

nd of t bout

vith Ray God,

loser? in?" h

id. "Lik s stron

ce body e on C

lly, he l I eve

up to t any id

staking e san

, I coul ery lo

ood rac ne sw

ng with e in s

we go behir

ill see in pu

ed?" he vent to

rivacy. grabb

hard. I

k, traci t, so f

ed it, ha

with m bing

bbing, I n cocl

he sound of unzipping filled the small space. I don't know who's h

, but before I knew it, I had his rod in my hand, and mine was in hi

it to do?" he asked, his tone challenging. I knew exactly, and sank